# RANDOM BULLETS

## Joy Mutter

This book is dedicated to everyone who ever encouraged me to write and publish books, especially Diane and my daughter.

# Contents

# And so it begins – 13:47 15th June 2015

Claire would have shrieked if the bang had been any closer. However, it goes off near enough to where she is sitting on her favourite park bench to make her jump and slop hot coffee into the lap of her brand new, apple-green skirt.

'Damn it!' she says, more concerned over the ruination of her newly-purchased garment than with working out what has caused the bang. She wants to swear more graphically but the park is busy due to it being a gloriously sunny day. Sitting on the bench next to Claire is a plump, middle-aged woman puffing self-consciously on a vape. The lady glances sympathetically at Claire and passes her a crumpled tissue to mop up some of the offending beige liquid.

'Thanks for that. I've only just bought this skirt on my way to work today. I'm supposed to be going out for a special meal with my fiancé this evening to celebrate the anniversary of the day we met. Now it's all ruined. I knew I should have changed back into my old clothes after trying on this skirt,' Claire tells the woman, who now seems less of a stranger after the coffee fiasco.

'Oh, what a shame,' replies the friendly lady in the dowdy clothes. 'It looks like that coffee is sadly going to stain. You might have got away with it if it had been a patterned material.'

'There's not enough time to buy a replacement before returning to the office. I work across the road from here. I've only got fifteen minutes left before I have to get back on the treadmill,' Claire says, although she loves her job in the illustration department inside the thriving advertising agency.

As a sun-lover, it has always been a struggle to drag her lithe, petite body away from her favourite park bench. She thinks of the bench as her personal property and heads for it every lunch break when the weather is inviting. It faces the sun and is situated in the perfect position to bronze her limbs as she eats her sandwiches and attempts to drink her coffee.

Having a park set only a two-minute walk from the London advertising agency where she works is one of the perks of her job.

Whenever heading towards it, if she spots interlopers sitting on her bench, she curses inwardly and glares at them before reluctantly seeking out an inferior bench. On this particular day, Claire is the first to claim this paragon of benches. She has managed to eat her tuna roll before the plump woman sits next to her, fishes around in her handbag, pulls out a vape and self-consciously puffs on it. Claire tries not to breathe her fishy breath over her and is relieved that the woman is large enough to prevent anyone else from joining them.

'You work in one of the buildings across the road from here? What a coincidence! Yesterday, I started working in the accounts department of an advertising agency,' says the older, mousy-haired woman.

This slightly scruffy, out of condition, maternal-looking woman is not really Claire's idea of a typical accountant. She looks like she would be more at home cooking delicious meals for an appreciative family. Claire inwardly scolds herself for judging books by their covers.

'You must have started working at the same place as me. I've been working in the illustration department at Bernard Wiggins Agency for over two years. My name's Claire, by the way. Dare say that we'll be seeing a good deal more of each other from now on,' Claire says in her usual friendly manner. A sudden, stiff breeze blows through the leaves of the nearby trees and just as suddenly dies away.

'It's lovely to meet you, Claire. I'm Pauline,' says the woman, thinking how she really must lose a few stones in weight if she is going to be surrounded by such lithe, pretty, young women in her new job.

## Pauline and Bob

Pauline had never been skinny, but her weight was now becoming a serious problem to her. She always tried to dress as attractively as her bulk allowed, but constantly wearing dark-coloured clothes with stretchy waistbands to mask the problem was depressing. Her excessive weight problem had begun after Pauline had resorted to numbing her unbearable pain by eating every food imaginable after the traumatic loss of their last baby. This bingeing was usually carried out in secret because she knew how much it would upset her husband, Bob to see her gorging.

Bob worked long shifts driving his taxi around London, which left Pauline with many empty hours to satiate her taste buds with regular trips to the fridge and kitchen cupboards. Her surviving children, two teenage boys, always kept to their bedrooms in the evenings, chatting online to their friends.

Crisps were Pauline's weakness. She would guiltily polish off four packets of the greasy, crunchy morsels at a time as she sipped red wine whilst watching television in solitude. After despatching the crisps, an urge for something sweet quickly followed. After risking her fillings with a handful of toffee éclairs, she would demolish a slab of cake, disdainfully avoiding the fruit bowl. This would trigger a desire for something savoury, so back to the kitchen she would waddle for chunks of various cheeses and a pile of assorted buttered biscuits. Riddled with guilt, she would then rush to the bathroom and vomit.

For years, she had been filled with self-loathing for the damage inflicted on her body and mind by her eating so much, although she understood why she did it. She took some comfort from having recently given up smoking and switching to vapes, although she was still addicted to the nicotine in the water vapour.

Four days before starting her new job, Pauline and Bob

were lunching at home on one of his rare days off from working at the taxi rank. Pauline said to a miserable-looking Bob, 'I feel and smell so much better after quitting the evil weed, Bob. I wish you'd consider knocking it on the head too. The family would be at least four thousand pounds better off each year. Your early morning cough is bloody atrocious. It sounds like you're just about to cough up a lung.'

Bob hated being nagged, especially when he knew that she was right. He gazed at the ceiling as his wife continued, 'There's not much point in me thinking my clothes will ever stop stinking of ciggies whilst you're still puffing away. Your smoke is still making everything in my wardrobe and the rest of the house smell foul. The living room's cream wallpaper is turning a disgusting nicotine yellow colour.'

'Tell you what, as a special favour to you and the kids, I'll agree to only smoke in the garden and not inside the house,' he conceded heroically.

'Hallelujah! Thanks, babe. The kids and I'd all really appreciate it,' she replied, genuinely thrilled that their house might soon be a smoke-free zone. 'It's such a shame you don't enjoy using vapes like I do. I've not fancied smoking a single ciggie since swapping over to my lovely vape.'

'I might switch to vapes one day, but I feel like a bit of a poof puffing away on one. You know how much I've always enjoyed a smoke, whereas you weren't really enjoying it anymore,' he said, picking up his pack of cigarettes and a lighter from the kitchen table before heading out of the kitchen door and into the back garden.

'Shit,' he thought to himself with outstretched hand. 'It's drizzling. I'll have to stand under the tree at the end of the garden. I must clear a space in the shed and put an old chair in there for when the weather's crappy. I might as well suffer in comfort.'

As Pauline stood looking out of the kitchen window as she washed up the dishes, she felt guilty watching Bob shivering under the flowering cherry tree. Eventually the guilt became overpowering, forcing her to weaken and call him back into the house. After Bob had gratefully settled back indoors with a cup of tea and a cigarette, she fast forwarded her thoughts to four days into the future when it would be time to start her new job in the accounts department in Hammersmith. When she had visited the offices for her interview, she was pleased to notice a sprawling park opposite the building where her return to working life would soon take place. Although not a sun worshipper, preferring to hide her bulky body under camouflaging layers of clothes whenever possible, Pauline welcomed the prospect of enjoying fresh air in pleasant surroundings during lunch breaks.

'I'll be able to sit on a park bench, plug myself into my audio book collection and eat my sandwiches in the sunshine,' she informed Bob on the day she opened the letter advising that her job interview had been successful.

'Sunshine? My arse! This is England we're talking about here,' Bob reminded her. 'But I'm chuffed for you. I know that area of Hammersmith really well and have even eaten my sandwiches in that very park a few times. The boating lake is fun to sit and watch. At least there's no danger of that lake running dry with all the rain that pisses down on it, ha!'

'Oh, stop! Don't rain on my parade,' she replied with a chuckle. She was well used to him winding her up and she loved him for it.

# Bob's other career

Although Pauline believed that her husband loved her, she also knew that Bob would certainly appreciate it if she dropped a few dress sizes. He had made a few unsubtle, jokey remarks as her weight piled on over the years, but her grief at losing their last baby in childbirth had made comfort eating escalate into an addiction for his wife. Bob had naturally also been grief-stricken after their daughter was still-born, but his grief had come out in other ways, unbeknownst to his wife.

He had been driving a black cab for over fifteen years and the job had opened his eyes to the seedier side of life. He was a good-looking, burly, cuddly bear of a man, with twinkly, mischievous, blue eyes and a wicked sense of humour. His thick, black hair had turned an attractive shade of silver early in his life. It complemented his all-year tan, courtesy of as many winter breaks in Tenerife with Pauline and their boys as the family budget allowed.

Bob was highly popular with most of the other drivers, one of whom, an Indian called Divesh, had approached him with an unusual proposition seven years previously, when Bob was in his mid-forties.

'Hey there Bob, mate. How's it going?' Divesh had asked at the end of another long shift. They were sitting on a low wall enjoying a smoke before heading back to their respective homes.

'Could be better, Divesh. Pauline wants a new kitchen, so I need to put in extra hours in the cab to pay for it all. Where the hell does all the money go, Divesh?' Bob asked mournfully.

'If you want to lay your hands on some quick, easy money, I could let you in on a little scheme I've been involved with. Promise to keep it under your hat though. It's a bit suss,' Divesh replied, searching Bob's face to ensure that his friend could be completely trusted.

'I'm intrigued. Tell me more. I promise to keep it secret

from everyone,' Bob said eagerly.

'I've been meaning to mention it to you for a while, but had to be certain you'd be receptive to the idea. Well, I know that you like looking at porn now and again. No doubt you've seen porn where a cab driver picks up a sexy tart and through various ruses talks her into having sex with him. All of the sex action is captured on a secret camera,' Divesh whispered conspiratorially, warming to his theme.

'I'd have to be blind not to know what you're talking about. I think I can guess where you're going with this,' Bob replied, giggling with nervous excitement.

He had always enjoyed watching the taxi driver porn when Pauline was out or in bed and had often imagined that he was the taxi driver in question. The story always ended in the same way, with the girl in the back of the cab put through various sexual activities. The face of the driver was always blurred out. The girls involved had no such consideration paid to them.

Divesh continued, saying, 'I've been involved with one or two of the shoots and have lent my cab out for a tidy sum. I've obviously always stipulated that my cab should never be identifiable. I've even hung around on one of the shoots and was involved in a bit of the action after the camera stopped rolling. It was awesome, although the girl was fairly worn out after what the fake taxi driver had just put her through. I've even asked to be considered to play the part of the taxi driver and might get a test run in a few weeks to see if I'm up to it. I'm not entirely confident of performing to order, although I'd love to give it a damned good try.'

'Count me in. It'd beat driving round London all day, although the shoots probably don't happen that often,' Bob said, already imagining being between some voluptuous, young blonde's legs. Divesh was unaware that Bob could perform sexually to order, or at least had been able to before married life and the still-birth had taken the edge off his rampant sexual appetite. 'I'd even be up for performing in a shoot, as well as allowing my cab to be used,' Bob added.

‘I’ll let my contact know that you’d be interested. As your financial need is greater than mine, I’ll let you take the next gig if you like. You look pretty fit for a guy of your age. You never know, you might be on the brink of a sparkling new career,’ Divesh observed. They almost fell off the wall with laughter at the thought of the impending excitement.

For a man in his mid-forties at the time of his debut performance in front of the camera in his cab with a dark-haired, vivacious girl, Bob proved to be a natural porn star. Divesh was envious of his friend’s sexual prowess and popularity with the crew and female talent. However, he could not really complain too much because he managed to pick up some action after the cameras stopped rolling. He had ensured that it would be part of the deal.

Pauline had no suspicion that her husband was now indulging in such a sordid side-line. He had always worked long, unsociable hours, so when he was spending a few sweaty hours ravishing whichever girl had been booked by the production company, Pauline just assumed that he was driving his passengers around London. She received her new kitchen earlier than expected. She neither complained about that nor questioned how it had suddenly become possible. When the money started rolling in, courtesy of Bob’s regular pornographic activities, the couple’s holidays became more exotic than they might otherwise have been.

Bob’s guilt over his betrayal of Pauline often brought him to the brink of giving up the porn work, but he enjoyed the sex and the money too much to cease. He fervently prayed that his wife and children would never find out what he was up to and had taken strict measures to ensure that his anonymity was maintained. There were no distinctive tattoos on his powerful body and images of his face were always meticulously blurred before the finished article was uploaded onto the porn site. He had horrors of his teenage boys watching their father humping some busty babe if they were ever to log into a porn site. The fear never prevented him from carrying on with his shady practices.

'I'm doing this for the future of my whole family,' he thought one day, whilst the cameras started filming in his cab. He had then grabbed the hips of the near naked redhead girl and in a minute or two he was back to full power, all thoughts of family banished.

Bob's sense of humour and prodigious libido kept everyone smiling. There was always a friendly twinkle in the eyes of whichever girl he was partnered with. After a year of internet porn shoots, Bob recklessly branched out into the televised adult channels, risking appearances in non-taxi situations where his face was clearly visible. As the chances of his secondary career being discovered increased, his guilt and anxiety worsened. He contemplated calling a halt to appearing in porn films but after giving it up for three months, he was missing the adrenaline buzz from doing unspeakable things to young, often breathtakingly beautiful females.

During those three months of abstinence, he also missed having the extra money and taking pleasure from watching his wife and offspring enjoying a better quality of life. Returning to endless hours of driving his taxi around crammed London roads depressed him, especially when he was reminded of the porn shoots every time an attractive young girl stepped into the back of his cab. The back seats of his cab had seen more action than his marital bed ever had and whenever he lovingly polished its leathery surface, Bob would smile as he recalled particularly memorable encounters.

'Are you crazy? Why on earth would you want to give up all the fun and money?' Divesh had asked him when Bob had first turned down a request to star in another backseat romp.

'It's different for you, mate. You're single, not married with kids like I am. You don't get to display your arse on camera when you're banging a girl for everyone to see,' Bob had replied whilst gazing reflectively into a puddle on the pavement.

'Okay, don't rub it in. We can't all be Super Stud. I tell

you what, if I had your sexual stamina, you wouldn't see me for dust. I'd be making porn fulltime,' Divesh said. 'I really miss being on set with you, even if I'm never filmed.'

'Yeh, this is what's really behind all your whinging at me. You miss the free bangs after I've done my bit with the girls,' Bob replied with a knowing laugh, tapping the side of his nose.

Divesh laughed, jokingly punched Bob's arm and said, 'I can't deny missing sharing the wild life with you, but I'm also thinking of a better lifestyle for you, Pauline and your boys.'

'But at what price?' Bob asked.

Divesh ignored his friend's question and said, 'I can carry on getting my end away anyhow at other shoots because I'm still letting them use my taxi, but it's not half as much fun when you're not around. The girls are really missing you too.'

'Oh, how sweet of them,' Bob replied sarcastically.

'Let's be honest, you've only got a few years of messing around on a porn set left in you. You might as well make the most of it whilst you can. Think of Pauline and your retirement. It won't be that many years before you're both wetting yourselves and playing bingo in some care home. You should stick a few quid away for a rainy day. Not everyone has your enviable sexual talents. The production company have been bugging me to see if I can get you to return to them as you were great for their business,' Divesh said.

'Soon you'll be rattling out the tired old 'sex sells' phrase. I'll be frank. I'm struggling with my decision to quit and really miss it all, but I can't carry on being such a prick to Pauline. I admit I'm totally dissatisfied with endlessly driving around London and my temper is beginning to flare up at work more than it ever did before I got into making porn. I've even started losing my rag with Pauline and the kids,' Bob admitted.

'Do everyone a favour and come back to the fold,' Divesh replied, guessing that if he kept the pressure up then it would not be long before Bob would cave in.

Bob could stand Divesh's nagging no longer. His resolve snapped and he phoned the porn production company. They were delighted to welcome him back because he had been sorely missed, having made a name for himself in a comparatively short time. There was an endless stream of porn stars hammering on their doors for employment, but Bob was such a likeable, popular, salt of the earth chap who just happened to also be able to fornicate for England with style.

Bob still carried on with his regular taxi driving career, but after a year or two, his porn activities increased to such a degree that he considered himself to be more porn star than taxi driver. He was addicted to everything about it and yet he loved his wife with all his heart, although the passion had died off years before. Walking away from his marriage in order to devote his life completely to porn was never a consideration. He would have been as devastated as Pauline if she ever discovered his secret. She would have certainly thrown him out of their comfortable, Kilburn home if it ever came to light. He would not have blamed her in the slightest.

Pauline was the opposite of all the girls that Bob worked with, but he would never love them like he loved her. Her self-loathing at the way her body looked made her keep her husband at arm's length in their bedroom. She was as comfortable as his favourite, old jumper, good-hearted, intelligent and made him laugh. He knew that she cherished him in her own, platonic way. He also admired her prodigious accountancy skills and self-sacrificing dedication to him and their surviving children. Despite being fully aware of all of the wondrous, positive benefits that his marriage to Pauline brought to his world, Bob selfishly wanted to have his cake and eat it too. Pauline just wanted cake.

# Edward – 13:47 15th June 2015

The first loud bang that rends the air apart down a road close to the Hammersmith Park, heralds Sam's instant death. He has been shot at close range by his uncle Edward. The young man's brains now decorate the grimy, London pavement. A couple of curious pigeons that have flown skyward at the noise are now bravely advancing to investigate.

Seconds before, Sam's sixty-two-year-old uncle had managed to sneak up unnoticed behind the heavy-set youth. Edward had shot him in his spiked up, strawberry-blond hair during his walk to the park to enjoy a lunchtime break in the sun. Edward has been lurking in wait for over an hour behind a bank of large wheelie bins in a narrow side road, attempting to blend in with the shadows.

On the verge of aborting his mission, Edward's heart lurched on finally seeing a door open and Sam heading alone down the steps of the management training building where he has been honing his management skills. Sam had reluctantly signed onto the course in order help him now that he owned his recently deceased father's restaurant in Cornwall.

Edward had been stalking his nephew for the past two days, trying to work out the best time and place to execute his plan. He had always realised, despite his intense brain confusion, that he stood little chance of escaping unscathed after the hit.

Although the street is now almost free of pedestrians, Sam's murder is naturally not going unnoticed. A couple of young, French holidaymakers have been approaching the tense crime scene, intent on spending a relaxing few hours in the nearby park. As soon as they hear the loud bang, they struggle to take in what's happened. The man grabs his girlfriend's arm, wrenches her around and screams, 'Vite! Sauve qui peut!' They disappear in confused terror back from whence they came before Edward can raise his arm to fire at them.

‘Bugger it! Let them go. There’ll be plenty more bastards to choose from,’ Edward mutters. He has always hated the French for no reason that he could articulate. On hearing them shouting wildly in French, he regrets not firing into their fleeing backs. ‘Those bloody snail guzzlers! I should have bumped them off whilst I had the chance,’ he shouts as the traumatised couple run for their lives.

Edward looks up at the towering, smart buildings flanking the narrow street. Inquisitive, anxious faces of office workers slide into view at most of the windows, intent on finding out what has caused the sharp explosion. From the building directly opposite where Sam’s lifeless, bloodied body lies with the top of its skull missing. The windows are quickly lined with more agitated, horrified faces. It is the office of a rival advertising agency to where Claire and Pauline work. Within a few seconds, dozens of hands stretch out to grab telephones to summon the emergency services.

More than half of the workers lining the windows are filming the murder scene on their smart phones, intent on posting them on social media, it being the modern-day, knee-jerk reaction to every event. Most of the people who have filmed the body of Sam think better than to download it, but some keep it as a personal record of the closest they have come to a murder. They are sensitive enough to be mindful of the feelings of anyone who might have known the dead stranger not to post it in public arenas like Twitter, Facebook or Instagram.

Two male, amateur filmmakers have no such sensitivities. They shock and appal their online followers on their social media with their gory video clips of dead, horrifically damaged Sam. Contrary to what the two men have wished for, namely more followers, they lose many of their more squeamish followers.

Several of the more sensible, alert witnesses take accurate videos of the gunman. Their swift action comes in very handy when the police eventually arrive to resolve the tense situation.

It gives them a good idea of the weapon that Edward carries, although, at this point, they are unaware that he has a second, loaded, handgun in the pocket of his beige, baggy shorts. However, they know that this could be a possibility.

# A bit about Edward

Three days before the shooting, Edward had been doing a great deal of muttering to himself on the train from Manchester to London. 'It doesn't matter a hoot whether I escape afterwards or not. My fucking life is fucking over in anyway,' he jabbered, loud enough to be heard.

His behaviour caused a middle-aged, Indian woman in an expensive suit to frown and look at him accusingly. Edward met her disapproving stare and refused to let it go. She was finally forced to lower her eyes in submission.

The woman turned to her husband and said in Urdu, hoping that the strange man opposite them would not understand, 'This is where care in the community seriously falls short.'

Her husband whispered back in Urdu, 'I agree. Too many mentally unstable folk are left to wander wherever they like to upset the rest of us. Better be quiet, just in case he's an expert in speaking Urdu.'

'I doubt that very much. He doesn't look like he knows what day it is, let alone understand what we've just said about him,' she replied.

'He might be playing it cool. Phew! He really stinks of stale sweat and mouldy clothes. What a pong! So glad we're getting off the train soon,' her husband said, taking a peppermint out of his pocket to try to mask the smell of the gibbering stranger. Eventually, they made their escape and were able to breathe marginally sweeter air; the outskirts of London can be fairly malodorous.

On his first night in London, Edward had booked himself into a cheap, rundown bed and breakfast establishment near to where his nephew was attending a management course. He badly needed a shower, but the water pressure was pathetically weak so he did not bother. On the second night, he booked into a hotel, knowing there was every chance that he would no longer need his limited cash after wiping out his money-grubbing nephew. He felt that he would most likely soon be dead. He wallowed in the depths of a luxurious bubble bath, emerging smelling fresher than he had done for months. His body's sweeter odour sadly did not last long, as he was soon sweating with nervous energy, knowing what lay ahead of him if all went to plan.

It was essential that Sam should not spot him as he monitored the youth's movements to try to work out the best place and time to destroy him. If Sam were to notice him then the game would be up. The penultimate meeting of nephew and uncle was when Edward had stayed briefly at his half-brother, Charlie's house down in the depths of Cornwall. He had visited them a few months after they had discovered that their mother, Florence had as good as stabbed Edward through the heart by unexpectedly disinheriting him.

To Edward's fury, when his mother's Will had been read out, it was clear that his crazy mother had disinherited him because his name was never mentioned. However, she had chosen not to disinherit Charlie, who had always been her favourite son by far. In the Will, it was made clear that in the future, Charlie was to eventually be heaped with even more bounteous gifts.

Marcus was Edward's stepfather and Charlie's biological father. On Marcus's death, Florence had decreed that only Charlie should inherit the sprawling family home set in its own woods in one of the most popular parts of Jersey. Naturally, Marcus would not be cruelly thrown out onto the street now that his wife was dead, even though he was wealthy enough in his own right to have afforded his own comfortable pile. The property was in slight need of modernisation, but because of its enviable position overlooking a picturesque bay and the fact it was a very large plot of land, the property was worth at least a couple of million pounds. It could even be demolished and a hotel constructed on the site, making the property even more valuable. Space has always been at a premium on the small island and its sandy shores are a haven for many millionaires, pricing the ordinary, Jersey-born natives out of the house-buying market.

Like lemmings, both Edward and Charlie had left the beautiful yet overstuffed island in their late teens to seek further education and to find their fortunes in England, as do so many of the island's youth.

On Marcus's death, the spread in Jersey would become the property of Charlie, with Edward never to be allowed a look in. Any children that childless Edward might have sired in the future would also have been automatically disinherited by their vicious grandmother. Charlie's children and grandchildren would prosper, whereas Edward and any of his future heirs would all remain comparative paupers. Charlie had been given a hand up in the world, with all of his financial worries immediately ended.

By contrast, Edward and any of his future heirs had been given a powerful kick in the genitals. Edward had no intention of producing offspring. However, the injustice of what had happened to the future prospects of his imaginary, unborn child at Florence's dead hand eventually, drop by poisonous drop, drove him further out of his already challenged mind. A potent cocktail of hurt, envy, injustice and anger will eventually do that to a person.

The losing hand dealt to him by his mother became too much for Edward to endure. 'It's the principle of the thing,' was a phrase oft repeated when he told anyone brave enough to listen to his life story, detailing the life of purgatory that his mother had sentenced him to.

'I am the disowned, the dispossessed,' he would rant. His reluctant audience usually looked at him with concerned pity whilst his eyes sparked with anger. They could usually tell that he was becoming unhinged and opted to give him a wide berth in future. Florence's cruel actions gnawed away at his innards, no matter how hard he tried to push the hurt from his mind. 'It can never be rectified, because my mother is now dead. How can I now argue with her to convince her of the enormity of her actions on my life?' he would ask, his guts churning with bitterness.

'You should put it all behind you and move on. You can't let it ruin your life. Don't forget, the best revenge on someone is to be happy,' were all phrases often trotted out by caring, positive-thinking folk who could not stand to see Edward's pain.

'Easier said than done,' he would say.

Even if she had remained alive, he knew that his mother had been such a heartless sadist where he was concerned that she could never have been persuaded to bequeath him his rightful dues. Florence had planned to cause trouble in death as effectively as she had always revelled in causing mischief whilst alive.

Her sadistic streak was an integral part of her complex, undiagnosed mental condition, a psychosis that had transferred to her eldest son, Edward. It had lain mostly dormant inside his brain, popping out increasingly over the years. The mental illness had erupted full force after he was disinherited and disowned in his late forties.

Although Edward's disinheritance was unexpected by everyone, especially Edward, it was the sort of irrational, hurtful behaviour that his mother had displayed towards him and his father, Gregory. Edward's father had realised that his young wife, Florence was emotionally unstable early on in their marriage. She had wrongly accused him of cheating with one of her best, long-suffering, female friends whilst brutally attacking his head and shoulders with a heavy, ornate hairbrush in their bedroom.

'Ouch! Lay off me, you mad mare! I was only talking to Mags about her holiday in Sardinia. I've never cheated on you in my life,' Gregory had said, trying to grasp his wife's wrists as the blows rained down on his upper body.

'That's a likely bloody story! I've seen the way you look at her,' Florence had screamed, her green eyes flashing dangerously. Gregory could see no love in those eyes, only a ferocious, burning hatred and something else that he could only identify as insanity.

'Calm down, woman. You're literally foaming at the mouth,' Gregory had replied, managing at last to take the brush away from her. He had looked at his beautiful, blonde wife as though she were a stranger, something he did increasingly as her paranoid fancies worsened over the few, unhappy years that they were married.

As her jealous, unfounded rants and physical attacks escalated, her husband had sought solace from her vicious tongue-lashings and physical assaults in the welcoming arms of a local, sympathetic barmaid. Megan was a buxom wench who opened her legs to many of the misunderstood husbands in the locality. His adultery only came to light after Gregory picked up a nasty dose of Chlamydia from Megan, which he unfortunately spread to his wife, who naturally became incandescent with rage.

His doctor's examination of his genitalia during Gregory's STD appointment unearthed a large lump on his patient's testicles which proved to be advanced case of virulent testicular cancer. Watching his father disintegrating daily had cruelly affected Edward. Although he had only turned five at the time of his father's death, he never forgot the image of that once strong, handsome man who he loved so much, lying in bed with pale, paper-thin skin, lack-lustre eyes, his thick, black hair gone, annihilated by the chemotherapy treatment.

Still livid with her husband for cheating, Florence had been put in an awkward position now that he was ill. She had wanted to throw him out of the house when his affair with the barmaid had been unearthed, but she would have looked ruthless in the eyes of society if she had cast a dying man out of the house. She made his last months on earth hellish, showing no warmth and doing the bare minimum to keep him alive.

Although only a small child, Edward would spend far more

time than Florence ever chose to spend in his father's airless bedroom. Gregory had reclined, suffering horribly in his sweat-soaked bed. Edward had often spent the night cuddled up in his father's double bed after Florence had taken over the guestroom as soon as Gregory's cheating had been exposed.

Edward had only been nine when Florence had thrown his father's adultery in Edward's face during one of their many rows. Her son was growing increasingly similar to her now deceased husband, a fact that riled Florence greatly, not that her son could do anything about the resemblance. Edward had the full mouth, thick, dark, curly hair, large brown eyes and hooked nose of his father and his tall body was as skinny as Gregory's had been.

With almost indecent haste after her husband's death, the new widow had seduced and remarried another wealthy man called Marcus. He had been an enemy of Gregory's from their school days on the island. The newlyweds had swiftly procreated and Charlie was soon born for Florence to dote on and worship. Five year-old Edward was mostly ignored, side-lined for being a product and reminder of Florence's past, unhappy marriage that had ended so grimly.

Marcus was corpulent due to his genes, a situation made worse by indulging in too many expensive restaurant meals with clients. The extra food treats that Florence foisted upon Charlie did her precious son no favours. Charlie soon became a chubby, docile boy who was bullied at school because of his size. Less favoured Edward did not experience that problem, although he had many other, far more damaging problems foisted upon him, courtesy of his neglectful, spiteful mother and hostile step-father.

Edward had not helped matters and further failed to endear himself to his mother and step-father by behaving like a young, argumentative hooligan, acting out his pain at the loss of his biological father and the subsequent lack of parental love and attention. His relationship with his mother and new father became increasingly toxic. It was made worse because

Florence wanted to spend all of her time pleasing her new husband, who was as selfish and self-indulgent a human being as his new wife. Marcus had no time to spend on the offspring of another man who he had never liked.

## Fried brain

As Edward entered the minefield of puberty, he acted much like many teenagers in the seventies. He identified with all of the tortured, mysterious loners throughout history, believing that he was a misunderstood, social outcast. He sought out likeminded peers and disappeared during school holidays and weekends to smoke cannabis and drop tabs of acid.

Drugs had a far worse effect on his inherited mental problems than it had on the brains of his companions. Edward's already imperfect brain never recovered from a particularly bad acid trip that he had dropped when he was seventeen.

One Friday evening in late summer, seventeen-year-old Edward had met up with Carl his closest school friend. Carl was a self-proclaimed outsider, although he had grown up in the care system after his parents died in a house fire that he had only just survived. He bore the scars from that fire both mentally and physically. Carl would have been a more attractive, young male if it were not for the burn marks down the left side of his face, neck and upper body. He was a tall, tanned, well-muscled youth with long, fair hair that he let flop over his face in an attempt to cover his scars.

That summer evening in the seventies, the two, teenage boys had planned to meet up on a nearby beach with two girls from their school for an illicit, drug-fuelled party.

'Trust the girls to be late. Typical! I'm not dropping the tabs until they arrive,' said Carl, sitting down on the dry sand under the high, pink, granite wall that sheltered them from the prying eyes of any motorists using the coast road.

Both boys wore identical blue, flared jeans and long-sleeved tie-dyed tee-shirts that barely reached their navels. A warm breeze blew through the boys' long hair and the warmth of the granite wall felt comforting against their backs as they casually laid up against it to wait for their female companions.

‘I’ll be back in a tick,’ said Edward, getting to his feet and strolling nonchalantly over the crunching pebbles towards the lapping, salty waves. Hidden from the view of motorists by giant rocks, he unzipped his jeans and urinated into one of the rock pools.

‘Too lazy to walk to the public toilets over there are you?’ Carl called out as Edward returned to where Carl was still lounging.

‘Rebel, that’s me,’ Edward replied, laughing mischievously. Edward rarely laughed, having little reason to, but Carl occasionally brought a more humorous side out in him.

As the sun gradually died away, the distant rocks looked more and more like dinosaurs or mythical monsters. Soon, the most visible object on the beach was the glowing tip of the joint that the teenagers were passing back and forth to each other.

‘At long, bloody last! I think that’s Tracy and Moo walking down the slipway. I can see the glow of their ciggies. Moo’s wearing that white top again, so I reckon it’s them,’ said Carl, waving both arms above his head so that the girls could see where they were.

He did not want to shout out to tell the girls where they were, as it would not have seemed cool in front of Moo, Carl’s love interest. He had high hopes that Moo would let him feel her up again like she had once before when she had worn the same white, cheesecloth, halter-neck top on her first date with him.

Giggling with anticipation, the two girls reached where Carl and Edward were leaning against the wall. The citrus smell of Tracy’s Aqua Manda perfume mixed with the strong odour from the seaweed bordering the shoreline. The tide was moving its relentless way up the pebbled sand. However, from years of experience the teenagers were confident that they would not be chased off that particular Jersey beach by the incoming tide. They only chose to meet up on that beach when they were certain the weather would be dry because there was nowhere to shelter if it had rained except a nearby smelly toilet.

It was usually a nightmare for the youth of the island to find places to meet up in Jersey during winter or when the weather was uninviting. At seventeen, Carl and Edward often risked being caught breaking the law whilst they drank in pubs or danced in the island's discos, but they had little option. Youth clubs were anathema to the friends because they smacked of goody two shoe adolescents. These clubs were too main stream and suffered from too much adult, often religious, interference. For the two teenage boys, excitement usually came at the expense of breaking the law.

That late evening was perfect for a night of drug taking under the stars and also for trying to persuade their two, female companions to have sex with them. All four teenagers sitting on the beach were virgins, but each was deeply curious about the mysteries of sex.

'I brought my travel rug, just as you asked,' Tracy said to Edward, removing the large, tartan rug from her plastic bag and laying it onto the sand.

She sat cross-legged next to Edward, her long, hippie skirt covering her bare legs. Similarly dressed Moo also sat next to Edward, with Carl on the other side of her. If by some miracle anything sexual was about to happen, it was thought that it would probably occur between Moo and Carl. Edward and Tracy would be coupled, by default, even though they had not yet kissed, although they both secretly believed that kissing, and probably more, would happen that night.

Carl was already eying up Moo's tightly-packed, white top. He remembered how thrilling she had felt a week before when she had graciously allowed him to grope in the back row of the Forum cinema during a screening of recently released film, 'Easy Rider.' He had caught Moo waving and smiling at one of the boys sitting with a group of equally rough looking males in the back row during intermission and was livid.

'What did you go waving at him for? If you'd rather be with him than me, then go ahead, feel free,' Carl said angrily to her through gritted teeth. 'Wait until those yobs have gone. I don't want to run into trouble outside the cinema.'

He barely kissed her before she caught her bus home alone feeling miserable. However, they grew friendly again over the following days and arranged to meet up that Sunday at Anne Port Bay for a double date with Edward and Tracy.

On the moonlit, empty beach, Carl was already groping Moo when Edward rather petulantly said, 'Are we going to drop the acid tabs now or not even bother?' He was feeling angry after Tracy had coyly pushed his hand away when he had tried to copy Carl's bold, exploratory move on Moo.

'Yeh, why not? You girls are game to drop a tab of acid each, aren't you?' Carl asked, realising that his friend was getting nowhere with his designated girl.

Not wishing to appear to be spoilsports, both girls nodded their approval in the moonlight, although they were secretly slightly scared by what might happen after swallowing the tabs of acid. It was always hit or miss whether they would be lucky enough to experience a good trip, or unlucky and be thrown into what could be a waking nightmare. From the quartet's recent conversations with more experienced drug users, the type of trip one could expect seemed to depend on the state of mind of the person at the time of ingesting their LSD-soaked blotting paper.

Edward was the most anxious person of the four before they all swallowed the drug. A few hours before, he had endured a particularly upsetting row with his mother, who had picked a fight with him over the state of his bedroom. She had picked on him just so that she could scream abuse at him and slap his face to make herself feel better. Self-harmers gain relief from their tension build ups and stresses by perhaps slicing their inner thighs or arms with razor blades. Florence gained her stress relief by hurting Edward emotionally and physically.

As the four waited for the drugs to kick in, they lay on their backs on the travel rug, smoking cigarettes because they had sadly run out of cannabis to roll more joints. Tracy had brought along a bottle of wine and a corkscrew that she had stolen from her father's drinks cabinet. They took turns at swigging from it. The cannabis had worked its magic on Moo and she was only partly aware that Carl had pulled her top up. With Edward lying as close to Moo on the rug as Carl was, he could not believe his luck at being offered a free show.

Moo offered no resistance, much to the surprise of her more reticent girlfriend, who was beginning to feel rather left out and neglected. Judging by Edward's heavy breathing, Tracy could tell that Edward was enjoying the sight of his friend playing with Moo's breasts. Tracy sensed that Edward would probably soon give up trying to get anywhere with her and join Carl in playing with Moo if the ice queen did not loosen up a tad.

Scared of being completely ignored, Tracy decided to up her game and whispered to a transfixed Edward, 'So, when am I going to get a look in?'

Edward was shocked but delighted because he had never expected Tracy to be bold enough to bestow on him much more than just a kiss. As she lay back on the rug with her arms folded behind her head, he tentatively rolled her blue, flowery top upwards until it was scrunched up under her chin to match Moo's top.

Edward sat up and leant on one elbow. Soon, he was mimicking what Carl was doing to Moo. Not wanting to be outdone by her friend, Tracy decided to go one better and lifted her long skirt. Inexperienced, virginal Edward discovered to his surprise and confusion that his hand had been placed in between her bare legs.

'This is all getting a bit out of control. I'm not entirely sure what I'm supposed to do next,' Edward thought.

Both girls seemed to be trying to outdo each other, as were both boys. All four of them were pretty clueless about what sex entailed but they seemed to be discovering together at the same time, loosened up by the drugs. It was as though they were still in class at school, all learning human biology the practical way.

As Carl and Moo were far too preoccupied with exploring each other's bodies to pay attention to him, Edward unzipped his jeans, slid them off and threw them onto the sand next to Carl's discarded flares.

Strange thoughts were brewing inside all of their brains as the acid gradually took effect. Edward sensed that Tracy's breasts seemed to be growing and taking on a life of their own. He looked down the beach and was alarmed to see that the dinosaur rocks near the water's edge seemed to be ominously moving towards them.

Before he could stare at them any longer and run from danger, Tracy pulled him down onto the rug and pushed his shocked face towards her naked pubic area. Even though it was now night time, the sight of her nakedness suddenly terrified him. The acid in his body made her look like some unknown threatening, fabled beast, fearful to behold.

'I'm sorry, I can't do this,' Edward said solemnly, jumping to his feet and pulling on his jeans. He started running up the beach towards the slipway which led onto the pitch black, winding coastal road.

'Where the fuck is he going?' shouted Tracy at Carl's moonlit face. To Tracy's drug-confused brain, Carl's scarred face looked robotic, shining silver in the moonlight.

Carl said, 'I'm too messed up by this acid to go chasing after the fool. I'm sure he'll be fine.' Not content with playing with just Moo, Carl's hands started to wander in between Tracy's legs. He wanted to reassure her that he had no intention of making her feel left out and because he felt he could get away with it.

By the end of that night Carl, Tracy and Moo could no longer call themselves virgins. Edward, however, was still very much of one, although he had experimented more than he had ever done before with any girl. Whilst Carl experienced his first threesome at the age of seventeen, Edward went on to endure one of the scariest nights of his life.

The sight of Tracy's naked body had triggered a very bad trip indeed inside Edward's brain. As he trudged away from his friends along the moonlit beach, everything around him took on a hostile aura. A large rock on the waterline morphed into a disembodied head to his terrified eyes. The crunch of the seaweed sounded like the shattering bones of baby birds. By the time he reached the coast road above the beach wall, the sight of the trees lining the sweeping, narrow road, rooted his feet to the spot.

'Oh no, more monsters,' he cried out loud to the moon that looked down like a disapproving wraith.

The road was not much used, even in the daytime, but it was completely deserted that night. The only illumination shone down from the ghost above. Edward stood shakily on the high, granite wall above the beach, looking towards where his three friends should have been. He could see the moving shapes of their naked bodies and could hear distant moans as they climaxed in turn. To Edward, they sounded like a Minotaur, devouring maidens in its labyrinth.

As he stared in horrified fascination down at the troubling, erotic scene below him, he suddenly felt a hot rush of energy flood into his brain. His penis was a writhing serpent. Tracy could see his silhouette against the moon and shouted out, 'Come back and join in the fun, Ed. You don't know what you're missing.'

He could not immediately make out her words. Once he understood her meaning through his drugged state, he decided it might be safer back on the beach with them rather than up on the roadside surrounded by all the dark, swaying tree monsters.

In keeping with ancient legends, Edward believed that he might be Mercury, the winged messenger. With a confident smile, he spread his wings and launched his body upwards into the darkness, intent on flying down onto to the sand. There was a shriek from Tracy followed by a dull thud as Edward landed flat on his face fifteen feet below the wall, gritty sand forcing itself into every facial orifice. He was lucky that there had been no rocks beneath him, but even so his hooked nose felt broken and one arm was twisted at an impossible angle beneath his twitching body. The pain was intensified and muddled by the drugs.

His naked friends rushed towards him where he lay in the sand. In a flash, their acid trips had switched from glorious to horrible.

'Christ, are you alright? Don't move. It looks nasty,' said Carl, his stomach churning at remembering the thudding sound Edward's body had made as it walloped the ground.

Tracy had been feeling disgruntled because Carl had paid Moo more attention than her. She had been on the edge of a bad trip and Edward's accident pushed her and her friends over the edge into nightmare territory. It had felt euphoric during the early stages of the beach orgy, but now she started to laugh and cry simultaneously, until Moo slapped her friend's face to break the hysteria.

'Shut up, Tracy. You'll wake the people in that house opposite. There's a call box further up the road. You two, stay with Ed, whilst I go and phone for an ambulance. There's no way we can walk him home with his arm busted up like that. Do either of you girls have a tissue for his nose in your bags? It's pouring blood,' Carl asked.

'I've only got a sanitary pad in my bag, but that'll have to do,' said Moo, taking one from its wrapper and dabbing the blood away. The three, naked teenagers rapidly dressed, struggling to cope with the situation made even more challenging by the group being in the powerful grip of LSD.

'I can't move. I think I've buggered my back up as well,' said Edward, rightly guessing that his back injury would cause him permanent difficulty.

Edward was so badly injured and flying so high on drugs that he did not recognise his friends or realise where he was.

When the ambulance drove up onto the slipway, the teenagers all tried to act as normally as they could to hide their drug taking activities. However, it soon became clear to the ambulance crew who were carrying Edward on a stretcher up from the beach and into the back of the ambulance that all four teenagers were tripping out of their skulls on acid.

'More damned hippies. These hot, summer nights always bring them out of the woodwork,' the ambulance driver moaned to his colleague as they delivered a screaming, gibbering Edward to A&E. He had badly damaged several vertebrae which prevented him from walking for six months and delayed him sitting A-levels until the following year.

His mother was livid that she had to endure her least favourite son lazing around the house for months. It took a supreme effort on her part to act maternally towards him to nurse him back to health. Just as she had acted with his dying father, Florence did the bare minimum to help her eldest son's recovery. What little she did was carried out with ill grace and large doses of martyrdom.

Edward was left in no doubt that Florence hated every minute of her enforced role as a somewhat sadistic Florence Nightingale. His right arm was also badly broken and took months to recover. Edward's already hooked nose was now permanently bent at an odd angle after his attempt to fly, which did nothing to improve his dealings with the opposite sex.

His mother had been incandescent with rage with him after learning how Edward had received his injuries. Every time she looked at him, he reminded her of Gregory, her cheating first husband, returned from the grave to torment her. She was not the only person to notice her eldest son's behaviour becoming increasingly strange after his drug-fuelled flight from the top of the beach wall. It was an indication of just how bizarre Edward's behaviour must have become, if a mentally disturbed woman thought him odd.

The worst of Edward's damage was invisible to the naked eye. His brain came off worst on that night on the beach, with frequent flashbacks and visions of hostile monsters cropping up in his head at random times. When his rebellious brain allowed Edward to think lucidly, he bitterly regretted dropping acid on that fateful night. He had been tipped over a precipice into an abyss, both in reality and metaphorically. He developed debilitating, embarrassing, panic attacks which appeared out of nowhere in any place at any time. These panic attacks made his heart race, his body sweat and his mouth go dry. Sadly, they never left him and added to his difficulties with integrating into the world, like an ill-fitting jigsaw piece.

Florence and Marcus were grateful when Edward eventually recovered sufficiently from his injuries to resume his habit of spending his waking hour away from their house. It meant an end to having to deal with his moods and tantrums, leaving them free to self-indulgently wallow in their considerable wealth on the so-called millionaire island. There were always plenty of empty bottles of alcohol for the bin men to remove from outside their property from all the lavish dinner parties with likeminded people.

Edward and Carl had left school forever months earlier and still felt light-headed with the heady taste of freedom. Carl joined Edward at Manchester University to also study electrical engineering alongside his friend. It was miraculous that they had gained high enough grades to be accepted to study anywhere but they had scraped through their exams after doing the least amount of work possible to achieve their goal.

'Do you fancy going to the pub this evening, Carl? My parents are having another crappy dinner party tonight. They've ordered me to stay out of the way, not that I want anything to do with their vacuous, fake friends in any case. What a bunch of tossers they are,' Edward asked his friend as they left the island's main library after taking out set books to prepare for their forthcoming university courses.

'Sure, mate. You can hardly blame them for wanting you out of the house after what you did to their posh friend's car a few weeks ago,' Carl replied, chuckling as he remembered

Edward's animated retelling of the incident.

'Yes, it was pretty spectacular,' Edward said with a wry grin, reliving how he had wedged some of their Alsatian dog's excrement inside the shiny exhaust pipe of the silver Mercedes.

The car belonged to his mother's best friend, high-fashion store owner, Camille and her insipid, chinless husband. Edward had always hated the couple and had waited for years to burst their self-satisfied bubble.

'That'll teach mum and Marcus to keep on asking me and not Charlie to pick up all of our dog's stinking shit from the lawn. They know how bending down to scoop it up hurts my back. They gave me such a bollocking for my little prank, but it was well worth all of the grief,' he added as they both rolled around laughing.

# The good boy

Unlike Edward, Charlie never caused his parents a moment's worry. He was always studious, well-behaved, obsequious and home-loving. One of the many reasons that Edward often kept away from the homestead was so he did not have to stomach witnessing his younger half-brother's sycophantic behaviour when around their parents. Charlie had always attended the only public, all-male school on the island, whereas Edward had been sent to the mixed, local, state school.

Marcus had refused to pay for the education of another man's child, especially Gregory's child, a man that he had despised. Charlie's many academic successes were rewarded and praised far more than Edward's average achievements, which went mostly unnoticed by their parents. Edward's large, now bent nose was pushed increasingly out of joint as he progressed through life. He wished that his fragile mind would not rebel against him, which happened more frequently and violently since dropping acid at Anne Port Bay. His back caused him constant pain, but he knew that he had nobody else to blame for that damage except himself.

If, years later, Edward had not become so mentally destroyed by firstly being ostracised then eventually disinherited by the woman who should have cared for him, there might have been a chance of holding down a job. However, it was doubtful that he could have ever gained as lucrative a role as Charlie had landed. Charlie became the owner-manager of a Cornish seafood restaurant, partly bought with the money bequeathed to him in their mother's Will. Like Edward and most of the youth on Jersey, Charlie had crossed the narrow strip of water to further his education and establish a career.

As a student, Charlie had met Lara on a night out in Exeter with the other lads on his business management degree course. She was a flirtatious, statuesque, blonde woman who could smell money when she sat on his lap and sniffed Charlie's aftershave at the nightclub. She set about the task of sinking her painted talons into him. He had been flattered by such an attractive woman, who had a hint of Scandinavia about her, throwing her bosomy body at his portly frame. On the first night that they met, after much teasing and flattery she managed to manoeuvre herself into his bed and later into his heart. Sadly, he never won hers. Lara always had a green eye peeled for flirty fun outside of her relationship with besotted, boring Charlie. The only attractive part of him was the money and the expensive gifts that he showered upon her.

All too soon, Charlie realised that he could no longer do without Lara in his bed. He suffered a moment of weakness and married her. The newly-weds moved to one of the most popular, moneyed areas of Cornwall where he put his business management degree into action. He bought a seafood restaurant with money loaned to him by his parents.

Years later he poured more money into the business after he was named main beneficiary of his mother's Will. The same document wrenched the guts out of Edward's body and left him a bitter, bubbling cauldron of resentment.

Edward could never stomach eating at his brother's Cornish seafood restaurant because it reminded him of how badly Edward had always been treated. He sadly could not always avoid visiting Charlie's home which nestled on the Cornish coast.

Edward had no time for Lara because he sensed that she had no real love for his half-brother, but was merely using him to live the high life. She had deigned to half-heartedly help him to launch the restaurant, occasionally working front of house, but never anything too strenuous. She enjoyed lording it over the restaurant staff and particularly appreciated spending time with the male staff. She ensured that easily manipulated Charlie always employed attractive males for her to flirt with in order to spice up the few hours that she worked there.

'Perhaps Lara will be Charlie's punishment for being the

spoilt, over-privileged, favourite of the family. Bloody well serves him right,' Edward thought on one of his rare visits to Charlie's home.

He was conscious of Lara's eyes appraising his body as he lay on a sun lounger by their pool. Chunky Charlie was suffering with prickly heat on another sun lounger; his strawberry-blonde hair and fair skin did not respond well to the sun. Swimwear did not suit his wobbly, bulging belly as much as it suited Edward's taller, leaner frame. Lara was well aware of that fact and enjoyed flirting with her brother-in-law whenever he stayed with them. Charlie only ever witnessed the playful flirting and so he saw no real harm in it. However, he would have been horrified to have heard the lewd comments that his wife made to Edward when Charlie was out of earshot.

# Hardly a love story

From an early age, Edward had not actively shied away from working during the school holidays. He needed the money and it helped to keep him away from his mother. To his dismay, each time that he landed a job, either his erratic behaviour, or, later on, his damaged spine and drug-frazzled brain made it impossible for any employer to keep him on their pay role. Despite his best efforts, he would argue with anyone for little reason, be they colleagues, customers or even his employers. From the age of twelve, he tried his hand at many of the usual holiday jobs that schoolboys opted for on the island during the long, summer holidays.

His stint at working in the beach café near to his family's home lasted all of two days. He lost his patience and was sacked for shouting at one of the Portuguese staff for putting sandy trays into his clean cutlery water. He took the rest of that summer off, too angry over the sacking. Another summer holiday job only lasted a week when he lost his temper with the ice cream he was trying to scoop out of tubs for customers in a local freezer centre.

Edward told Carl what happened as they rode on the top deck of the bus into the main shopping area in St Helier, the capital of Jersey. 'The bloody ice cream was far too solid and wouldn't scoop out quickly enough for my liking. Trying to dig it out of the tubs made my arm muscles ache and I swore a fair bit. A few of the customers complained about my swearing to my boss and he showed me the door. The sacking made me swear even more, right into my employer's fat face.'

'You're becoming a bit of a legend, you badass,' Carl said, laughing uproariously at his friend's antics.

Edward sat stony-faced then said, 'I did not plan to be sacked. It just sort of happened.'

'Lighten up, dude. At least we get to chill for a couple of months rather than working our butts off in this heat,' Carl replied. He was often confused by his friend's response to situations. What Carl found funny, Edward would occasionally take the wrong way. If Carl had not been almost as much of a social outcast as his friend, he might have avoided him, but they were dependent on each other for emotional support.

There was much the same disastrous outcome when Edward had started studying towards an electronic engineering degree at Manchester University when he and Carl were in their early twenties. He lasted only two months on the course after an unfortunate incident with Janine Polson, who was studying for an English Literature Degree at the same university.

Unlike Jersey-born Edward, she was a native of Manchester and had chosen a university that was close to her parent's home. Janine could have picked a university in another county, but her father was very ill with motor neurone disease and she wanted to be close to him.

Edward and Janine had met one evening in the student union bar of the university, the scene of many a budding student romance. Like most men in their twenties, Edward's male hormones were a raging cauldron of desire that needed to be satisfied. His black, straight hair was long and he sported a moustache and beard as many young males grew in the seventies. His thin, tall frame suited his wardrobe of tie-dyed tee-shirts and frayed denim jeans. He had taken to wearing a midnight blue, velvet cloak, which gave him a travelling vagabond look, one which was attractive to many females in the seventies.

When Janine spotted this flamboyant, eccentric figure from across the smoky bar, she assumed from his bohemian appearance that he must be enrolled on an arts course just as she was. Being a confident girl, she tossed her long, dark locks over her bare shoulders, pulled her clingy, sleeveless top further down in order to reveal more of her ample, creamy cleavage. She sidled up next to him where he stood talking quietly to his only friend, Carl.

‘As it’s Fresher’s week, I thought I’d be proactive and come over to say hello to you. I’m Janine,’ the buxom, dark-eyed girl said confidently, targeting Edward and ignoring his more physically attractive, but less enigmatic companion.

Edward was taken aback by the attractive, tall girl’s bold entrance, because approaches by good-looking females never happened to him. He was much shyer and more introverted than Janine but he was delighted to be singled out for her special attention. He had always loved looking at big-breasted girls although he had only once managed to progress slightly further than just looking. He had managed to bag only one girlfriend in the past, which was very unusual when, at that time, he was living in the age of free love and sexual freedom.

His odd, aggressive manner had soon put paid to his relationship with his first and only girlfriend. He was still technically a virgin on his first day at university, although he had gratefully fumbled around with his only date since the Tracy debacle. The girl had devastated him by calling a rapid halt to proceedings after only a few kisses.

Whilst at school in Jersey, Edward had nervously asked a few girls out on dates, but their friends usually warned them off dating him with tales of his strange, disturbing behaviour. With Jersey being so small, rumours spread like bush fires. This led to Edward’s label of ‘weirdo’ being almost impossible to shake off. It sentenced him to spending hours upstairs in his bedroom, browsing through well-worn copies of Playboy and other similar magazines available in the late sixties for sexual relief.

His mother had found his secret stash under his socks inside his bottom drawer and waited for him to return from school. As soon as he had strolled in oblivious to what lay ahead, Florence had viciously hit her son twice across his startled face and triumphantly shoved the lurid photographs of naked women under his nose. She then belittled him in front of Charlie and Marcus before angering Edward by cruelly forcing him to stand next to her and watch as she set fire to his collection in the garden incinerator.

'You disgusting little pervert! You're as bad as your father was. Don't ever let me catch filth like this in your bedroom ever again,' she had screamed in his face, so that the rest of the family and the neighbours could hear his humiliation.

As the smoke from the magazines stung his dark eyes, Charlie and Marcus could see there was a red hand print on his pale cheek and a deep cut below his lip where her wedding ring had caught him. The small scar gradually faded over the years but never entirely vanished, making him feel as though he had been branded by his mother, marking him as her property to use, abuse and discard whenever she chose.

Edward remained self-conscious of the scar below his lip, especially when around attractive females. He had grown a beard and moustache as soon as he was physically able to in order to hide the disfigurement. In reality, the scar was barely noticeable, but to insecure, paranoid Edward it always felt enormous and he was certain everyone was staring at it.

Forgetting that the scar was now hidden behind his dark beard, habit and nerves forced Edward to automatically lift his hand up to his mouth when he replied to Janine. 'Hi, Janine, my name's Edward,' was all that he mumbled with the faintest of smiles on his lips. Another of his crippling insecurities was the appearance of his top teeth because they crossed at the front, so he often shielded them with his hand when he felt that a smile or laugh might be brewing.

A lesser girl would have given up and walked off after working out that the lanky youth seemed to be a fairly useless prospect, but Janine found Edward's appearance and manner intriguing. If he had not been wearing the cape, she would not have been quite so excited to unearth more about him. She was much encouraged to notice that Edward smelt strongly of patchouli oil, just as she did. There was a Byronic aura about this student to Janine's book-loving eyes. Her eyes had devoured much of Byron's work before she had applied for the English Literature course in her hometown.

Sensing that this shy, reticent youth would need to be drawn out of his protective shell before she could talk easily to him, she prodded him with further questions. She asked, 'So Edward, which course are you on? I'm studying English Literature. It's going well so far, although it's early days. The amount of reading that I must do by next week is pretty daunting.'

'Electronic engineering,' Edward replied, too tongue-tied by the sight of her large, pale breasts bursting from above her skimpy top.

The tall, buxom brunette had also not gone unnoticed by Carl and several other randy young males in the bar. Harry, a rugby playing, ginger student studying French, had dated her the previous week. However, she had told him that sadly he was not her type of boy, being too clean-cut and sporty. Janine had ever since avoided the disappointed, flame-haired student as much as was feasibly possible.

Harry was now watching her mournfully from across the bar as she attempted to talk to Edward, desperately wanting to repeat the delicious experience of their first date, followed by some passionate, urgent love making if only she could be persuaded. He looked enviously at Edward, wondering what Janine found so attractive in his new, odd-looking rival.

Leaning closer to Edward to deliberately treat him to an even more expansive view of her deep cleavage, she remarked, 'Electronic engineering? How dull! I pictured you being on some kind of arts course like I am. All wrapped up in that cloak, you look like an artist or a writer or something similar. Aren't you sweating hot wearing it? I'm boiling down here in the bar and that's with me wearing hardly anything.'

'My cloak comforts me,' Edward replied. He could have told her much more about his cloak, but he prudently kept quiet because his ramblings would probably have alarmed her.

Edward had been tempted to inform Janine that it was really his cloak of invisibility, which was how he liked to think of it. He would have been ecstatic if the deep-blue, velvet cape really had made him invisible to the world, but sadly this was not the case. He had bought it from a second-hand shop the year before leaving Jersey. When his mother shrieked loudly with derisive laughs on seeing him wearing it, he vowed to wear it all the more, just to rile her.

'Who the hell do you think you are flapping around like some deranged Dracula?' Florence had mocked, making Marcus and Charlie roar with laughter. Edward had merely glowered at them and walked off to his room, his cloak swirling dramatically behind him. In the solitude of his bedroom, he had lifted one arm, with elbow crooked so that only his dark, pained eyes showed dramatically over his cloaked arm. He stared into the mirror whilst utilising his best Dracula pose and said, 'I wish that I had no reflection, like a true vampire. I am indeed one of the un-dead.'

He became so attached to the cloak that he rarely went out in public without it slung over his shoulders. He also wore it indoors, even when alone. Given the chance, he would have slept in it, like Dracula wrapped in his daytime coffin. Only fear that the material might become smelly and damaged prevented Edward from wrapping himself in it like a shroud each night. At night, it would reside majestically over the back of his bedroom chair, so that Edward could gain some comfort from glimpsing it if he ever woke up in the early hours.

In essence, his cloak became a glorified security blanket, although he looked far more like Dracula than Linus. It was one of his many, increasingly strange eccentricities, all tell-tale signs of the burden of his mother's deep-rooted, psychotic genes that lurked inside the body of her eldest son. As he aged, Edward often wondered whether the mutual, enduring hatred between his mother and himself was due to their psychological similarities more than to their differences. He looked so much like his cheating father, Gregory that everyone expected him to also have his father's character traits, not his mother's. Charlie was more like Marcus in every way, body and nature. This meant that Florence had no cause to clash in the same way with her youngest son, not like she constantly clashed with Edward. She felt no guilt whatsoever for her favouritism; on the contrary, she revelled in it.

'Hey, wakey wakey, love! You look as though your mind is a hundred miles away,' Janine said in her broad Manchester accent.

Edward was in fact hundreds of miles away, inside the kitchen of his childhood, listening to his mother's shrill voice admonish and deride him as the rest of the family looked on. Neither Charlie nor Marcus ever stood up for Edward, who would become angrier to see Charlie gloating over his sibling's distress. From early childhood and beyond, the word 'unfair' figured evermore frequently in Edward's vocabulary and thoughts. He disliked his own self-pitying attitude, but from his experience, life had indeed been very unfair to him, increasing to unbearably high levels of unfairness and inequality as time progressed.

'Oh, sorry, I was just thinking about something,' Edward replied, smiling guiltily, conscious how greatly his southern accent differed from Janine's northern twang.

He snapped back into the present, mindful that an all-too rare opportunity with this attractive girl might be squandered if he did not pay her more attention. She had called him 'love' which had made his ears straightway prick up and warmed his cold heart, despite him knowing that 'love' was a word Manchester women often called strangers. His immediate problem was that he did not know exactly how to deal with unexpected attention from such an attractive female. He prayed that she would take the initiative, which, luckily for him, is precisely what she did.

'This music is total shit, isn't it,' Janine observed, as The Sweet's latest record blasted out of the juke box.

'Totally! What fool decided to choose to play this bilge when they could have stuck on Hendrix or The Who?' Edward replied. He was glad to see that Carl had moved off to talk to a group of students by the door, leaving the coast clear for him and the luscious Janine.

'You've just mentioned two of my favourite groups,' she said. 'I knew that I was right to talk to you. Fancy going to sit at one of those tables over there?' She pointed towards an empty bank of tables in the shadows across the dimly lit room.

'Yes. Why not? I'll buy us both a couple of drinks as these are nearly done,' he said. He ordered a couple of half pints of ciders, as he did not yet know if it would be worth spending too much of his small grant on her.

'I'll buy the next refill,' she offered, much to Edward's relief.

He watched how invitingly her pert buttocks moved inside her tight, flared jeans as she walked in front of him to her chosen table and chairs in a dark, well-hidden, unpopulated corner. When he sat opposite her, she leaned forward and placed her bare elbows on the sticky table top, making him very aware of how close she was to him. His automatic reaction was to move backwards, retreating to the security of the chair back, unconsciously signalling that she was invading his personal space.

'I don't have B.O. you know, love,' she remarked with a snort of laughter.

Realising that he might appear unfriendly, he leaned forward, his intense, brown eyes meeting her larger, hazel, mischievous eyes. When she smiled widely at him with her perfect teeth, he nervously smiled back, trying not to display his crooked front teeth. When her hand later rested on his thigh under the table, he did not shift his leg from her grasp, although his first instinct was to snatch it out of her reach.

'My God, she's a fast worker,' he thought, startled to find himself praying that she would move her hand further up his thigh. His facial expressions betrayed his thoughts, as did his heavier breathing. Janine laughed quietly and slid her hand slightly further up his thigh. Edward could scarcely breathe with excitement.

'Shall I come and sit next to you rather than opposite you?

We can talk just as easily and it could be fun,' she said, grinning wickedly and unbuttoning the button on her jeans, much to his puzzlement. Then the penny dropped with a clang inside his brain.

Hoping that she meant what he thought she meant, he struggled to sound casual despite his rising excitement and said, 'Please yourself! It's a free country.' She stood up and slid onto the bench seat next to his quivering body.

It did not happen immediately. It was a full five minutes before her cool hand took his sweaty one and slid it under the table. There were no students nearby because it was early in the evening and many students were still eating in the university canteen. Nobody witnessed her placing his hand on her crotch. To his great surprise, his fingers touched bare flesh. Edward looked at her quizzically.

'I unzipped my jeans. As you can feel, I don't like wearing underwear,' she whispered, thrusting her hips upwards and sliding the jeans all the way down her slim thighs to below her knees. Luckily, the chairs opposite them were blocking the vision of anyone in the bar who might have glanced their way.

Edward needed no further prompting. As he talked gibberish to her so as to detract from what he was doing. On realising that nobody could see much in their dark corner, he became bolder and explored further.

'You're a wild one, aren't you, Janine?' he said as she struggled to keep a look of extreme pleasure from her pretty face.

After a few minutes of joint heavy breathing, she said, 'Wow, that was great!' Her hand grabbed for the button on his jeans and she whispered, 'It's your turn now.'

'No bloody chance! Not in here!' he said. The bar's music drowned out their voices so that fortunately only they could hear each other's passionate words.

'Do you fancy going to my room in the halls of residence?' she asked, confident as to what Edward's reply would be.

'Yes,' was all he managed to say, his desire making it too

difficult to utter anything more expansive.

He felt as though everyone on the planet knew exactly what he and Janine had done and were about to do. They walked quickly from the union bar out into the drizzle and across the campus towards the halls of residence. So many other students seemed to be milling about and Edward was conscious that each student could smell Janine on his fingers.

Janine seemed to delight in embarrassing him. She kissed him in a dark, narrow gap between two buildings, uncaring whether anyone could see her hand stroking him through his jeans. He was torn between asking her to stop and saying nothing. Words refused to escape his mouth. To his combined horror and delight, she slid his jeans and boxers down to his knees.

She asked, 'Do you like that then?'

'Don't touch me. I'm going to explode,' Edward groaned. 'Is this really happening to me?' he thought, delighted that it seemed to be very much happening.

Janine could clearly see that he meant what he said, but wickedly chose to ignore his desperate plea.

'I've got you where I want you,' she said, mischievously bending down. The erotic tableau was lit solely by the weak, yellowish light of a street lamp from across the quadrangle.

'Jesus Christ, God Almighty!' Edward moaned, trying with every fibre not to explode.

The girl knelt down as he peered anxiously from their inadequate hiding place up the alley, praying that nobody would spy them, especially a tutor. Janine quickly pulled up her skimpy top and lacy, black bra high under her chin so that he could admire her. Edward needed no further invitation. He lasted barely thirty seconds.

He leaned back against the wall, all strength deserting his shaking, pale legs. Suddenly remembering that his bottom half was still exposed to the world, he rapidly pulled up his boxers and jeans. Janine did not seem to mind being exposed and placed both his hands on her bare breasts, now slippery from the drips of rain and glistening under the street lamp.

'I love having sex in public, don't you?' she asked, looking down as he played awkwardly with her.

Edward kept quiet, not wishing to admit that it was his first public sex act and that he had almost collapsed with fear. He was far too occupied with worrying whether anyone could see them to reply.

The cold drizzle suddenly made Janine's half-naked body shiver. She said through chattering teeth, 'I'm bloody freezing. Let's hurry along to my room right now so we can continue this in private. You should hopefully have recovered your strength by then. I really need you to give me a thorough seeing to,' she said.

She kissed him, slightly irritated that he had not taken the initiative and kissed her first. 'Reckon I've bagged myself a bloody virgin. I'm not entirely sure whether that's a good or bad thing, but let's see what he can do for me,' she thought. Janine usually preferred more experienced males than Edward.

Janine was still keen for action, so she led him back to her small, single room and stripped them both naked. She pushed him backwards onto her single bed and handing him a packet of condoms.

'I'm not on the Pill after I had a bad reaction to taking it. I hope you don't mind using a condom,' she said, noticing his worried look as she handed it to him. He had to use all of his concentration as it was the first time he had ever been fortunate enough to have occasion to wear one.

'There's no way on earth that I'm admitting to this obviously experienced girl that this is my first time,' he thought, suppressing a cheer when he succeeded in penetrating her mysteries.

They used all three condoms that night, the final one splitting when they had enjoyed particularly vigorous sex on waking the following morning.

'Oh, shit. The damned thing's split!' they both thought, but they kept their concerns to themselves, not wishing to destroy the erotic, sexual mood with depressing discussions of possible pregnancy.

They each told themselves that there would be nothing to worry about. However, when Edward left Janine's room later that morning, proud to no longer be a virgin, fears about the repercussions following the burst condom niggled them both as they went about their studies.

Edward and Janine spent the next month regularly having sex in her bed and several times in his room. During the second month, he noticed a subtle change in her attitude to him. He would have been content to carry on the way it had been progressing. Sex with Janine was joyous, unashamed and he loved every minute of his time with her. At Janine's insistence, they even returned to the alley to repeat the experience. Public sex was extra arousing to her, although Edward was far less enthusiastic.

'I might lose her if I don't go along with her kinky ideas,' he told himself as she dragged him back up the alley and hitched up her long skirt.

On that particular evening, the newly-initiated ex-virgin had counted himself lucky that his identity was hidden by Janine's long, multi-coloured, hippie-style skirt. His personal tutor happened to be walking past the secluded alleyway with its two lust-fuelled occupants. Little did Edward realise that his tutor had indeed recognised Edward's distinctive black and white, snakeskin ankle boots poking out from under Janine's skirt.

'Nice work, Ed! Give her one from me,' the tutor thought whilst running a hand through his long, ginger hair.

When the flame-haired tutor had finally walked by, after first meeting Janine's stare and winking, Janine breathlessly said, 'Oh God, some tutor with a long, ginger mullet just walked by. He had the bloody nerve to wink at me as you were busy down there. I know he's a tutor, but I can't think of his name.'

'Shit! That sounds like it could have been my personal

tutor, Mr. Gillespie. Was he quite tall with a hooked nose?' Edward asked. He was certain that it must have indeed been Mr. Gillespie, because he had never noticed any other ginger tutors at the university.

'It's quite dark up this alley, but I reckon that he had a hooked nose a bit like yours, but it did not bend to one side like your conk,' Janine said, relieved that her top had been in place when the tutor had walked by.

'Well, in any case the guy would not have recognised me because my face was hidden up your skirt. It must have been embarrassing for both of you,' Edward replied, walking her further up the alley away from the street lamps to gain them more privacy.

Aroused and emboldened by almost being caught, he bent her over, pulled up her skirt and slid on a condom.

'Wow, what's got into you? You didn't have to be so rough. Now you've split the condom, yet again!' Janine said tetchily

'Stop moaning! I can't help myself when you're around,' he replied as they both rearranged their clothes before heading off to the bar. For a second time, the bursting of a condom played on their minds. Back in her room, they even argued over it when she accused him again of having been too rough in the dark alleyway.

With a scream of rage, he punched the door, bloodying his knuckles. Janine sat open-mouthed in stunned disbelief.

'Get out. You're crazy,' she screamed, flinging the door open then silently waited as he marched off to his own room in the Halls of Residence.

His angry over-reaction during their row had terrified her. His rages continued to crop up over the following weeks, particularly after he spotted her chatting at length to Carl in the canteen. Her bare arm was resting on Carl's shoulder as she bent and whispered in his ear. Edward was as annoyed with Carl as he was with her because he could tell by the leer on Carl's face that he was taking the opportunity to grab a lingering look down Janine's loose-fitting, skimpy top as she bent over him.

'Those are mine alone to look at,' Edward thought, giving Carl a killer stare as he approached the couple, quickly weaving his way through the canteen tables. Seeing the look of guilt on Janine's face provoked another raging row between them in her room that night.

'I'd finish with him completely if the sex wasn't so good,' Janine thought as he forced her head down into the pillows so that she could scarcely breathe.

The earlier look of hatred in his eyes as he berated her for flirting with his friend had turned her blood to ice through fear. 'The guy may be insane,' she thought, 'But he feels so good.'

Edward usually thought of Janine in loving terms and considered her to be his girlfriend, his property. Janine however, was finding him weirder the more time that she spent with him. It was increasingly unsettling her.

One day in the canteen, after a particularly upsetting argument with Edward the night before, Janine confided in her best friend, Penny, saying, 'I can't stand Ed's long periods of silent pondering. It creeps me out whenever he just sits for ages staring into space or at me. All of his angry, jealous outbursts are really freaking me right out.'

'Cut him loose if you're unhappy with him. You're a great looking girl. Let's be honest, you could do so much better than Ed. He's way too intense,' Penny replied.

From under her long, black lashes, Janine cast her huntress gaze around the canteen, settling in the direction of a group of rowdy male students which included Carl. Sensing that the girl he had always fancied was staring at him, Carl broke off mid-sentence and smiled back at her with a provocative flick of his long, fair hair. She licked her lips suggestively and smiled back, sealing the deal.

Whenever Edward arrived late at the university bar, he was often disturbed and suspicious to find Janine giggling in corners with random male students, most of them far more handsome than him. One evening, Edward entered the bar over half an hour later than Janine due to being held up in a deep discussion with Mr. Gillespie. His tutor had often smirked at Edward following the embarrassing incident with Janine up the dark alley. His tutor's knowing looks unnerved Edward.

However, the envious, older man had decided not to admit to Edward that he was fully aware that it had been Edward who had been busy performing a public sex act on that attractive, dark-haired girl. Mr. Gillespie himself had not been averse to bedding several female students during his time lecturing at a previous university, so he had nothing but respect for Edward for landing a female so far out of his league.

Still wondering why Mr. Gillespie had been acting so oddly, Edward spotted a scantily clad Janine sitting side by side with Carl at the same table in the dark corner where Edward had first made his girlfriend climax. The couple was so engrossed that they failed to notice him as he stared from across the bar. She appeared to be whispering into his friend's ear, but on closer inspection it was her gasps, not her words that Carl was listening to so intently. Edward's heart sank. With his midnight-blue cloak billowing out behind him, he marched angrily up to their table.

Janine and his friend looked up in guilty surprise. Edward stood menacingly in front of them and demanded, 'Shake my hand, Carl.'

'What are you talking about? That's an odd thing to ask me to do. We've already met, you fool,' Carl replied, making a feeble attempt at humour to lift the tension.

Through gritted teeth, Edward repeated, 'Shake my hand, Carl. I'm deadly serious. Shake it now!'

Slowly taking his hands from beneath the table top, Carl tentatively stretched out his right hand to shake Edward's proffered hand.

Instead of shaking the hand, Edward grabbed Carl's wrist and roughly jerked it upwards, pulling his friend's fingers to his nose so he could sniff them.

‘Well, just as I feared. Fish fingers! You bastards!’ Edward shouted, slamming Carl’s hand down onto the table in disgust.

Edward threw over the small table, spilling drinks onto the bar’s dingy carpet. Janine scrambled to her feet, buttoning up her flared jeans that she had so willingly unbuttoned for Carl. When he saw her re-buttoning action, Edward reddened with an even greater rage. He pushed Carl roughly to the ground and kicked him in the side, badly winding him. Edward stormed towards the exit of the bar, slinging over tables and punching anyone who challenged him.

When the barman yelled for him to stop, Edward picked up a barstool and threw it with all of his might at the bar area, smashing bottles, glasses and cracking a large, decorative mirror on the back wall.

The next day, a deeply lovelorn but still furious Edward was unceremoniously thrown off the course, accused of physical violence on a fellow student and extensive damage to the bar. He had neither the energy nor the will to challenge his expulsion. He was far too devastated by Janine’s betrayal, especially as it had taken place with his closest friend, Carl. In the time that it took to sniff a finger, Edward had lost the two people closest to him in the world, his girlfriend and his only companion, Carl. Edward knew that Janine would probably by now have taken his ex-friend back to her small, bare room in the Halls of Residence. It tore him apart.

The evening after his meltdown in the bar, he waited for them both to emerge from the Halls of Residence building, guessing that she would have enticed Carl there to continue whatever they had enjoyed the night before. It pained him to note that he had to wait over two and a half hours before they staggered out. As the hours ticked by, Edward was driving himself insane with imagining what the couple were doing on her bed.

As the new couple headed across the quadrangle to the canteen, Janine spotted Edward lurking threateningly in the shadows and said to Carl, deliberately loud enough for Edward to hear, 'Keep walking Carl. That scary weirdo over there seems to be stalking us.'

Carl felt too guilty for betraying his friend to reply. He walked on without saying a word to Edward, remembering the devastation his former friend had caused in the bar the previous night. His guilt had not prevented him from fully enjoying his filthy sexual exploits with Janine on the night of the pub fiasco. Carl took full advantage of her sexual expertise and refreshing lack of inhibition. Several other male students and one ginger-haired, hooked-nosed lecturer also took full advantage of Janine during her short-lived university career. Edward had no desire to talk to Carl ever again, but fate decreed that he was to talk to Janine Polson in Manchester many years later, with far-reaching consequences.

## After the bar brouhaha, a death

Understandably, Edward's mother and step-father back in Jersey were immensely disapproving of his violent behaviour that had led to the university discarding him. Far from trying to cure whatever ailed their son, they cut him off without a penny.

He was forced to sign on in Manchester whilst trying to find a job during a depressing time of high unemployment. Any job that he managed to procure lasted less than a few weeks, just as had happened with every school holiday job he ever applied for. It was not as though he ever aimed high when looking for employment. Employers in the newsagents, the fish and chip shop and shoe store all had taken exception to his rudeness with staff and customers alike. He was then rapidly dismissed from a furniture store after he had kicked over a nest of tables on sale in a fit of anger over a delay in his wage payment. The incident was almost a replay of when he had kicked over the tables in the university bar.

Edward's shock over Janine and Carl's betrayal and his rapid expulsion from his degree course had triggered his most severe episode of mania and anti-social behaviour to date. It rendered him completely unemployable and very much alone.

Nobody cared enough to suggest to Edward that he should seek professional, medical assistance for his increasingly obvious mental issues. He would not have followed any advice anyhow because he would not, could not admit that he behaved and thought differently to most other people. His ailments prevented him from holding down any job that might have allowed him to integrate properly into society. In any case, it was never his wish to integrate, being more of a loner than a people person.

Back in Jersey, the unexpected death of Florence came about rather oddly, as befitted her eccentric character. Wearing only her swimsuit and carrying a shrimp net, she had followed the tide down alone, to fish for prawns under the seaweed in the many rock pools. It was an unusually low tide and the merciless sun was blisteringly hot. Although she was well used to low-water fishing, she had never been so far down the beach as on that day. She had managed to bag an impressive quantity of large, green-grey, translucent prawns and was congratulating herself, looking forward to the prawn supper that she and Marcus would be enjoying later that day. The beach at low tide was like a moonscape, deserted except for dozens of gulls, a few oyster catchers and whatever mysterious creatures were lurking under the seaweed in the limpet-studded rock pools.

Now in her late sixties, she was beginning to feel achy after the long walk out to the tide's edge. To restore her depleted energy, she foolishly decided to lie out on an unusually flat rock under the fiercely hot sun. She closed her green eyes and listened to the plaintive, monotone cries of the gulls circling above her head, trying to banish thoughts that the birds might dive bomb her to protect their nests. As the sun's rays warmed her fashionably thin body through her expensive swimsuit, she drifted into a deep sleep.

She was jarred awake by a freezing sensation. Her bathing suit was drenched through from the spray of the waves that were crashing against the surprisingly comfortable rock on which she had accidentally fallen into sleep.

She glanced at her watch and discovered to her horror that she must have been asleep for well over an hour. Florence suddenly realised that she had committed a huge error, one more typically made by holidaymakers and not by people born and raised on the island. Residents respected the sea and its capricious ways.

'Shit! I'm totally cut off by the tide. I didn't mean to fall asleep. I'm usually the one to warn holidaymakers about getting cut off by the tide, now here I am, cut off by the sodding tide! Shit, shit, shit and fuck!' She stood on tiptoe atop the rock, waving her arms like a demented windmill, but she was too far from shore for anybody to see her. The magnetic pull of the tide's current eventually made standing impossible. The rock was soon covered completely in sea water and she struggled to keep her bare feet on the rough surface of the submerged rock. As the waves whipped up around her, she thought, 'There's no other option except to swim for shore. Shame I must leave my bag of prawns behind, but the wind has come up and I'll need all of my strength to reach safety.'

The ice cold of the water made Florence gasp as she pushed her aging body off from the rock that she had been sleeping on. The tide's powerful current was pulling her further out to sea, much to her increasing alarm. As waves crashed over her head, with the salty water stinging her eyes and pouring into her mouth and nose, Florence panicked more than she had ever done before. She was making no headway, cursing as seaweed wrapped around her limbs. The cold was making her hallucinate, with the grasping clumps of seaweed taking on the appearance of sea monsters.

Although Florence could swim, she had never been a strong swimmer. Battling against the current and freezing cold water gradually sapped every ounce of her strength. Slowly losing consciousness through hypothermia, she sank below the surface, her lungs filled with water and she drowned.

The split second that Florence's heart stopped pumping, she was whisked upwards through the water and high into the air. Something was pulling her effortlessly over the sea wall and across the road to her home. She landed effortlessly in the branches of a flowering cherry tree in her garden, just above the heads of Marcus, Charlie and Lara.

Charlie and Lara had been visiting his parents' house in Jersey as they often did, leaving the Cornish seafood restaurant in the capable hands of his restaurant manager. The trio all sported swimwear and were drinking cider as they sprawled indolently on sun loungers around the pool. Florence screamed at them for a solid ten minutes to try to gain their attention, but they just kept on talking between themselves, oblivious to her distress.

'I wish mum would hurry back with the prawns. I really fancy a prawn salad tonight,' said Charles sulkily.

'I'd have thought you'd be fed up with the smelly things, what with us owning a seafood restaurant,' Lara chipped in with a slight sneer.

'Oh God, the prawns that I caught will all be washed away by now. What will they eat for supper?' thought Florence, unaware that she had far greater problems to deal with, and yet no problems at all.

Whilst her spirit was struggling to acclimatise to being up in the cherry tree, Florence's discarded shell was washed up on the beach hours later. Her body was deposited like a large piece of driftwood amidst the other shells, seaweed and litter, much to the horror of a couple of paddling middle-aged holidaymakers that had stumbled upon her corpse.

Florence pondered a while. 'How is it possible that I can think if my brain is lying washed up on the beach with the rest of me? It makes no sense. I must be in another weird dimension that nobody ever imagined existed. I'll hopefully get used to it, eventually. The best that I can do to contact those three fools below is rustle a few leaves. It's taking far too much energy even to do that, so I'm not going to bother trying any more. It is probably for the best, because communicating with the living will neither solve my problems nor theirs. All that's left for me to do now is to observe. Hmm, that's a thought. Observing could turn out to be interesting. It means that I can spy on Marcus without him being aware that I'm watching his every move. I'm sure that he's been talking online to tarts whenever I wasn't around. I doubt that he'll be in the mood to do it tonight once he's been made aware that I'm dead. Hang on! He's looking at his phone now whilst the other two are busy swimming in the pool. I'll swoop down next to him and have a gander at what the old fool is looking at.'

In a flash, his invisible wife was leaning closely over Marcus's shoulder as he scrolled through his phone with a secretive smile on his weather-beaten face.

'Just as I thought, he's got his earpiece in and looking at some porn site. Disgusting!' Florence screamed into his ear, although he could not hear his dead wife.

'I'm just going inside for a top up,' Marcus shouted to his son and Lara. He took his phone and walked upstairs, intent on watching more porn in the bedroom until he was satisfied.

'Flo won't be returning back home for ages, so there's plenty of time to play,' Marcus thought, sliding his swimming trunks off and reaching for his wife's pink bottle of baby lotion.

Despite herself, Florence found it strangely erotic to watch him watching porn. She now saw a different side of her husband that he had never felt comfortable to show her. As the years passed, she even looked forward to watching him in the bedroom they had once shared whenever he brought back random women that he had either hooked up with online or were one-time friends of Florence's. She strangely enjoyed cheering him on, unheard, from the end of the king-sized bed.

'That's right Marcus, bend her over and spank her hard. That's it, Marcus, she can take it. Mary Beth always was a tart.'

Marcus's sexual exploits after her death became a surprising source of titillating distraction to Florence. It gave her something to do during the endless days of being dead. She might have felt more jealous about watching him if she had not fallen out of love with Marcus soon after the birth of Charlie. She sometimes attempted to join in, but Marcus and whichever woman he was with at the time obviously knew nothing about it.

'It's really chilly in this bedroom,' was a phrase often mentioned over the years, but nobody ever suspected that it was because of Florence.

## Funeral fiasco

On the fittingly drizzly day of Florence's funeral, Edward was the only family member who did not cry.

'If it had been left up to me, I wouldn't even have bothered attending the evil cow's funeral,' Edward told his friend Tommy in their local pub back in Manchester on the evening of his return from his recent distressing time spent over in Jersey.

However, Marcus had insisted that his half-brother should show their deceased mother some respect. He insisted on paying for Edward's flight over from Manchester to attend her funeral. Florence's eldest son reluctantly agreed to come, despite having zero respect for his mother after suffering a lifetime of her neglect and emotional abuse.

After a gap of so many years, being forced to stay in his mother's home felt uncomfortably strange to Edward. It messed with his brain to be back in his old bedroom which was stuffed with mostly unhappy memories. He could sense his mother's malevolent energy within the sombre, rambling house. It was clear that she did not want him to be in her house any more now that she was dead than when she had been alive. When he walked along the corridor to his old bedroom on the night before the funeral, he could have sworn that he could smell her perfume. An icy shiver slid down his back, despite it being a stifling hot, stormy night.

'This must be what an out of body experience feels like,' Edward thought as he stared into the eyes of his dead mother. The woman that he had always hated in response to her always irrationally hating him was staring down imperiously at him from a large, professionally-taken photograph that hung high on a wall. Her tanned face had been made up to the nines and her blonde hair was swept up in a stylish, French pleat. But it was her cold, green eyes that froze his soul.

He failed to sleep that night. Every creak and slightest

sound convinced him that his mother's powerful, negative energy was intent on ejecting him from her precious house. A ferocious thunderstorm in the middle of the night did not help matters. The crashes of thunder and flashes of lightning transformed his bedroom into the perfect setting for a gothic, horror movie.

'The sooner I'm bloody well out of here the better I'll be pleased,' he thought, awaiting the appearance of the spectre. Florence's hostile spirit actually was sitting at the end of his bed, but mercifully he could not see it. However, he could only sense it, which was almost as bad. If he had been able to see her ghost, he might have stood a chance of either being heroic and dealing with it, or of running away from her malevolence as his terrified screams rent the air. He was very much trespassing on her territory and so the latter option would have been more likely.

Considering how she had been such an unpleasant woman, Florence's funeral was surprisingly well-attended thanks to the efforts of Charlie and Marcus. Edward had shown no interest in becoming involved with any of the funeral arrangements and could not give a damn which mourners showed up. As the brothers sat side by side in the creepy crematorium, Charlie was blubbing into a tissue as he whispered in Edward's ear in a shaky voice, 'At least try to look as though you care, Ed. You did nothing to help organise the funeral. I guess you consider you've already done more than enough by merely attending.'

'Got it in one, bruv,' Edward said under his breath.

Edward would really have much preferred to be wandering around Jersey, reliving his private memories of the island, memories that did not include his mother. Memories of her would only be painful to relive. He had tried to obliterate her memory by mooching on beaches, watching boats bobbing in the harbours or strolling along narrow lanes that bordered onto fields. He once stood and stared at a herd of attractive Jersey cows that were chewing the cud in a field near his old home. He was mesmerised by their huge, brown eyes which seemed to be encouraging him to tell them all of his woes. The beasts were startled and moved away when he started to rant at them.

So much had changed for the worse on the island since he had left two decades previously to study at Manchester University. However, enough of Jersey's heart remained intact to remind him of the rare, happy times before his mind disintegrated.

There was limited time before his flight back to Manchester airport, so he resented having to waste an entire precious day saying farewell to a woman that he knew had detested him. Edward comforted himself with the thought that the day of the funeral would not have been suitable for reminiscing on his travels around the island. Thunder and lightning as ferocious as the previous night's had theatrically returned, just as the crematorium was filling up with mostly expensively-dressed mourners. Edward was the most shabbily dressed by far, much to Charlie's embarrassment.

As Florence's coffin drifted past him decked in wreaths, Edward felt nothing, which worried him. 'Shouldn't I feel at least a faint flicker of emotion on the day my mother gets fried? There's nothing inside me, zero, zilch. I might as well be in a supermarket or on the toilet for all the emotion that I'm feeling right now. Bloody Charlie is sobbing like a baby next to me, trying to impress Marcus no doubt. Even mum's next door neighbour is bawling. I can't even squeeze out a single, measly tear. I'd be a hypocrite if I did, wouldn't I? I can't and won't fake emotion,' Edward thought as the lightning flashed. 'The sickly scent from all these flowers in the wreaths makes me want to heave. Trust Charlie to have gone overboard with his wreath. Bloody show-off! It's not my bloody fault that I couldn't afford a humungous wreath like his. My disability benefit hardly allows for such extravagances.'

At the back of the gloomy room, a sudden loud crash made all the mourners jump.

'That's not thunder,' thought Charlie, turning around to see who dared to be disrespecting his mother. There was confusion amongst the mourners, caused by one of them falling, twitching to the floor.

'Oh Christ! It looks like one of Marcus's friends is having another one of his epileptic fits. Bloody typical! I guess his attack must have been triggered by all of this thunder and lightning,' wet-faced Charlie whispered to Edward, who was desperately trying to stifle a subversive giggle.

Edward bit his lip and ground his nails into the palms of his hands to prevent himself from exploding into an enormous belly laugh. Conscious that Charlie had spotted his animated struggle to stop laughing like a deranged hyena only worsened his predicament.

'If the laugh escapes, I'm lost,' thought Edward, raising his hand to his mouth to hide the facial contortions that he was forced to make to hold back the hilarity. 'What a farce this damned funeral is turning out to be. Let me out of here,' he thought, suddenly leaving his seat and rushing out of the crematorium into the pounding rain. Once safely outside, he bent over and bellowed with laughter, unaware that his guffaws could be heard by all of the affronted mourners still inside the crematorium.

Edward decided not to bother returning to his mother's funeral. Instead, he chose to take the coastal road, walking for hours along the deserted beaches through the driving rain back to his mother's house. He stooped, picked up a large, flat pebble and threw it at a large group of darkly sinister crows that had congregated on the beach. As they flew skywards cawing loudly, their dark feathers reminded him of the sombre garments of the mourners.

'Take that, you bastards!' he shouted at the crows, wishing that they were the mourners.

He ignored Charlie, Marcus and all of the sniffing, disapproving mourners who had congregated back at the house by the time he had returned. He did not respond when Charlie berated him for leaving the funeral early but marched past him and up the stairs to his old bedroom. Packing his small suitcase, he walked back outside into the rain without a backward glance or a word to anyone in the crowded living room.

'That's my crazy half-brother for you. What a nut job,' Charlie said to Marcus as they watched him disappear into the gloom.

'The death of a parent can have a strange effect on some folk,' said Marcus, who had never liked Edward anyway and was mighty relieved to literally see the back of him, leaving them to grieve in peace.

'You know as well as I do that dear Edward is as mad as a hatter and getting progressively worse,' Charlie replied.

'God only knows what he will do after he finds out about his mother's Will,' Marcus said before stuffing a greasy sausage roll from the wake's buffet into his bulging face.

'What do you mean?' Charlie asked anxiously, a mirror image of his father, both fat in black with slicked-back, strawberry blond hair, both chomping on jumbo-sized sausage rolls.

'I guess I ought to warn you because it will inevitably also impact on you. Your mother and I discussed her Will, as is only fitting between married couples. She decided to write Edward out of her Will several years ago after that stand-up row the two of them had when he paid us one of his rare visits. She has naturally bequeathed the house to me during my lifetime, but on my death, she chose for only you to inherit this property and all remaining assets,' Marcus replied, brushing crumbs off his protruding belly onto the expensive cream carpet.

'Oh, my good God! What the fuck?' Charlie said, genuinely stunned by his father's words. 'I've become used to mum's spontaneous, capricious nature over the years, but this really takes the bloody biscuit!'

'Language, Charles! Please remember that we cremated your mother today!' Marcus scolded, eying up the rest of the buffet and singling out a large scotch egg to devour, despite knowing it would probably give him terrible gas.

'Sorry about my language, but what you just said is totally shocking. Edward will be bloody livid. He's got a huge chip on his shoulder already. He doesn't really need another reason to feel so hard done by. I honestly fear for my safety when he finds out what she's done to him,' Charlie said, too shocked to eat.

His father chomped down on his massive scotch egg then took a large swig of finest wine as Charlie continued, saying, 'I won't be able to look Edward in the eye from this moment on, even before he discovers that he has been disinherited and disowned by our mother. Hopefully he won't return to Jersey or visit me in Cornwall too often because I couldn't take the strain of keeping that information secret from him. It will be more than awkward for all concerned. Your news does not sit at all comfortably with me, dad,' Charlie added, planning what he might do with his future inheritance.

Charlie was already financially comfortable, but his future inheritance from his mother would push him to a level of luxury that made him drool to contemplate. Riches were heaping upon riches in his world.

'Once dad is dead, I really will be rolling in clover,' he thought, mentally rubbing his podgy hands together before silently reprimanding himself for being so callously mercenary.

'Edward brought this all upon himself for rowing so forcibly with his mother, although I do admit that they could each be as bloody awkward as the other at times,' Marcus replied shaking his head.

The widower had pinpointed far too many unfortunate character similarities between Florence and Edward over the years. He had been grateful that her vicious, venomous tongue had mostly been used against his stepson and not against him. Marcus had discovered long ago that his wife was unhinged, but she had managed to hide her weirdness well in public. He was forever grateful that Charlie's corpulent body had contained more of Marcus's own genes than Florence's genes. His doting son seemed to be as normal a person as one could ever wish to find, if somewhat dull. Even his own father had to admit that Charlie had turned being dull into an art form, taking pride in his normality, which incensed his adrenaline-junkie wife, Lara.

Edward's vile temper would explode like a fire cracker, even more unpredictably than Florence's used to. 'Florence and her damned first-born are anything but dull, or were, in Florence's case,' thought Marcus.

By now, Marcus sensed that his beloved wife would probably now be nothing more than cooling dust waiting to be poured into an urn ready for collection. Her meagre remains would then ceremoniously be poured into the sea off Geoffrey's Leap, a craggy pinnacle high above Anne Port bay. Ironically, it was the same bay that her scorned son, Edward had permanently damaged his back whilst flying off the seawall whilst tripping out of his skull. Florence had always loved the sea, yet the sea had killed her and she would soon be returned to its chilly embrace.

Jersey legend has it that the cliff was named Geoffrey's Leap after a criminal called Geoffrey who lived in distant times. Nobody is sure what terrible crime this man had committed, but he was nonetheless sentenced to death by being thrown from the cliff onto the jagged rocks below. Geoffrey survived the fall much to everyone's surprise, including his own. The watching crowd was split into two factions; those who wished him to be set free and more bloodthirsty members of the audience who called for him to be thrown off the cliff a second time. Encouraged by the crowd, Geoffrey decided to leap a second time to show how easily he could do it. He did not survive the second fall and perished on the punishing rocks. The moral of the story is: Don't be a show-off.

It had appealed to Florence's warped sense of humour to be sprinkled from Geoffrey's Leap cliff top and into the glistening sea that lapped onto the pebble-studded sands of her favourite beach. She had this wish written into her Will, along with her ultimate, evil joke on her first-born, the insult of disinheritance. Not once did she even mention Edward's name in the document. It was as though he had never existed in her cold, green eyes.

As soon as Edward heard about his mother's watery death, he soon worked out that the event would considerably ease his circumstances in years to come. He guessed that Marcus would inherit the Jersey house, but he had no reason not to assume that the property would eventually be split between him and Charlie after Marcus died. Edward's massive financial pressures would then melt away.

'If I can just struggle on, it'll all eventually work out fine for me, not before time,' he would often think when times were particularly challenging.

He frequently went to bed hungry much earlier in the evenings than he would have liked when he had no money to feed the electricity meter. Edward never once considered that his potential lifeline would fail to materialise. He was counting on it to rescue him from relentless, soul-destroying penury.

Edward was sitting alone as he usually did inside his depressing Manchester room when he heard several envelopes plop through the letterbox and onto the mat outside his room. As his room was on the ground floor, it was always easy for him to hear when the postman delivered the post, although the letters were rarely addressed to him. He had been expecting the arrival of a solicitor's letter concerning his mother's Will at around this time, so he decided to collect his neighbours' letters and junk mail from the mat, knocking on doors to deliver their post.

With excited trepidation, he reverently took his envelope back to his small room and ripped it open. On closer examination, he thought that the handwriting on the envelope looked very familiar. It was not the official-looking envelope that a solicitor might use.

'That looks like Marcus's handwriting. How odd because

he never writes to me,' Edward thought.

Although the envelope had been handwritten, the letter inside was typed, making it feel cold and impersonal, symbolising Marcus's relationship with Edward. The letter informed him that Marcus was terribly sorry, but Florence had not seen fit to even mention Edward in her Will.

With disbelieving eyes, Edward read, 'Your mother has naturally ensured that I can continue to live in the property, but on my death it will be passed down solely to Charlie and his descendants.'

The room seemed to spin and Edward's stomach lurched violently. All around him swirled a white mist, every colour draining out of his surroundings. As the awful truth hit him like a sledge hammer, on the brink of fainting, he dashed to his sink, rapidly removed a dirty plate and cutlery from it and vomited violently. Clutching the edge of the sink for support, he leaned and stared into the mirror above the sink, gibbering indecipherable questions at his reflection. Gaining no reply, he poured cold water over his head to try to regain his mind. Dripping wet, he staggered to the bed and lay flat on his back, staring up at the ceiling until his heartbeats slowed down.

'Nothing, zilch, nada,' he repeated, over and over.

He could not move, stunned into total immobility. He felt as though he had been shot through the brain, needing to recover from what pained him, as if it had been a physical wound. He did not stir from the bed all that day because he could not see the point of moving. He had no strength. Edward's head swarmed with thoughts of how smug Charlie's face must be looking after hearing how much wealth would eventually top up his already luxurious lifestyle.

Edward was in complete disbelief at how cold-hearted his mother had actually been to him. To have snatched his only chance of salvation so cruelly out of his hands illustrated perfectly just how devoid of any maternal feeling towards him that she had always been. It was a fact that Edward was to be reminded of daily by the arctic-cold icicle twisting deep inside his guts.

'That spiteful old witch must have written me out of her Will years ago for some unknown reason. She may possibly have done it after that horrendous row we had when I told her to fuck off and die. As emotionless as a robot, she has disowned and disinherited me with a few sweeps of a biro,' he thought bitterly.

Like the motherless child he was, he turned his death mask of a face into the wet pillow and cried angrily, thumping it with his fists to try to release some of the pressure building up inside his head.

To heap more coals onto his burning rage, Edward only had to contrast the two homes that he and his half-brother were inhabiting on the day the contents of his mother's Will were disclosed. For years prior to her death, Edward had been struggling to survive on his paltry disability benefit payments. He had been forced to stay on in Manchester after his ignominious expulsion from university because the cost of living was, and probably always will be so much lower in the north of England than in the south.

Jersey is so far south it is no longer even in England, although it is still part of Great Britain. Edward could no more afford to return to the island than fly to the moon in a balloon. He would have much preferred to move back there to live out his days in the island's warmer clime, to wander its familiar beaches and absorb all of the island's comforting beauty. However, it now seemed that his fate was to be banished forever to the punishing rain and depressing gloom of the north of England in the soul-destroying Moston area of Manchester. He had lived in Manchester for over twenty years, yet he still felt like an interloper. So deep was his depression after being disowned that he did not have an ounce of drive left in him, let alone enough money to make a return to Jersey even possible.

'Inheriting some money might not have transformed me into a normal, contented human being if I'd returned home to live in Jersey, but at least I'd be in with a chance of combating these black dog moods. Living in more picturesque surroundings than this dump would surely help,' he thought as he limped along the grey streets in the rain to the corner shop to buy milk. 'I might have been able afford to put my back right, or at least do something to ease this chronic pain.' He had a strong suspicion that the constant pain in his brain and heart could never be cured, even if a solution was ever found for his back problem.

# An unpleasant trip to Cornwall

Edward's small, damp room in a depressing area of Manchester had served to increase his clinical depression, sense of isolation and huge resentment. He battled alone with his mind and spinal problems. The only highlight of his week was when he received his disability benefit money and could walk slowly, painfully to the shops to buy essentials and pay off any outstanding bills. It was a hand-to-mouth existence without treats or added excitement.

No woman wanted to know a man with no money who had mental and physical problems, plus a bad attitude which, since the Will debacle, included a massive chip on his shoulder. As the years dripped by and his problems worsened, his chances of finding any romantic connection were wafer slim.

Edward was all too well aware that Charlie was living the high life in Cornwall with his beautiful, if somewhat immoral wife, Lara. Out of a bout of guilt that had been brought about by his good fortune, Charlie had given his half-brother a gift of ten thousand pounds from his inheritance pot, but that had long since disappeared.

Edward had managed to buy a decent television and a second-hand car with the money, which were his main forms of entertainment. He had no reason to venture out and it was never a pleasure, as his back would soon ache if he walked for more than the shortest of distances. Driving soon became less of a joy because his damaged vertebrae had caused sciatica which made driving painful. Besides, once the ten thousand pounds ran out, he could no longer afford the petrol. Eventually, the car broke and as he had nothing left of Charlie's money to mend or replace it, the car was scrapped.

'I might as well jump up on the scrap heap with it,' he thought.

Decades of mostly staying at home to help save money had helped to slowly drive Edward insane. The genes bequeathed to him by his mother were making him act even crazier, but unlike her he could not control his strange behaviour in public. Just as had happened to Florence, the older he grew the more the wiring in his brain deteriorated. Like most madmen, he was not fully aware of his mental decline. However, it would not be too long before Edward would be certifiably insane and only interested in revenge and retribution. He started to think of himself as a Saint George figure, out to slay the dragon of injustice. Right felt so much on Edward's side that it was smothering any clear thought, pushing him ever closer to the edge of a precarious, dangerous precipice.

After their mother's death, Edward had kept in sporadic contact with Charlie, not because he wanted to or because he had much liking for his half-brother.

He believed in the saying, 'Keep your friends close, but keep your enemies closer.' Edward would have preferred to never see Charlie ever again because he felt so hugely aggrieved and wounded by being disowned and disinherited for scant reason. He was so perpetually annoyed by it all that he did not discuss the situation with Charlie for over a decade, lest he say too much and completely alienate him.

Eventually, he decided to broach the subject of inheritance whilst on a visit to Charlie's family home in Cornwall over the Christmas period. However, Charlie was not in the mood to discuss the subject and so Edward reluctantly dropped the thorny subject.

Despite acknowledging that Lara was attractive, Edward had never warmed to his sister-in-law, especially after she had made a drunken pass at him in the kitchen of the Cornish house when he had attended his nephew Sam's christening. Having a new baby had not seemed to calm Lara's libido down as she had expected it to have done. She did not really bond with the baby and was more interested in palming him off on Charlie or her mother whilst she went out gallivanting with her girlfriends.

It was the day after Sam's christening and Edward was due

to return to Manchester the next day. It was always a horrendous journey that made his back ache for weeks afterwards, so he was not looking forward to it one bit. It was one reason that he rarely visited his brother's home, although he loved the Cornish beaches and country lanes because they reminded him of the Jersey beaches and intricate landscapes of his youth. As it was such a great distance to travel, he would never stay at Charlie's home for less than a week. Being signed off work with his back problem, let alone his depression and anxiety, meant that he had no time constraints. The train fare from Manchester to Cornwall cost him a fortune, money that he could ill afford to spend.

'At least I won't have to pay for my room and board whilst I'm staying at Charlie and Lara's place. It's the very least Charlie can do for me,' Edward had thought as the train journey dragged on interminably. His back pain was making him squirm and wriggle which he could tell was irritating the suited man sitting beside him. Edward shot him a laser beam glare to silence the man's tutting.

Whilst he had been helping Lara out by washing up the dishes in the spacious kitchen after lunch, he was staring out of the window at the sunshine glinting on the swimming pool when a feminine arm wound round his waist and made a grab for him over his ancient swimming shorts.

'What the fuck, Lara?' Edward had said under his breath, in case Charlie heard his words.

He could feel her hot breath on his bare neck. Shocked into immobility, he could feel her trying to gain entry inside his shorts. He turned his head and quickly whispered, 'Stop right there! You've obviously drunk far too much wine at lunch. What the hell are you thinking? You're married to my brother for fuck's sake!'

'Spoilsport,' was all she said, tossing her long, blonde hair provocatively over her shoulders. She sashayed off into the living room as if nothing had happened.

Edward felt violated by this unwanted, sexually

provocative invasion of his personal space. He was confused as to whether he should mention the incident to Charlie. Over the next few hours, he weighed up the pros and cons of ratting on Lara to Charlie, wondering whether it was just a huge mistake due to her being drunk. If she had shown the slightest remorse, he might have forgiven her trespass on his body, but she seemed far from remorseful.

Later that day, Edward was walking up the stairs to change out of his damp swimming shorts after a swim in the large, kidney-shaped swimming pool. He had to pass by Charlie and Lara's bedroom to reach the guestroom. Their door was half open and he was greeted by the sight of Lara's naked body as she rubbed herself dry after her swim. Charlie could still be heard splashing in the pool. Far from hiding her nudity, Lara turned fully towards her brother-in-law and posed provocatively with a wicked grin on her face.

'I look pretty hot for a new mother, don't you reckon?' she asked, cupping her breasts in both hands and placing one foot on the bed. Despite himself, he could not help staring at her.

'Fancy a quickie whilst Charlie's swimming?' she asked shamelessly.

Edward's heart was beating impossibly fast and it took all his will-power to resist her invitation. Eventually he gained control of the primeval urge to jump on her and said, 'Oh, grow up for Christ's sake, woman! The swim obviously hasn't sobered you up yet,' Edward said, slamming the door so hard that it woke the baby Sam in the nursery.

'That bloody well serves her right! Now she'll have to go and see to the baby,' Edward thought. His mind was now definitely made up to tell Charlie about his wife's uncalled-for, crudely seductive behaviour. If she carried on with her campaign to provoke him, he could not guarantee to be strong enough to resist. There was nothing left to do but to tell Charlie so that Edward could protect himself.

Whilst Lara was taking a shower before bedtime, Edward sought out Charlie who was watching television in the living room. Taking advantage of them both being alone, Edward whispered, 'I don't really know how to put this, but Lara has just come onto me, big style. I've been debating whether to mention it to you because I really don't want to upset the boat. On balance, I think you ought to be made aware of the situation. From what you've told me, she's played around a fair bit with other men over the years. It seems like she's now trying to keep her dalliances in the family.'

'Eh? What happened exactly?' Charlie asked. He was unsure whether he really wanted to hear what Edward had to relate.

Charlie was still besotted with his pretty wife, especially after they had recently become parents. Before marrying her, he had wondered whether her flirtatious nature might become too much to handle. It was becoming increasingly apparent that he had good reason to have been worried.

'I'll spare your feelings and won't divulge the details, but suffice it to say that she acted in a gross way. She came onto me in the kitchen and then made sure I saw her fully naked in your bedroom after our swims,' Edward said, saddened to see a look of horror appear on Charlie's meaty face.

'Oh God, no! I apologise for my wife's shocking behaviour. She can never hold her liquor, but I know that's no excuse. I hoped that having the baby might slow her down but it seems that she's worse than ever. I'll have a strong word with her. Be assured, my wife's trashy behaviour is now at an end, at least as far as you're concerned' Charlie said as a red flush of hurt and anger spread over his already florid cheeks.

'I hope you grow some balls and have more than a harsh word with the silly bitch. You've got to make her stop behaving like a whore. It's not fair on you or Sam. You'll not be married for long at this rate,' Edward replied, fairly sure his words were going unheeded.

Charlie had already forgiven Lara for far worse behaviour, so desperate was he to hold onto her. It pained Edward to hear the way that she spoke to her husband, not caring who heard her belittling him as she mocked him, usually over his appearance. Edward had always been slightly better looking than his half-brother and it was painful to see Charlie being made a fool of by such an unpleasant woman. It reminded Edward of how belittled he had felt when his mother used to cruelly mock him in public out of purely sadistic pleasure.

Charlie could still do something about his promiscuous wife situation, whereas Edward had never been free to berate his mother for her nastiness, being the child in the twisted relationship. Because of his troubled history with his mother, it particularly irritated Edward to see Lara triumph. Although acknowledging that Charlie loved the silly woman, Edward firmly believed that she deserved to be banished from Charlie's life. Sadly, it would be harder to make the split from her now that unplanned baby Sam had appeared.

Edward never heard the ferocious row that ensued between Charlie and Lara because his half-brother had the decency to wait until the next day to challenge her disturbing behaviour. He waited until shortly after Edward had set off on his challenging train journey back to his run-down Manchester flat. Charlie had been decent enough to stump up a hundred pounds towards the travel costs. The guilt over his financial good fortune, courtesy of his mother, had made Charlie hand the cash over. Edward felt like a charity case, but he took the money anyway.

'If I'd been given what was my birth-right in the first place, I wouldn't have to keep feeling beholden and unnecessarily grateful every time he coughs up a bit of cash,' Edward thought as his already aggravated back pain from the journey to Cornwall became even more excruciating on his return home.

The screaming match between Charlie and Lara had resulted in stalemate, so Lara was free to carry on with her philandering ways for fifteen more years. Apart from his attempted molestation by his sister-in-law, Edward's time spent in the uplifting surroundings of Cornwall improved his mental state for a few days, but eventually being trapped in his flat amidst the red-brick urban sprawl of Manchester pushed Edward's spirits even deeper under the chill waters of despondency.

# Dealing with Lara

Time drifted by. Sam was now a podgy, spoilt, fifteen-year-old public schoolboy. He looked so much like his father that it was comical. He had a ruthless streak in him, unlike Charlie, although Charlie did show some spirit on one day in particular. It occurred during a busy lunchtime at his restaurant in Cornwall, when Charlie walked into the wine cellar and was shocked to find an interesting tableau. His topless wife was on her knees in front of Geraldo. The Portuguese waiter seemed to be missing his trousers and underpants. Understandably, it finally all became too much for Charlie to tolerate.

Geraldo had been enjoying Lara rather too much when his boss had burst into the cellar. 'Shrink! Disappear you bloody thing!' Geraldo inwardly screamed, to no avail. It was not easy to switch his passion off.

'Put your fake boobs away and get out of here right now, you disgusting whore! You'd better be gone from our house by the time I return this evening. I'll teach you not to mess around with one of my bloody employees! I'm going to pick Sam up from school and take him for a burger. Make sure you're out of both of our lives for good by the time I return,' Charlie screamed at Lara, who was guiltily trying to refasten her bra as her red-faced lover attempted to shield his nakedness from his employer.

'I hope that you think my wife, soon to be my ex-wife, was worth losing your job over, you slimy Portuguese bastard!' Charlie spat venomously at his flustered employee who was wishing he had not completely removed his trousers before enjoying Lara's body and sexual prowess.

'Yes, boss,' Geraldo replied, too confused by what was happening and too unfamiliar with the English language to understand what was coming from his own mouth.

'Yes, boss? Yes, boss?' Charlie screamed sarcastically, grabbing the waiter around the throat. He met no resistance because Geraldo's hands were too busy attempting to hide his lower half.

'I mean no, boss,' said Geraldo just prior to Charlie's fat fist catching him square on his chin.

'Get dressed both of you and fuck off out of my restaurant. Geraldo, you're obviously fired and don't expect me to pay your wages this month. I never want to see you or Lara ever, ever again,' Charlie yelled, suddenly aiming a kick at Geraldo's groin.

Luckily for Geraldo's future fatherhood prospects, Charlie's aim fell short and slammed into the waiter's naked, hairy thigh.

'I can't think what she sees in you, to be honest,' the cuckolded husband sneered, pointing at the now flaccid organ hanging forlornly between Geraldo's hairy thighs.

By insulting his manhood, Geraldo's Portuguese blood started to boil. He glared at his now ex-boss whilst hurriedly retrieving his black work trousers and scrambling into them. He left his underpants on the dusty cellar floor in his haste. As he fled the cellar, he pushed Charlie so hard that he fell heavily against a rack of wine bottles. Luckily, only two bottles smashed but, much to Charlie's annoyance he later discovered that they were amongst his most expensive, vintage wines.

'And take your smelly boxers with you,' Charlie screamed, lobbing the colourful underpants at Geraldo's fleeing head, where they lodged to comical effect over his eyes.

Neither man saw the humour at the time. Diners at the restaurant were treated to the sounds of shouting coming from the cellar. They then enjoyed the sight of the still almost topless wife of the owner with red lipstick smeared over her cheeks, her usually immaculate blonde hair dishevelled as she teetered on her high heels out of the restaurant. They looked on open-mouthed as Lara jumped into a sleek, black sports car and drove away at high speed. Minutes later, a less than smartly-dressed waiter clutching something colourful in his shaking hands that looked like underpants, ran full-pelt through the restaurant and into the car park.

'What the hell's going on in here today?' said one of the regular diners to his astonished wife, his forkful of lobster poised halfway to his mouth.

'With all that shouting coming from the cellar, and with what we've just witnessed running through the room, I'd put money on the waiter having been caught messing with the owner's wife. Any fool can see that,' said his wife, salivating at the thought of adding such salacious gossip to her armoury.

The couple stared out of the window at the distraught waiter. Geraldo was miffed at being deserted in the car park and was pacing around the cars gesticulating like a lunatic. He reached into his trouser pocket and hooked out his mobile phone and shouted at Lara.

'Jesus, Lara, why did you drive off and leave me here?' he asked petulantly, conscious of many eyes burning into his back like laser guns.

'I'm so sorry, darling, I panicked. I'm turning the car around right now. Just stay there and I'll drive back to collect you,' Lara said as her car screeched in protest at being thrown into a rapid volte face.

A few minutes later, the diners were delirious with excitement to see the car belonging to the owner's wife pull hurriedly into the car park. Fingers were pointed at the waiter as he flung himself into the car, accidentally dropping his colourful boxer shorts onto the tarmac. Laughter rang out in the restaurant as Geraldo awkwardly scrambled back out of the car to retrieve his underwear and then fling his body back into the car.

'You should have just left them there. Now I'm a laughing stock,' Lara shouted at her bumbling lover.

'They were my favourite underpants and cost me a fortune. It would have looked worse to have left them there. Don't forget, I'm not made of money like your husband,' Geraldo replied.

As the shiny, black car sped off like something out of the

'Knight Rider' television series, the highly entertained diners discussed the farcical cabaret show that had played out that lunchtime. All discussion was halted by the sudden presence of the restaurant owner. Charlie had stayed in the cellar for twenty minutes, even cracking open a bottle of wine to calm his fevered, confused, murderous thoughts. Eventually, he emerged into the sunlight of the restaurant as if nothing had happened. He had a quick word with his restaurant manager to ask him to hold the fort and drove off to collect Sam from his expensive school.

'Mum won't be coming home anymore,' Charlie said to his portly, sulky, teenage son.

'What's the stupid woman done now? Actually, I can probably guess,' Sam said, well used to his mother's disreputable ways.

Normally Charlie would not let his only son get away with speaking about his mother in that manner, but he had been so destroyed by Lara that he did not bother to reprimand the boy. 'I won't go into the gory details, but you're correct in your assumption,' Sam's father said tersely, struggling to keep his muddled emotions under control.

'Well, good riddance to her,' Sam replied, pulling open a bag of caramel popcorn and calmly offering his father some as they sped home.

'Don't eat too much of that rubbish. I'm treating us both to a burger and fries whilst your mother collects her possessions and leaves the property,' Charlie warned.

Sam just ignored him and poured another handful of popcorn into his slack mouth, then another and another until there was an empty packet. He still managed to clear his plate in the burger joint and even polished off a large dessert. Charlie had found the cheap burger had made an unexpectedly pleasant change from the restaurant food that he was more used to.

'That's my boy. We must do this again,' Charlie said, ruffling his son's spiky hair, which was the identical shade of strawberry blonde as his own. The boy shrugged his father's hand away just as any self-respecting teenager would do in public.

'Get off me, for fuck's sake, dad,' Sam had whispered angrily, trying to rearrange his hair back into its sculptural spikes in case there were any good looking girls around.

His father turned a deaf ear to his son's disrespectful cursing. On top of his own personal pain at being cuckolded, he also felt guilty that Sam would now be without a mother, although he felt that the abrupt end to the marriage had been entirely Lara's fault. He took no responsibility for the fact that his boring nature had made her turn elsewhere for the excitement she craved.

Reckoning that his current motherless situation might play to his advantage, Sam continued in a wheedling voice, 'Dad, is there any chance of a sub on my allowance this month?'

'How much are we talking about here?' Charlie asked, dreading to hear the answer. He thought, 'How will I be able to refuse Sam anything now that he is virtually an orphan?'

'Well, I really, really need about three hundred quid. There's so much course equipment to buy now that I'm in the sixth form. My allowance just doesn't cover it,' Sam replied. The actual reason for wanting the money was his desire to buy cocaine for a few parties that he and his friends were shortly planning to attend. His request had nothing whatsoever to do with school course work.

'That's pretty steep, son, but if you need it then you shall have it,' Charlie said, who could easily afford shelling out such sums of money.

'Cheers, pops!' Sam said, laying back in the luxury of his father's car, dreaming of all the girls that he could pull at the parties.

He looked forward to being transformed into a rampaging sex monster by the cocaine. Sam had sniffed cocaine several times before and he had felt invincible under its influence. He had almost wrecked his underage girlfriend whilst on the drug, but she did not complain or seem to feel any pain, having sniffed several lines of coke herself. Sam was taking the drug partly in the hope that it would make him thinner and therefore more attractive to girls.

Fortunately for everyone concerned, before Charlie and Sam returned to their home, Lara had managed to hurriedly pack as much of her expensive clothes and jewellery as she could carry inside her car. She had time to make several car journeys to and from her marital home to her lover's flat. Before she shut the front door behind her for the last time, she desperately scanned the living room for the highest value item that she could find.

Charlie had a liking for buying antiques and art. Lara remembered him buying an ancient, Chinese vase that stood about four feet tall on the real wood floor. 'That's worth a few thousand pounds but I'd never fit it into the car. I know that there's an Edmund Blampied original on the landing. That'll do,' she thought, rushing up the stairs and unhooking the painting by the famous Jersey artist from the wall. Lara knew that it would hurt Charlie to lose the painting, because of its financial and sentimental value. He had bought it to display in their home in Cornwall as a reminder of his Jersey roots.

'My need is greater than Charlie's right now, so I'll take this painting to sell and this carriage clock too. I know it's worth a fortune,' she thought.

She staggered in her high heels towards the front door, awkwardly baring her plundered items. After a sudden, vindictive rush of blood to the head, Lara launched a powerful, angry kick at the Chinese vase, which swayed backwards and forwards tantalisingly before crashing to the floor and smashing into several large chunks. 'Serves you right you miserable, boring, fat bastard,' she shouted, although Charlie was nowhere to be seen.

As she drove away, Lara regretted smashing the vase because it meant she risked possible prosecution, although she planned to say that it had been an accident if she was ever challenged. As it turned out, Charlie thought it a small price to pay to be rid of her and never even mentioned the theft and breakage.

Luckily for Lara, Geraldo cared enough for her to eventually marry her after her divorce from Charlie was finalised, or else she would have been in a much trickier situation. Having upped sticks to live with Geraldo near his family's home in a small, Portuguese village, she missed her life of comparative luxury in Cornwall that she had enjoyed courtesy of Charlie. However, she was selfish and heartless enough not to miss Charlie or their son in the slightest. The feeling was mutual.

## Philippe – 13:48 15th June 2015

When the first bang cracks the warm air, Philippe's body involuntarily jerks as he sits on the park bench waiting nervously for his interview. He stifles a grin when he sees a blonde girl accidentally spilling coffee onto her skirt. He would have preferred to be sitting facing the sun, but the best bench has already been taken by the now soggy, diminutive, blonde girl and her bulky female companion.

He assumes that the two women know each other in some way judging by how comfortably they are talking, although they had only met ten minutes previously. Philippe's nerves are already in tatters because he is waiting in the warm sunshine for the time to pass before setting off for his important job interview in one of the offices opposite the park in Battersea.

The fiery Spaniard had stormed out of his previous job five months earlier after his male manager had propositioned him. That incident had caused quite a storm at the store, because Philippe, who had been deputy manager, had been very popular with customers and everyone who worked in the store. Everyone who met him had always appreciated his wicked, flirty nature. His lover, Neil would have been mortified and livid to have witnessed the sexual banter that Philippe indulged in during his working day. It was hardly surprising that Philippe's boss had misread the signals and propositioned him in his office.

If his boss, Ray had been more attractive, Philippe might have acted differently and reciprocated. Ray had occasionally made dubious sexual innuendos to his deputy manager in private, but Philippe had brushed them off and ignored his behaviour. Manhandling him was a step too far and could not be tolerated.

'But I've seen you flirting outrageously with Deepak from the canteen. I thought you'd be up for a bit of fun.' Ray whined as Philippe looked murderously at him.

'Have you actually seen Deepak? He's gorgeous. Need I say more?' Philippe said in a huff.

In truth, he and Deepak had done very much more than mild flirting, but surely Ray could not have known what they had indulged in whilst huddled together inside a toilet cubicle, could he? If Deepak had not been forced to return to India for family health reasons, Philippe would gladly have continued with the seedy, clandestine relationship. This was despite already being in a steady relationship with Neil, an insecure but wealthy art gallery owner.

After his embarrassing encounter with Ray, Philippe had felt too uncomfortable, embarrassed and ashamed of possibly leading his boss to continue working at the store. 'I was thinking of going after a job with greater responsibility anyway, but all of this nonsense from you just makes me want to leave immediately,' Philippe told his boss. Now that Deepak was back in India, there was no reason for him to stay on at the store. He assumed that it would be simple to land a new job.

'I'll make sure that you're paid in full to the end of the month. Don't fret. You don't have to come in to work after today. In fact, I'd much prefer it if you didn't,' said Ray, whose feelings had been very badly hurt by Philippe's rejection and the way he had cast aspersions on Ray's appearance.

Ray had another reason for wanting his deputy manager to never continue working at the store. The out of shape, balding, bespectacled, fifty-five-year-old had been married to equally plain Gail for twenty years and they had two, unattractive, teenage boys. If Gail was ever to find out about Ray's dalliances with men, the consequences would have been unthinkably dire.

'Ugly produces ugly,' one of Ray and Gail's children's less pleasant, young male teachers had observed to a sniggering colleague when Gail and Ray had attended a parent teachers evening. 'Thank God their two kids have brains. They'll need them with faces like that,' the reluctant teacher had added, as his colleague nodded sagely.

Ray's wife was totally unaware that her husband had been indulging in sexual relations with various men and one very unattractive woman throughout their marriage. Ray knew that it would probably end their marriage if it ever came out that he enjoyed sex with men as much as he enjoyed it with women.

Losing his children would have destroyed Ray, which was why he wanted to remove Philippe from the store as quickly as possible. Gail often popped into the store to briefly visit her husband when she was out shopping and Ray could not trust that Philippe, out of his usual devilment would not hint at what her husband had done to him. It was far too dangerous to have the target of his failed seduction remaining at work a minute longer.

Like some secretive bi-sexual men the world over, Ray was filled with self-loathing because of his sexual desire for men when everyone in his family and social circle believed him to be a happily married, heterosexual father. It is, and always has been, a fairly common story rarely told, where genuine feelings are buried deep lest they be discovered and all hell is let loose. For this reason and for many other reasons too numerous to mention, the fabric of family life could be said to be hanging by a thread, like a wobbly tooth.

'Naturally, I'll make sure that you receive glowing references from this store. You're also owed two weeks leave, which you'll be paid for in lieu,' Ray added. With Ray's agreement, an affronted Philippe left the store that evening, never to return.

If Neil had not been wealthy, Philippe might have decided to grit his teeth and stay on at work. However, the young Spaniard knew that Neil was completely besotted with him and had no objections to keeping him for a while whilst he searched for a new job in male fashion retail.

'Just because I'm gay doesn't mean I'm easy or should tolerate being sexually harassed,' Philippe had complained to

Neil, his older boyfriend on the evening that he had angrily flounced out of the department store. Philippe thought it best to play the affronted, innocent party to ensure that Neil never discovered the whole, unsavoury story.

'You are too good for that job anyhow,' Neil said, carefully removing his birthday cards from the mantelpiece, as a week had now passed since his fiftieth birthday. He was being particularly cautious, not wanting to knock any of his expensive ornaments onto the marble hearth. Philippe had already destroyed a rare piece of Dalton pottery after a fit of youthful exuberance when he had made a paper airplane and let it loose in the living room, much to Neil's horror.

'I'd like to thump that creep for what he tried to do to you,' Neil said. This remark sounded ludicrous as he had never thumped anyone in anger before. It was not his style.

'He didn't try to do it to me. He actually went ahead and did it. If I'd not had my wits about me, he'd have had these trousers unzipped in the blink of an eye,' Philippe replied, which was precisely what he had done to Deepak in the toilets at work the first time they had secretly hooked up.

'Don't give me ideas,' Neil said. 'Are you sure you don't want to have him prosecuted for sexually harassing you? He shouldn't be allowed to get away with such gross behaviour.'

'I honestly can't be bothered. I'm glad Ray was too embarrassed to force me to serve out my notice. I could not have put up with seeing his stupid, slimy face ever again. You know that I prefer a simple life and don't want any unpleasantness. My mother would be so upset if she ever heard about you and me. Our relationship might have come out if there ever was a court case or tribunal. I've been trying to fly under mum's radar ever since we met and I don't want her to find out about us, or that I was propositioned by my boss. As a strict catholic, Spanish mother, she wouldn't take kindly to discovering her son is gay,' Philippe replied, hauling his naked body from the bed, walking over to a small table with a drinks tray on it. He poured two, large cognacs and handing one to his silver-haired fox before climbing back onto the bed.

'Well, you know that it's absolutely fine for you to stay here at my place for as long as you like. I earn enough money to keep us both in some style,' Neil said proudly, looking around the large, tastefully decorated, well-appointed bedroom.

Its style was echoed in the rest of his property. In Neil's eyes, the most attractive, valuable object in the room was obviously his darkly handsome, curly-haired lover who had been born in Barcelona. Philippe's family had relocated to London as a young child when his father gained employment as head chef in a large, London restaurant. Philippe's father had naturally brought his family over with him, to the great disappointment of his wife who had not wanted to leave her family and friends in Barcelona.

'I'm not sure that I can easily adapt to becoming a kept man, but I'm very grateful for your kind offer, babes. I'll start looking for a new job tomorrow,' Philippe said, stroking Neil's soft back without realising that he was doing it. Neil turned over and mischievously smiled into Philippe's warm, brown eyes.

'Oh, you're a devious devil,' said Philippe, laughing. His hand wandered down Neil's pale, hairless chest, down and down. 'You're such a randy old goat!' he added wickedly, knowing that they would soon be setting off again on another sweaty journey towards mutual sexual gratification.

'Hey, that's enough, you cheeky young whippersnapper! I'll show you who's an old goat!' Neil replied.

Half an hour later, Philippe was lying next to Neil and thought, 'There's definitely nothing wrong with our sex life. It's such a shame that he makes me feel like I can't breathe in our daily life.'

As it turned out, Philippe did not start looking for a new job for over four months, due to having such a wonderful time living the high life with Neil. However, guilt and a certain amount of boredom set in and he eventually registered with an employment agency. The agency had found him a few job possibilities suitable for a man with a background in male fashion retail. He had attended six interviews to no avail and was starting to panic that he might never find a suitable job. This is the reason why he now finds himself sitting on a wooden, Battersea park bench, sweating with nerves because he really needs to be accepted for this job.

This will be the second and final interview and is to take place at the company's head office in Battersea and not at their large, Oxford Street store where his first interview had been held. The vacancy is for a top managerial position, a level that he has never previously aspired to.

'At thirty-six, I feel that I'm now mature enough to assume greater responsibility. I'm too old to be employed as a mere shop assistant,' he told Neil as they lay in bed the night before the second interview.

'Age is the eternal enemy of gay men, so don't wish yourself to be as old as me,' Neil said, who always became prickly whenever age was mentioned. He regularly spent a fortune on treatments to prolong a youthful appearance, but knew that he was fighting a battle that he could never ultimately win.

Philippe knew that if he was offered the job, it would be a welcome step up and would gain him greater respect and kudos from Neil. Philippe had enough pride to feel irritated by Neil's playful quips about him being a kept man. He knew that he had to equalise the balance in their relationship if they were ever to have any chance of a long-term future together. If he managed to land the managerial job, the increase in wage would help to restore his sense of self-worth which had been trickling away as the months passed.

Neil had enjoyed an easier passage through life than Philippe, having come from a wealthy family whose fortune had spread back for centuries. Neil had managed not to fall out with any of his relatives and so he had inherited the family wealth without a hitch in due course, unlike Edward's experience. Neil had been blessed that his wealthy parents had been surprisingly supportive when, at the age of sixteen he had confided in them and told them that he was gay. Not for him the bitter pill of disinheritance. His parents had long suspected as much in any case and so his revelation had not surprised them. They had been happy to provide the funds to pay for his top-notch education, which then led to him gaining a strong foothold in the world of art. Although never an artist, his art history degree led to a deep appreciation of art, plus an ability to tell a valuable, commercial art piece from trash.

When he had first set eyes on Philippe in a crowded, gay club in Soho, Neil had been running his prestigious, successful art gallery in Hampstead for over a decade. After not being keen to take his eyes off the tall, attractive, dark-haired, younger man standing at the bar, Neil had taken his courage in both of his elegantly manicured hands and approached him, saying, 'May I buy you a drink? You look like you're in need of a top up.'

Not having previously noticed the stylishly-dressed, elegant man with the sleek, grey hair, Philippe had looked him up and down and found him to be the type of elegant, older man that he particularly favoured. He replied, 'That's very decent of you. I'd love a spiced rum and ginger ale if that's alright. A bit of an odd choice I know, but I really fancy one.'

'Have whatever you like. My name is Neil, by the way. We could split a bottle of champers if you prefer,' said Neil in the faultless accent of an English gentleman.

He always enjoyed flashing his wealth and wanted the young Spaniard to realise that he was talking to a man of substance. He found that his money often turned his male conquests on as much, or maybe more, than his physical appearance.

'Hi Neil, my name is Philippe. It's a pleasure to meet you. I'd actually prefer rum and ginger ale if you wouldn't mind. I'm not too keen on champagne to be honest. It gives me heartburn,' Philippe replied, instantly more interested in Neil now that he had worked out that Neil had considerably more money than he did.

He could tell from the upper-class mannerisms, accent and from spotting the bulging wallet when he paid for the drinks, that the man eying him lustfully had huge potential. 'He's attractive in a gentle, David Niven kind of way,' Philippe thought.

They stood flirting at the bar until Neil pointed to a table and chairs in a dark corner of the club and politely asked, 'Can I tempt you to sit down with me over there where it's more private?'

'That's fine by me, Neil,' the younger, more handsome man replied. A shiver of illicit delight had run down Philippe's spine when the words 'more private' had been said in such a suggestive way. Neil's voice sounded as smooth as melted chocolate and Philippe loved chocolate.

From all of their easy conversation and flirtatious banter, it was clear that Philippe would be accompanying Neil back to his luxury home. After several drinks, much meaningful eye contact and Neil's hand boldly wandering up Philippe's firm thigh, they stepped into a black cab and crawled through the traffic towards Kensington. Neil wondered if he had died and gone to Heaven when Philippe unexpectedly squeezed Neil's expensively clad thigh.

'Keep the change,' Neil hurriedly said to the taxi driver before rushing his night's entertainment through his heavy, elegant front door.

Without any preamble or hesitation, Philippe asked, 'Where's the bedroom?'

'Follow me,' Neil replied, already unbuttoning his exclusive designer shirt. He grabbed a bottle of chilled, white wine from the fridge plus a couple of crystal glasses and headed up the stairs.

They scarcely talked as they skilfully made love to each other all over the crumpled sheets. After several hours, they fell into a deep, satisfied sleep, wrapped in each other's arms.

Next morning, a bleary-eyed Philippe was awakened by Neil standing over him wearing his bath robe and carrying a couple of bone china mugs full of top quality tea.

'I feel like I need to sleep for a week. What the hell did you do to me last night?' Philippe asked chuckling. 'I'm really impressed. You're quite a revelation for an older guy,' Philippe said, stretching like a lazy lion.

'That's a tad condescending, Philippe. Experience is a very valuable commodity, despite what you young bucks might think of us older men,' Neil replied.

He was used to getting what he wanted precisely when he wanted it. A life of wealth had treated Neil very well. His young, handsome personal trainer ensured that Neil's lithe, well-preserved body was more toned than muscle-bound as befitted his sensitive, aesthete temperament. Neil's tailored suits would not have looked so svelte if they had to be worn over bulging muscles. He could have had huge, bulging muscles all over his body if he had wanted them, but he chose not to bulk up. Regular sex kept him fit and he considered himself to be blessed with the libido of a twenty year-old. There were so many of his peers that could not make the same claim.

'I'm also very grateful for my genes. My grandfather was a famous lothario,' Neil boasted.

'Cheers to your granddad!' quipped Philippe, raising his cup of tea. 'But enough about you, what about me?' he asked, pulling back the duvet so that Neil could admire him. 'I think this is all going rather well. Bagged myself a rich one this time,' Philippe thought, turning over to snooze.

'You're all mine,' Neil whispered into Philippe's ear, thinking that he was asleep.

'That sounds a bit creepy. I'm my own man,' thought Philippe, who had only been resting his eyes.

## Mungo chills – 13:45 15th June 2015

Without even looking for an empty bench to sit on, Mungo sprawls out on the grass with his head resting on his large, leather bag that he had made from a leather skirt purchased from a charity shop. He hopes that he has not missed spotting any dog excrement when he had quickly checked the grass before laying his tall, tanned body onto the prickly, green blades.

His stash of dope, E's, cocaine and other illegal paraphernalia are packed securely inside his leather bag. He dreams of how much money will shortly be his after he offloads the gear in a couple of hours. His first customer, Jules, should be along shortly to take Mungo back to her flat to seal the deal.

'I just hope Jules doesn't want to try to seduce me again whilst I'm round at her flat like she did the last time I sold her some gear. I'm not feeling up to fighting her off today,' he thinks, as the sun makes him ache to drift off to sleep.

He barely notices the first, loud bang because he is so stoned and exhausted as he sprawls in his shorts and sleeveless t-shirt on the dry grass. He plugs his headphones into his smart phone and selects shuffle mode on his music library. Hendrix's 'Voodoo Chile' blasts into his dozing brain and Mungo smiles contentedly. The track is swiftly followed by one by the Foo Fighters. He drifts off to sleep on the warm grass, despite the cacophony assaulting his ears.

The reason for Mungo's fatigue is because he has just spent a virtually sleepless night in bed with his over-sexed girlfriend, Francesca who had invited herself around to his flat for a few days. He could barely walk to the park from his flat three streets away.

'You're going to kill me at this rate, babes,' he had moaned to Francesca.

'You know that I can't resist you,' she had replied,

flopping forward onto his naked, hairy chest. She smothered his tired, stubbly face and curly, dark brown hair with her sticky kisses.

'Just let me close my eyes for an hour or two, please, babe. I've got a big day ahead of me. I need to offload a ton of gear tomorrow if I'm going to be able to take us both to Ibiza next month,' he had said sleepily, feeling so tired that he could have cried.

He was beginning to feel irked that she was such high maintenance. Neither was he too happy with the way that she always expected him to treat her to meals, holidays and nights on the town. His previous girlfriend, Bernadette had been the reverse, content to pay for herself and often for him too. Bernadette had been twelve years older than Mungo and could well afford to help carry the financial burden. She had a highly paid job in the fashion industry which had made her financially secure. Mungo often missed the easier life he once led with Bernadette.

'Kill joy! Okay, you win,' Francesca had said reluctantly before turning away from him in a huff.

Mungo had not heard her words because he was already snoring. Francesca lay awake resentfully, although she fully intended going to sleep whilst he was out seeing to his shady business.

Francesca was a selfish, spoilt, young woman, whose looks rather than brains had managed to ease her path through life. She had wedged herself into Mungo's life four months earlier by stealing him away from his long-term girlfriend, Bernadette. Four months previously, Bernadette had been friends with Francesca despite them being completely different characters.

After a drunken party at Mungo and Bernadette's flat, Bernadette had been short-sighted enough to retreat to bed, complaining of a headache. It left the way clear for Francesca to seduce her boyfriend. Francesca had been lusting after Mungo for over a year, so when she saw her opportunity she grabbed it with both of her red-tipped hands.

Girl-code meant nothing to Francesca but she was punished to some degree by losing all of her best female friends who had been disgusted by her disloyal behaviour after they heard how she had stolen her friend's boyfriend.

Francesca consoled herself with the thought that she had bagged a good-looking, sexually adept male who was well off, albeit his funds came from his illegal activity. She was young enough and stupid enough to find it exciting to be aligned to a so-far successful drug pusher. She did not have the foresight to wonder what she would do if Mungo was ever arrested for drug-pushing or wiped out in the worst way by a rival, gun-toting, drug pushing gang.

## The second bullet

When a second bullet cracks the humid air closer than the first one had done a couple of minutes earlier, Mungo is oblivious to the sound. He is venturing deeper and deeper along sleep's dark corridors, accompanied by the beats of Metallica. His bag of assorted drugs is securely pinned beneath his mop of tightly curled, black hair.

Bernadette had once told him that his hair reminded her of a blackberry, but she had been very stoned at the time. He missed her quirky intelligence, something he could never say about Francesca whose good points were purely physical. His new lover's conversation was disappointingly banal.

From their bench, Pauline and Claire start to speculate as to the possible cause of the second bang. Claire has never heard gunshot in real life before, only on television or cinema screens, but this noise would be her idea of how gunfire should sound. Lurking at the back of their minds is the distinct possibility that the noise could be gunfire, but the idea seems so preposterous that they do not mention it to each other for fear of sounding alarmist.

'Maybe it's a car or a motorbike backfiring,' the older woman says to the pretty, blonde girl who is still dabbing at the coffee stain on her new skirt and inwardly swearing.

'Yes, you're probably right,' Claire replies.

She is being polite because it does not really sound like it has come from a vehicle. A toddler is screaming in her pushchair much to the annoyance of her young, clueless mother and everyone else in earshot.

The child's nappy is full and stinking in the heat, but the incompetent mother has no intention of changing it just yet. Money is short and she always tries to drag out the time in between nappy changes. The resulting nappy rash on her baby has been causing concern for her social workers for some time.

'Kids, eh,' Pauline says to Claire who nods knowingly.

Claire feels the urge to place her hand onto her swelling belly. She is four months pregnant, much to her delight and the delight of her fiancé, James. Claire feels a sudden rush of love as she thinks of how James is only a few hundred yards away, working hard in the literary agency office up the road from her office.

# A matching pair

Even as a young girl, Claire had always wanted a baby. The desire had increased now that all of her friends from her university years are either married or proud parents. She is planning to relinquish her job at the advertising agency to become a freelance illustrator once her child is born, working from home whilst James carries on working in the literary agency.

The couple had first talked two years previously during their lunch break on a similar sunny, summer's day in London. Several interested glances had been exchanged between them several times in the weeks leading up to the day when James had found enough courage to approach Claire. Their paths had sometimes crossed on the underground tube journey into work. Each time that it happened, they exchanged warm smiles and eventually even awkward waves of recognition.

The relationship would have blossomed much sooner if James or Claire had been bold enough to enter into conversation when they found themselves standing in a queue inside a local café. They had each inwardly kicked themselves for merely smiling at each other. They had walked off separately up the road clutching their tasty purchases. James had even shyly hung back slightly so as to avoid the embarrassment of walking side by side with the attractive girl back up the road to their respective workplaces.

As it was now becoming ridiculous not to talk when they both so desperately wanted to, James had finally gritted his perfect teeth and approached the petite blonde sitting on the sun-drenched bench.

'May I join you?' James had said, nervously flicking his thick, blond, floppy fringe out of his eyes, hoping that she would act as friendly towards him as her demeanour suggested.

Claire moved her handbag onto the ground and shifted

along slightly. 'Of course you can. It's not as though you are a complete stranger. I've seen you around and about for quite a while now,' Claire replied in a gentle, warm voice that melted him as she smiles sweetly up into his blue eyes.

They looked similar enough for them to have been related, possibly even brother and sister, both fair, fine-boned. They looked more cerebral than sporty, party animals.

'It would be rude for us to carry on not talking every time we bump into each other. It's happened to us quite a lot,' James said with a nervous laugh. He then kicked himself for making it sound as though that was the only reason he wanted to talk to her. This was far from the case because he had been longing to talk to her for weeks.

'I've seen you disappearing into Flemming, Upkirk and Kilbride's offices a few times, so I'm guessing you work in publishing,' Claire stated.

'Yes, I'm one of the many poor bastards slaving away in there. My name is James, by the way. What's yours?' he asked, starting to relax slightly.

'I'm Claire. You've probably seen me disappearing into Bernard Wiggins Advertising Agency, or B.W.'s as we like to call it. It's such a mouthful,' she replied.

'Using that logic, my agency would be called F.U.K.'s. They would have been better calling it Flemming, Kilbride and Upkirk if they had used a bit of forethought,' James said. Their easy laughter perfectly broke the ice and soon they were talking as if they had known each other for years.

On so many levels, they were destined to meet and deeply connect. They both had pointy, small noses and lightly tanned skin. In winter they became delicately pale, like bone china. Although James was a couple of inches taller than Claire, they were both shorter and thinner than average. Even without opening their mouths, they both had an intelligent air about them, yet both were blessed with enviable looks in understated ways. They were vain enough not to wear glasses socially, but both sported reading classes whilst working at their desks in their respective offices. The slight indentations in the sides of each of their small noses gave the game away.

'Sadly, I must head back to the office. I've really enjoyed our little chat. I hate to cut it short,' Claire said to James, who was glancing at his mobile to find out the time.

'Me too,' James replied. 'There's a writer coming into the office to see me in about fifteen minutes, so I'd better get a wriggle on and walk back with you. Hopefully I'll see you again on another lunch break, when the weather is as fine as today.' He felt the urge to ask her out for a drink that very evening after work, but thought it might seem slightly desperate.

They both slowly prised themselves off the bench and wandered back up the road together to their almost neighbouring offices. That afternoon, they both thought about their conversation on the bench, hoping they could continue with it the next day. James checked London's weather forecast on Google and smiled when he saw that it should be sunny and dry the following day.

That afternoon, Claire had plenty of opportunity to think about James. She was working on several watercolour paintings of board members of a large, financial institution that would grace their annual report. A mere headshot photograph was obviously not sufficient. It had been deemed that the company could spare the money from their overflowing coffers to pay the advertising agency for Claire's skill with watercolours.

Working from photographs, she had already produced two of the illustrations which she hoped that the clients would be satisfied with and was now working on the third. It was of a rather unattractive, overweight man that she knew would be a challenge to make look anything except rather repulsive, but she was doing her best. Claire smiled as images of James' face with his twinkling eyes and floppy, blond hair popped up into her mind, replacing the face of the florid, greasy-looking man looking up at her from the photograph on her desk.

At the end of the work day, James found himself seated on the wall outside Claire's office waiting for her to appear with butterflies fluttering in his stomach. During their lunchtime conversation, they had both had discovered that they were single. This news had secretly encouraged them both. He simply could not wait until the following day to see her again.

During the afternoon, he had thought how wonderful it would be to enjoy an after work drink with Claire in one of the local pub gardens. He felt nervous as he sat on the wall in the early evening sunshine, conscious of the inquisitive eyes of pedestrians walking past him.

'I feel like a bloody stalker sitting here like Humpty Dumpty. I wish she'd hurry up. She might be working late. Maybe I should go. I'll be able to see her tomorrow with any luck,' James thought.

He was just about to wander off to catch the tube home when the front door to Claire's office building swung open. Two, young women emerged chatting and laughing together. Luckily, one of them was Claire. James jumped eagerly from his perch.

'Oh, hi, James,' Claire called out warmly, surprised but delighted to see him. Her companion looked at him with interest, wondering if her friend Claire had been keeping secrets from her.

Seeing that she might be surplus to requirements and a bit of a gooseberry, Claire's friend said, 'See you tomorrow, Claire,' and marched off towards the tube station.

'Bye, Sharon,' Claire shouted after her friend, relieved that she would now be alone with James as he appeared to have something important to say to her, judging by the anxious expression on his face.

They stood staring at each other, both awkwardly waiting for the other to say something. Hesitantly, James eventually said, 'Um, I was wondering if you'd like to go for a drink with me this evening. It's been such a hot day, I thought it'd be lovely to sit with you in a pub garden near here and get to know each other a bit better, if you're not doing anything else this evening.'

Claire thought that his nervousness was endearing and her heart went out to him. She replied, 'Oh, that'd be great. I'm free this evening, as per usual.'

'Do you fancy going to the 'Magic Garden'? They do a great steak and ale pie there,' James asked.

'Oh, I love that pub. I had a few too many twisted apple martinis on my birthday in there, last month,' Claire replied, remembering the horrendous hangover she had experienced the day after her birthday drinks party with her friends from work.

'I didn't want to be presumptuous, but I'd also like to buy you a meal in there too,' said James, who was more than ready to eat after a busy day.

'How quaint! Haven't the days passed when men bought women meals? I'm more than willing to pay for my share of the meal,' Claire replied as they made their way in the direction of the pub.

The pavements were busy now that most office buildings were regurgitating their occupants into the outside world.

'I was just being polite,' said James, hoping that she was joking and was not a strident feminist, although she certainly did not look like one.

'And I was only joking,' Claire quipped, much to his relief.

By the time they reached the pub, it was heaving with a motley collection of mostly young folk enjoying themselves in the sunshine. They miraculously managed to find a small space outside. After placing their steak and ale pie orders with a waitress, they sipped their halves of lager shandy whilst waiting for their food to arrive. Eager to make a great impression on each other, neither of them wanted to become too drunk and ruin their first date, which is why they opted for a weaker drink.

'I guess this is an actual date,' thought James, who had not been on one for over a year and was feeling rusty.

Claire was thinking the same thing, although she had been

on a horrendous, first date two weeks previously with Doug, a garage mechanic who she had been chatting to on an internet dating site. As can happen all too often, the man had looked very different to his profile photograph, which he must have failed to update for over ten years.

Although he was still a tall, good-looking, dark-haired man, she noted there was a cruel coldness about him that made him not quite as attractive in real life as she had been led to believe. His powerfully muscled torso appeared to be trying to break out of his denim shirt. His intense gaze fell either on her bare legs or her breasts and spoke of his intentions. She felt trapped, like Bambi being stalked by a hungry lion.

Doug's creepy aura made her want to immediately make her excuses and flee the pub, but she thought that staying for one drink would not hurt. Unbeknownst to Claire, Doug had snorted several lines of coke before leaving his house and was feeling rampant. She shifted uneasily in her seat as his eyes kept wandering to her cleavage, making her wish that she had chosen to wear a more modest top. When he gripped her bare knee with one powerful hand, not wanting to cause a scene, she rapidly brushed it off with a nervous giggle, hoping nobody had seen.

Doug had wrongly assumed that Claire would be as enthusiastic to have sex with him as the other dating site females that he had met. As Claire talked about her job at the advertising agency, Doug's eyes glazed over as his mind shot back a month to a completely different first date he had been on with a sex maniac called Ruth. Hardly ten minutes had passed after setting eyes on the busty brunette for the first time at a pub, before Ruth was on the back seat of Doug's Vauxhall Vectra in the pub's car park.

'I should have realised that she'd be this filthy from the way she talked to me on the dating site,' Doug thought. He had to quickly wind up the windows mid-thrust so that her screams of ecstasy did not alarm the inquisitive drinkers in the nearby pub. Ruth did not seem to care a jot when a shocked, middle-aged couple walked by Doug's Vectra to collect their car from the crowded car park.

'Disgusting,' the woman said loud enough for Doug to hear her comment and cringe.

The disgusted woman's husband hung back for as long as he could in order to catch a better look at half-naked Ruth. His flat-chested wife called his name three times before he reluctantly dragged himself away. Before he was dragged off to his car, the desperately unhappily husband made eye contact with Ruth. She just smiled knowingly at him and winked, which made his year.

To his chagrin, Doug was discovering that Claire was much less forthcoming than Ruth had been. He could tell from her demeanour that she thought herself superior to him, probably because she was. Against all the odds, he managed to convince her to stay for a meal, much against her better judgement. He was drinking far more than Claire would have wished. In his drunken state, Doug pushed his luck much too far. Remembering all the fun that he had enjoyed with Ruth and the flame-haired girl, he decided to try to melt the blonde iceberg sitting opposite him. He leant forward and reached under the table. She looked quizzically at him, unprepared for what happened next.

With a drunken leer, Doug boldly slid his large hand roughly up Claire's short skirt. Claire was so shocked and affronted that she briefly froze in disbelief but then grabbed her dinner fork. Doug yelped as she speedily punctured the back of his hand with her sharp fork. The look of shock on his dark, swarthy face was comical, but Claire was not in the mood to laugh. Without a word to her wounded, swearing dining companion, she swept regally out of the restaurant, jumped into her car and sped into the night.

'I guess she won't be up for a second date then,' Doug said to a shocked elderly male diner who had witnessed the entire episode. Ignoring the specks of blood around the fork's puncture marks, Doug sighed and scraped Claire's leftover food onto his plate. 'Waste not, want not,' he slurred to the waiter who smiled back politely. The waiter was used to seeing drama between diners at his restaurant.

After a long soak in the bath to wipe the feel of her groper's hands from her body, Claire then angrily blocked Doug, aka Scrummyboy257's profile later that night. After some consideration, she then deleted her entire profile from the dating site where she had started talking to Doug. Internet dating was proving not to really be her style after discovering to her cost that there were such dubious people as Doug lurking on them.

Put off by her traumatic evening with Doug, Claire had rather overdramatically begun to fear that she might die a spinster. That was until James quietly infiltrated her life. After their meeting, life began to look distinctly rosier. She resolved never to disclose her experiences with Doug to her new love interest. Even she could scarcely understand why she had acted so violently and stabbed a fork into the back of a man's hand as though she was about to flip over a beef burger on a barbecue.

She smiled sweetly as she looked deep into James' blue eyes that peeped from under his floppy, blond fringe. All memory of her recent debacle with the ghastly groper, drunken Doug immediately vanished. She wiped Doug from her mind and snapped back into the present.

'So what did you get up to at work this afternoon?' James asked Claire. 'What do you actually do in the advertising agency?' James continued. He thought that work would be a fairly safe subject to discuss. Claire was looking so attractive, almost virginally pure, that she was making him feel tongue-tied.

'I was painting some ugly guy in watercolours for his company's report. I tend to handle the illustration side of any advertising work that comes in. It could be photographic, computerised or hand-done artwork,' she replied. 'I've worked there a few years and it's a fun company to work for, apart from my boss being a bit of an ogre. I'm pretty happy as they are mostly a great bunch of people.'

Her relaxed attitude, sprinkled with mild expletives gradually served to relax James and he soon discovered that he was revealing personal details that he usually did not discuss.

As they finished the last morsels of their delicious meal, he said, 'I'm almost ashamed to admit it, but I live at home with my mother. She suffers from multiple sclerosis and, as dad left us both a few years ago for another woman, I feel it's my duty to be there for her as she has nobody else to care for her. She's fairly independent, so I'm not too worried to leave her on her own tonight. She says that she can cope, but I wanted to be company for her after dad moved out to be with his tart.'

'I think that's a wonderfully unselfish thing to do and nothing to be ashamed of admitting to. It says a lot about you,' Claire said warmly.

'She's been nagging me to move out because she doesn't want to hold me back from making a life of my own. She's not wheelchair bound, but she uses a stick, which she hates because she's always been such an independent, strong woman. Her house is very near to a tube station so it is very convenient for my work. There seems no reason to move out just yet,' James said, feeling himself blushing at Claire's kind words.

'My parents are boringly normal and still happily married in Bournemouth. Like you, I'm an only child and they've spoilt me rotten,' she joked.

'You don't come across in the least bit spoilt I'm delighted to say,' said James.

They had swapped to drinking red wine after their thirst had been quenched. He was feeling pleasantly mellow as a light breeze wafted through his fair hair and that of his companion. As he gazed at Claire, he had an urge to kiss her but knew that would be pushing his luck too far. Their conversation was flowing easily as they talked about their past lives, but at the back of his mind he was pondering how he should act at the end of the night.

'Can I risk giving her a quick kiss on the lips before we set off for our respective homes?' he wondered, looking at the pale slick of pink lip gloss on her perfect mouth.

She caught him staring at her lips and being very perceptive, she knew just what he was thinking.

After their perfect evening together, it was Claire who slightly raised her head and kissed James as his tube arrived at the platform. A warm feeling flooded through her as she watched his smiling face whilst he waved her goodbye from inside the airless tube then disappeared inside the dark tunnel. She walked to the opposite platform and waited a few minutes for her tube to arrive.

She normally felt disgusted by all of the dead skin floating around in the underground for her to inhale, but her mind was too occupied with thoughts of her wonderful evening with James to be depressed and disgusted by her surroundings. His lips had felt so soft and warm.

'I can't wait for tomorrow when I can see him again,' she thought, as she cannoned her way through the rattling, dark tunnels towards her small, cosy flat in Camden.

'I wish that James had been bold enough to ask me for my mobile number. I'd have loved to have received a text from him now whilst I lie here in bed. I bet he sends the most wonderfully soppy texts. There's no way I'd ever offer my number to him without him asking me for it. I hope he has the courage to ask me for it tomorrow. Please, weather, be dry tomorrow lunchtime.'

As Claire looked through her bedroom curtains the next morning, it was a relief to find that the sun was beating down with barely a cloud in the blue sky. 'Perfect conditions,' she thought as she set off to shower. Refreshed, she slid a sleeveless, light blue, loosely fitting dress over her slim body and slipped some flat, blue, open-toed sandals onto her bare feet. Her damp hair was dripping onto her thin dress as she ate her cereal, but it would soon dry of its own accord. She took extra care with her makeup that morning and squirted her favourite perfume onto her slender wrists and neck.

Over in his Battersea home, James' mother said, 'You're looking extra smart today. You smell nice too. I reckon there's a female involved somewhere.'

'Oh, shut up mum. You're making me cringe,' James said affectionately. 'Actually, I met a great girl yesterday in the park. She works up the road from me and we got on really well when we went for a meal last night.'

'I hope that was gravy on your shirt and nothing more revolting,' his mother said, who had noticed the brown stain on his shirtfront when he had placed it into the washing machine that morning.

'Yes, it was my over-enthusiastic eating of steak and ale pie. Claire was so sweet; she never even mentioned the splodge to me. I was mortified when I looked into the bathroom mirror last night,' he said. 'I've squirted some stain remover on it. I'll wash it tonight.'

'I'm sure I can manage to switch the washing machine on. I'm not completely useless,' his mother replied, knowing that she felt completely useless most of the time.

'Up to you mum,' James said, grabbing the pack of sandwiches he had made, plus a bottle of still mineral water. He stuffed them into a carrier bag and lightly kissed the top of his mother's greying head as he shot out of the door to work. 'I might be back late. It all depends how it goes with Claire.'

'That's my boy!' she yelled after him with a giggle.

Although the young couple eagerly looked out for each other on the way into work, James and Claire were disappointed not to bump into one other. The morning seemed to drag, but eventually lunchtime arrived, brimming over with promise. They had agreed to meet at one o'clock at the same bench they had sat on the previous day.

'Damn, the bench is already taken,' thought James who had been clock watching all morning.

Claire was nowhere to be seen and he anxiously looked

around the park in case she was sitting somewhere else. He walked to the closest, empty bench, perched nervously on it and waited in a nervous sweat.

'Oh, God, maybe she's changed her mind and wants to avoid me,' he thought, knowing he was probably being overdramatic.

Sure enough, five minutes later, he saw a smiling Claire enter the park through the wrought iron gateway, looking like a blonde angel entering through the Gates of Heaven. He smiled broadly and waved.

'Sorry I'm late but I had to finish off an airbrush illustration. The joys of deadlines,' she said apologetically, sitting demurely next to him on the bench. 'You smell edible, if you don't mind me saying.'

'That must be my new aftershave. If we are giving compliments, so do you. Issey Miyake? Yes, I thought so. That's a lovely dress too,' James observed.

'Enough! Enough! We sound like a mutual appreciation society,' Claire joked as she unwrapped her shop-bought pack of sandwiches. 'They're egg and bacon, my favourite.'

'Don't make me jealous. Mine are home-made cheese and pickle. This time, I'll try not to drip pickle on my shirt like I did last night,' James said.

'Oh, you noticed it then. I didn't like to mention it last night,' Claire replied, laughing.

They chatted in the sunshine as they nibbled their sandwiches and glugged bottled water.

'I don't like the look of those big, black clouds drifting this way,' Claire said, pointing to their threatening trajectory across the sky.

It had been unusually warm all week with a close, thundery feel in the air. They ignored the few large plops of rain and the rumbles of thunder because they wanted to continue their chat. They were so engrossed with each other that they failed to notice that the other people were scurrying away from the park. By the time the downpour arrived, it was far too late for the couple to escape from the park without getting drenched, so they huddled under a spreading tree.

'Is it safe to be under a tree when there's a possibility of lightning?' Claire asked, soaked to the skin.

'There's just thunder so far, so don't tempt fate,' James replied.

Her skin was clearly visible through the dress material. He did not mind getting a drenching if it meant he had such a glorious, unexpected view. As they huddled under the tree for the worst of the shower to disperse, he bravely bent down and kissed her glossy lips, long and hard. He could feel her smiling with pleasure as they kissed, their tongues exploring the secrets of each other's mouths. It was not the most practical place for their passion to ignite, but ignite it did.

Claire whispered, 'I feel like we're castaways on a tropical island. Everyone else has wisely legged it from the park.'

They instinctively moved around the thick trunk of the tree to stand on the side furthest from the distant street, seeking a place where nobody could see them. As the deluge of water fell on them, he ran his hands up her wet, bare thighs, expecting to meet resistance at any moment, but it never came.

She knew that her inviting reaction was very different to her fork in the hand response to Doug, two weeks earlier, but the crucial difference was that she desperately wanted James.

Claire leant against the rough bark of the tree trunk as he looked deep into her eyes as she moaned and sighed as the thunder crashed around them.

Almost on cue, the thunder and rain died away. As they waited until the brief shower ended, they looked at each other and laughed with a tinge of embarrassment over what they had just done.

'You don't think anyone saw us, do you?' she said, looking around as though just waking from a dream.

'It's a bit late to worry about that, but I'm pretty sure nobody saw. You shouldn't look so gorgeous. It's totally your fault. I just couldn't resist you, and that's not usually like me,'

James said, wondering where this bold man had suddenly sprung from, one bold enough to indulge in public sex that he had only dated once.

He usually worked much more slowly with women. 'It must have been the influence of all of the electricity in the air or something. Whatever it was, I liked it,' he thought.

'It was wonderful and let me assure you, I don't normally go in for sex in public either. It felt like I was in the middle of some gothic fantasy movie. Heaven knows where it would have all ended if the sun hadn't come out as suddenly as it had disappeared,' she said as they walked back to the damp bench.

'That's British weather for you. Thank you, British weather! You played a blinder!' James exclaimed loudly, not caring who could hear him. He was giddy with happiness. 'We might as well sit on the bench as we're both soaked through.'

Claire looked down at the front of her dress and gasped. 'Oops! I never realised that this dress turns transparent when wet. Mind you, I'm actually glad it does as long as it's only you that's looking. That was such a mind-blowing experience. I'll never forget it.'

'I simply must see you this evening after work. Are you free? What's your mobile number?' James asked. They were all too aware that their action-packed lunch hour would sadly soon be drawing to an end.

'Yes, I'm free again tonight, although I can't promise sex in a thunderstorm again,' she replied, grabbing his mobile and deftly tapping her number into it. 'There's a great bistro near me. We could go there if you like.'

'Sounds perfect,' James replied, realising that if it was near her flat then there would be a good chance that he would be spending the night in Claire's bed.

They headed back to their offices with Claire self-consciously trying to hide her body which were still visible through her wet dress. Her awkward embarrassment made James chuckle, until Claire punched his arm playfully to quieten his laughter. They briefly kissed before Claire walked up the steps to her office.

Once inside his workplace, James sent a text to his mother. 'I mightn't be home tonight. I've got a date. Are you well enough to be left alone?'

'Don't be soft. Of course I'll be fine. I didn't feel too bad today. Enjoy yourself xxx,' his mother texted back.

'Oh, I intend to,' James thought, wondering if steam was rising from his wet clothes as he sat at his desk reading a disappointing manuscript from an aspiring young writer.

James and Claire watched their office clocks even more avidly that afternoon. Texts were zooming to and fro between them, mostly referring to their thrills under the tree.

They both managed to quit work early and rushed out of their buildings, meeting half way on the busy pavement. With a brief kiss, they dashed down the stairs to the underground station and caught the tube to Camden. James was disappointed to see that her dress had dried out.

They decided not to bother heading for the bistro, but rushed immediately to her tiny flat. Without any discussion, as soon as the door closed behind them they headed for her bedroom, grabbing a couple of glasses of red wine to take in there with them. They ignored the wine, so great was their haste to finish what they had started under the dripping leaves in the park.

'I really need some of that wine,' she eventually said, clambering off the bed and padding across the carpet to retrieve the glasses. They sat naked on the bed and sipped it, chatting contentedly as if they had known each other for years. By the time they had finished it, James wanted her again, much to Claire's surprise and delight.

'I seem to have bagged a sexual athlete,' she thought, as James expertly flipped her over onto all fours.

They suddenly realised that they were ravenously hungry, but this time it was for food. 'I know I mentioned that we should eat at the local bistro, but I'm not sure I feel up to getting all dressed up again to go out. I'm exhausted, but very,

very happy. Do you fancy a takeaway? There's a great Indian restaurant I know who deliver. I'll give them a ring if you like, unless you prefer a Chinese?' Claire asked. Even ringing the takeaway restaurant seemed too much of an effort.

'Indian food is perfectly fine by me. I'll eat anything,' James replied, feeling lightheaded from so much unaccustomed sexual activity and lack of food.

They slowly pulled their clothes back on. Whilst James sat in her small living room, Claire rang through their food order with the local Indian takeaway and then made them both a very welcome mug of tea in the small, galley kitchen at the end of her living room. She switched on her iPad in its docking bay and switched it to shuffle, hoping her new lover would approve of her music library selection. The comic tones of 'Yes, we have no bananas,' a tune from the distant past, boomed out.

'What the devil is that?' James asked in mock horror, as Claire doubled up with laughter.

'It's a long story. I bought that song on iTunes to make a Vine; one of my little hobbies,' Claire replied, rapidly switching the iPad from shuffle to a safer U2 album. 'That's better, unless you have an aversion to U2 of course.'

'U2 is fine by me. 'Yes, we have no bananas' would be fine by me too. I have very wide music tastes,' James said.

They chatted easily as they enjoyed their Indian meal, all barriers down. James stayed the night after double-checking that his mother was feeling well enough for him to sleep at Claire's. In the morning, they made love again, showered together and set off for work. It was a far more rewarding journey than usual because for once they were travelling together to their offices that were situated so conveniently close to one another.

Without having to state the fact, both parties knew that they wanted this new relationship to progress and endure. There were no troublesome exes to contend with, nor interest from prospective rival lovers, so the way was clear to be happy ever after. James's mother was very understanding, even eager, for her son to move into a new flat with Claire.

With both being in well paid jobs, James and Claire rented a small, neat flat very near where James had lived with his mother, so she never lost his support. She appreciated Claire's easy, open personality and was delighted when the young couple announced their engagement. The flat was more convenient for Claire, as it was much closer to work than her old place in Camden.

They enjoyed a far more exciting social life as a couple than they had ever experienced as singletons. They ate out at the plethora of London restaurants, leapt around at music venues, travelled to music festivals and spent idyllic holidays in Ibiza and Kos.

Over eighteen months later, Claire was surprised to discover that she had accidentally fallen pregnant. At first Claire and James were shocked and worried that a baby would not be a wise idea when they required both wages to pay the mortgage. After much discussion, they worked out a plan. Claire would work freelance from home because her illustration skills were sufficiently in demand for her to command a high fee for her work.

'My boss says that she will still use me when I'm settled into a routine with the baby. If we squirrel away money each month until I am ready to pop, we should survive for a few months until I can spare the time away from the baby to start illustrating again.  I can use the spare room as my studio as well as the nursery. It'll be a squeeze, financially and space-wise, but needs must. We can postpone the wedding for a while until we can afford it. The baby comes first, when it eventually arrives. I'm only a couple of months pregnant, so we have a few months to tighten our belts, although dare say my belt will be left in the wardrobe once my bump expands,' Claire said as James nodded.

'My word, you've really worked things out perfectly, haven't you, babes? Sounds like a perfect plan. We have cut back on meals out, now that your morning sickness, that seems to last all day, has kicked in. That'll save us some money. I'm glad we managed to get all the mad times at clubs and festivals out of our systems over the past year or so. Once our future child goes to nursery, you can consider returning to full-time work anyway, if you want. You never know, if your freelance work is really successful, you could just carry on working from home,' James replied.

'Just think, in less than a year, if everything goes well, we'll be proud parents. What an odd, slightly scary thought. I don't think I've ever even held anyone else's baby before, but I guess it'll all be fine as long as I don't drop it or something,' Claire said. She kept quiet about her substantial fears, almost amounting to a phobia, surrounding the actual birth. She did not want to worry James, who was also terrified at the prospect of witnessing the woman he loved suffering birth pains. He too was keen to spare his fiancée's feelings and tried not to voice his concerns. She had enough to contend with, suffering as she was from frequent bouts of pregnancy-related nausea.

# A significant meeting

'I'm sure that's Janine over there. It must be over twenty-five years since we last met. I'd know that face anywhere, even though she's chunkier now and she seems to have sagged a tad,' Edward thought.

He stared at his long-lost ex-girlfriend as she morosely shoved groceries into her shopping bags whilst the miserable-looking cashier scanned them. Her long, dark hair, now shot with strands of grey, was hanging limply around her lined face. It looked as though she had not washed it for a month. Edward had been waiting to be served in the adjacent queue with the depressed, mildly impatient expression on his face that most people in queues wear.

Adrenaline suddenly roared around his aching body after recognising Janine. Although their short relationship had ended badly after the incident in the bar with Carl, their time together had been one of the rare times in his life when Edward had felt alive and relatively happy. There was only a pint of milk, a pack of economy bacon and a small loaf of bread in his basket, so he was dealt with and despatched more speedily than Janine.

He waited outside for her near the exit to the supermarket with the early evening, summer sunlight, plus his excitement, overheating his unwashed body. He wondered whether she would speak to him, considering the dramatic way in which they had parted decades earlier.

'Janine? It is you, isn't it? It's me, err, Edward from university,' he said, tentatively walking towards her, wishing that he had phrased his introduction more eloquently.

Janine stared blankly at him for several seconds, but once it had dawned on her who this unkempt man was, she was visibly shocked. However, she pulled herself together quickly and replied, 'Bloody hell. It really is you, after all this time. I hardly recognise you without your velvet cloak. I bet the smelly thing disintegrated with the amount of times you wore it. Boy, it didn't half pong,' Janine said with a half-smile.

Neither of them quite knew how to react to the other after so long, although both were secretly pleased to see someone from their past, short-lived university life. The shoppers milling around them seemed to disappear as though they were both trapped in a bubble that isolated them from the rest of the world.

'You always were the joker, Janine. How's everything going for you these days?' he asked.

'We can't talk properly here. I live just around the corner. Fancy a cuppa and a catch up? No doubt too much has happened to us both since we last met for us to discuss in five minutes outside a grotty supermarket. You can pop your cold stuff into my fridge whilst you're at mine. You can meet Danielle, my daughter,' Janine said, seeming much keener to talk to Edward than he expected.

Edward rarely had anything interesting to do in the evenings, or daytime too for that matter. Without hesitation he said, 'That'd be lovely. I take it you're still single like me?'

She nodded. 'I hope she's not thinking of jumping my bones whilst I'm around at her place. Don't really fancy her much with all that greasy hair,' Edward thought, despite him being no oil painting himself and his body unwashed for a week.

With Edward walking nervously by Janine's side, they made their way to a small, drab, terraced house that looked the same as all the hundreds of others in the area. Dumping her shopping bags on the pavement, she wrestled with her cumbersome handbag to find her front door key. Eventually she managed to let them both inside the narrow hall and through to the cramped living room.

'The delights of rented accommodation,' Janine said, casting a disdainful eye around her cluttered abode.

'Tell me about it. I don't live around here. I rent a room in Moston, for my sins,' Edward replied. He watched from the doorway as Janine placed his meagre shopping items into her small fridge. She then spun around the small kitchen putting away her own purchases like a demented, inefficient, filing clerk.

'Lucky you,' she said sarcastically, knowing Moston well. 'Danielle won't be back for a while. She still lives here to help me out with the rent. She has a little job in a tanning salon and I work in a local pub. It's lucky that you've caught me on my day off.'

She handed him a chipped mug brimming over with tea and they nibbled digestive biscuits served on mismatched plates. Looking around the house, Edward could tell that although Janine might not be rolling in money, she must have more than him after he had been forced to live for decades on disability benefit. He was very aware of his shabby, unwashed clothes and unkempt appearance, but he relaxed when he looked at Janine's lank locks and old, worn tracksuit.

Catching him staring at her, she said, 'Pardon my scruffy appearance. It's my day off so I'm wearing my casual clobber. I scrub up pretty well though.'

'I'm sure you do,' he replied with a giggle. He spotted a photo on the mantelpiece that sparked his interest. It portrayed a pretty, dark-haired girl who looked remarkably like Janine when he had first met her at university. 'That must be your daughter. She's the spit of you.'

'Yes, that's Danielle, bless her. She will be twenty-seven in a few weeks. Frightening thought. Where does the time go, eh?' Janine said, looking deep in thought as though she was trying to phrase a difficult sentence but was uncertain exactly how to tackle it.

'Twenty-seven? She must have been born around the time you were at university. Did you fall for that so-called friend of mine, Carl then? Is he Danielle's dad?' Edward asked, remembering how Carl had betrayed his friendship by stealing Janine from him. Janine stared at the floor for an unusually long time. 'What's wrong Janine? You look really worried.'

'I'm just trying to work out the best way to tell you something pretty major,' she replied, chewing her nails.

'I think the best way is to just go ahead and tell me, whatever it is. Surely it can't be that bad?' Edward said, beginning to feel inexplicably jittery.

'Okay, here goes then. No, Carl isn't Danielle's dad. In fact, I'm virtually certain that you are,' she said, her dark eyes as big as saucers as she watched fearfully for his reaction, unsure of what it would be.

Edward sat bolt upright, unable to speak, mouth wide in disbelief. He placed his mug of tea onto the coffee table because his hands had begun to shake with a mixture of unidentifiable emotions.

'Say something. Don't just stare at me. Haven't you any questions to ask me?' Janine asked, although still frightened to hear whatever he might say.

'I'm totally gobsmacked. Give me a second to think,' he replied, risking picking up the mug of tea because his mouth had dried out from such an extreme, life-changing shock. His face was as white as a snowdrift yet felt flame hot. After a few minutes, he pulled himself together enough to ask, 'Are you sure that she's mine? What happened to you after I was chucked out of university? Why didn't you find me to tell me that I have a daughter? There are so many questions I need to ask.'

'I discovered that I was pregnant soon after you left so abruptly. I considered tracing you, but after much consideration I thought it would be better to raise the child on my own. You weren't the most stable person to care for a baby, were you, love?

'Possibly not,' Edward had to agree.

'After they chucked you out of university, I figured that you'd have more than enough problems of your own to contend with. I left university when I was about seven months pregnant. I saw no point in continuing studying towards my English Degree, although, like so many in my circle, I've got a novel on the go that I've been writing for years.'

He interrupted with, 'Well done, you.'

She brushed his congratulations aside and continued. 'I went home to my dad's house to look after him, have my baby and bring her up. Dad died when Danielle was two. He was piss-poor and so I was left with nothing. I put Danielle into nursery and took menial jobs to pay our way. Despite the crippling cost of childcare, we got by. So many other unmarried mothers are in the same boat as I was and still am, so I can't really complain. Oh, and before you think that she might be anyone else's offspring, Danielle definitely has your nose.'

'I can see that from the photograph,' Edward concurred.

Janine said, 'She looks so much like you from certain angles that it's unreal. I didn't sleep around at university as much as you might think that I did. Let's face it, we both weren't there long enough to bed many people, were we, love?'

'True. I'm happy to take a DNA test, although I doubt either of us can afford one. Fancy a trip to the Jeremy Kyle studio? It's not that far from here,' he asked, but he was joking.

Edward had forgotten how much he liked Janine calling him 'love,' although he knew most Mancunians call everyone that. Even after living in Manchester for decades, he was still very conscious of his southern accent. He had never lost it because he hid away most of the time, hardly ever talking to any of his neighbours in Moston, only the occasional shop worker. If he had been more sociable, his accent might have gradually morphed into something sounding more northern. His southern accent had served to make him feel even more of an outcast, lost in Manchester.

'I would rather have all of my pearly whites extracted without anaesthetic than appear on that Jeremy Kyle show,' she said with a harsh laugh, then nibbled another biscuit.

'Same here, but I thought I'd mention it as an option. I

can't wait to see Danielle. How do you think we should handle the situation with her? We'd better discuss what we should say before she returns,' he said, rushing his words in case his newly-discovered daughter walked into the house.

'It's totally up to you, love. I didn't know how you'd take my news, so I haven't yet reached far enough with my thought processes to have formulated what on earth to say to her. To be honest, I never expected to see you again, so I am as in the dark as you are about what to do next,' Janine said. An aura of panic descended on the room.

'Honesty is probably the best policy. Now I'm here, we might as well tell her. No, wait. Maybe we ought to wait until we have enough money saved up for a proper DNA test. It would be so bad to tell her that I'm her dad and then discover that I'm actually not. Maybe I should leave right now, before she returns. Oh, Janine, I don't know what to do. Fuck, I'm useless,' Edward said, all in a rush.

His back was hurting badly from earlier gallantly helping to carry Janine's shopping. It all felt too much for him to deal with. He sat impotently with his head clasped between his hands.

'Calm down, love. Danielle is a very chilled, young woman. We don't have to say anything today about you possibly being her dad. We can just say that we bumped into each other in the shop and that I invited you back for tea and biscuits to chat about our old times at university. It's not being dishonest, because until we organise a DNA test, we don't actually know the truth. When she sees you, she might notice the similarities between you both and guess. She's always been a smart kid. Her tanning salon job is only until something better crops up. I doubt she'll hang around downstairs anyway when she comes in. She'll probably just say hello, then take a microwave meal up to her room. She always likes to go online to chat with her mates,' Janine said as they both gradually calmed down.

'When is she due back here?' he asked.

'Probably in an hour or so,' Janine replied. 'Hey, that's enough about me and my boring life. How has life been treating you then, love?' Judging by Edward's old clothes, slight whiff of mould and his hangdog demeanour, she guessed that life had not been at all kind to him.

Edward sighed deeply then reeled off a list. 'Well, since I last saw you, the short version is: expelled from university, unable to get work because of my 'issues,' been on disability benefit for decades, hardly set foot out of grottiest parts of Manchester, never had a woman since you because of my 'issues,' disinherited by my mother....'

'What? Disinherited by your mother? That's a bit drastic,' Janine said, secretly preening her feathers for having been the only woman in his life.

He sighed again, deeper this time. 'It's a heavy burden that I'll never be free of. I will never fully understand why the bitch did such a horrible thing to me. Nor can I ever put it right. It's caused no end of trouble between Charlie and me. You remember me talking about Charlie, my half-brother?'

'Yeh, you once showed me a photo of him. A spoilt-looking, fat bastard with funny hair,' she replied, not caring whether or not she offended him.

'That's right, ha! He's got a son called Sam who is the spit of him. The kid's a nasty piece of work. At least Charlie isn't intentionally malicious, but Sam has a devious mind to go along with his spoilt nature. One thing I can never be accused of is being spoilt,' Edward said, feeling his hackles rising as the full force of the injustice done to him yet again washed through his body like an incoming tide.

'I can tell that you're not in the least bit bitter about it all, ha!' Janine observed smiling sarcastically, despite feeling sympathy for his misfortune. She had said it to try to drag him out of the deepening, depressed mood that he was visibly sinking into.

'I totally admit that I'm as bitter as hell. Who wouldn't be?' Edward said, his face glowering with a rising anger at his unjust lot.

Janine felt that she may have overstepped the mark and therefore softened her demeanour. 'Is there anything you can do about being disinherited? You're obviously on your uppers and could do with the money.'

Edward could see that he was frightening Janine and so he struggled to calm down. Eventually he said, 'I can't deny regaining my rightful inheritance would change my life immeasurably for the better. Through solicitors, I came to an arrangement with Charlie which means that, when mum's second husband, Marcus dies, Charlie and I will share the Jersey property. Marcus is living in there until he dies, then it should revert to us two.'

'Should? I don't know the guy but I kind of hope he snuffs it soon so that your life can be sorted out. I know you and I ended our relationship under unfortunate circumstances back in our university days, but I don't begrudge you any future happiness. You deserve it and it looks like you need some luck,' Janine said. A sudden thought whirred through her brain, one which could benefit her daughter.

The same thought suddenly simultaneously occurred to Edward. He looked at Janine intensely and said, 'Now I know that I am more than likely a dad, I find that I want my rightful inheritance all the more. My dear, fucking mother has not only disowned me but she has also disowned my offspring and all of their future offspring until the end of time!' His voice rose in volume and pitch until he shrieked, 'Oh, my God! I feel sick. How dare that witch disown Danielle and all of her future kiddies too? I've not even met Danielle and yet I feel a huge bond of blood with her.'

'Calm down, Ed, love. Danielle might come home any time now and I don't want her upset by another of your freak outs,' Janine said, placing a soothing hand on his arm.

On cue, the scraping of a key could be heard as it unlocked the front door. A pretty, elaborately made-up, dark-haired, orange-skinned girl sauntered into the living room. Surprised to see a scruffy-looking, male stranger sitting on the sofa with her mother, she looked at Edward and said, 'Oh, hi,' then waited patiently for an explanation from her mother.

Edward smiled and gave the girl an awkward wave, hoping that Janine would supply her with a credible reason for him being there. There were far too many emotions swirling around his body due to unexpectedly meeting his potential daughter for the first time for him to be capable of formulating a single, coherent word to her.

Fortunately for him, Janine came to his rescue. 'Hi, Danielle, love. I bumped into Edward this evening in the supermarket. We went to University together back in the mists of time, didn't we, Ed, love? We had oodles to catch up on, so I asked him back here for a cuppa,' Janine said, more calmly than she was feeling.

'Oh, cool. Nice to meet you Edward, love,' Danielle said to him in her broad, Mancunian accent with another little wave, flashing him a blindingly white smile. Her teeth had recently been whitened at a local beauty salon. Her orange, fake tan sprayed on her slim body at her workplace, along with her long, black hair, served to make her white teeth even more pronounced. They could have lit up a room in a power cut.

For a second, Edward forgot that she probably was his daughter and thought, 'At least her boobs must be real because they look as large as Janine's were at her age and Janine's were definitely real.' He gave himself a mental slap when he realised that this was an inappropriate thought to be thinking if she turned out to be his daughter. 'You too, Danielle,' was all he could manage to utter, hoping that she had not just read his mind.

'I'll leave you two to carry on nattering. I need to go online. There's a guy in America who is going through some shit that I must talk to. Don't mind me. I'll just microwave a curry and take it up to my room. See you!' Danielle said, heading into the kitchen. They soon heard the familiar, loud pops as a fork pierced the plastic film on a ready-made meal.

Janine and Edward wracked their brains for innocuous subjects to discuss until Danielle was safely out of the way. She was soon tucked up under her duvet, frantically typing on her iPad with one hand to a young, suicidal biker in Pennsylvania, whilst shovelling forkfuls of curry into her glossy mouth with her other hand.

Taking great care to keep her voice down to prevent Danielle from hearing their conversation, Janine whispered, 'I told you that she'd soon disappear upstairs, bless her. I think we did the right thing not to say anything to her just yet.'

'I'm pretty certain we did, although I obviously want to tell her the truth eventually, as soon as the 'you know what' result is known for sure. She's a lovely, young woman. She looks so much like you did when we dated. Even without a 'you know what' test, I can see that she definitely has my nose,' Edward said with a broad, proud smile.

'Don't go telling her that she's got the same nose as yours, for fuck's sake. She'd have a fit, ha!' Janine said, laughing as quietly as she could.

Edward laughed too and then an idea struck him. He said, 'I've just had a brainwave. What if I ask Charlie to lend me the money for the 'you know what' test? When he knows all the facts, he might even decide to give me the money outright, because I guess Danielle would be his niece. Since mum's death, Charlie has shown some guilt for the way he has always been treated as the golden boy of the family whilst I've been shunned and cast out into the wilderness. Marcus, my step-dad, never talks to me these days, but Charlie and he are always in each other's pockets. They're always staying at one another's houses and often holiday together. Surely he wouldn't begrudge me finding out if I'm a father or not?'

'You can only ask. Surely he'd not be so heartless as to deny you the money to discover the truth as soon as possible?' Janine asked in a whisper.

'With my damned family, you can never be sure about anything. I'll email him tonight and ask. He's rolling in money now that his restaurant in Cornwall is doing so well, so he doesn't really have any decent excuse not to help me out. Scribble down your email address so that I can keep in contact with you to organise the 'you know what' and anything else we need to discuss concerning Danielle,' he asked quietly.

'I'll give you my mobile number,' she replied, reaching for her sparkly mobile phone.

'Um, I sadly don't own a phone because I can't afford one. The internet café in town is the only place that I connect to the world,' he said, feeling ashamed to be so lacking in modern technology, because of his financial problems.

Visibly shocked by his admission, Janine replied, 'I couldn't function without my phone, although it's a luxury I can ill afford. They're so expensive each month but, as I never go out these days, I think I deserve it.'

'I don't go out much either, but I still can't afford a bloody phone,' he said, laughing bitterly.

Even his interaction over the internet with users of both sexes was limited by the internet café costs. This had increased his sense of isolation over the years which in turn exacerbated his mental issues. He badly needed to fill his days with thoughts other than his own solitude. He was a Robinson Crusoe, cast adrift on a hostile island, talking more and more to himself, answering his own questions and driving his brain increasingly crazy.

'I'd better make a move. I've really enjoyed speaking to you and meeting Danielle, to put it mildly. What a momentous day,' Edward said. His heart was fit to burst with the exciting realisation that his life had possibly been worthwhile after all, if Danielle turned out to actually be his daughter. 'I need to bomb down to the internet café to email Charlie about the possibility of a loan,' Edward said, standing up cautiously, the pain in his back making him wince.

'It had better be a gift. From what you've told me, he owes you big-time,' Janine replied. She walked into the tiny kitchen to pull out his meagre supermarket purchases. She scribbled her email address on a scrap of paper and handed it over to Edward. He looked at the paper as though it was made of gold, carefully folded it and inserted it into his worn wallet.

'Thank you so much for everything, Janine,' he said with feeling.

'Wait. I need to fetch you something,' she said, feeling almost tearful. She raced upstairs and handed him a photograph of herself standing next to Danielle on a sunny beach. Both women were wearing bathing costumes and were wreathed in beaming smiles as they posed for another ubiquitous selfie.

Tears welled up in Edward's dark eyes then poured freely down his face. With a trembling mouth, he said, 'Oh. How beautiful. Can you spare it? I'll treasure it forever.' He placed it inside his wallet along with the email address. There was hardly any money in the wallet, leaving plenty of space for his new treasures.

Not wanting to further distress Edward, although they were happy tears, Janine said, 'I've plenty of spare photographs and so I want you to keep it, love. That photograph was taken in Benidorm last year. We had saved for ages to go somewhere foreign for once and we had a bloody good time. We were pissed every night, ha! We're very close, with me having brought her up on my own.'

'If I'd known that she existed, you'd both have not been forced to be on your own and neither would I have been so alone. I guess you had genuine reasons for not telling me,' Edward said, wiping away his tears.

Janine did not want to divulge to him all of her reasons for keeping Danielle's birth from Edward for fear of upsetting him further. She was well aware of her ex-boyfriend's mental instability from having dated him for two months all those years ago. The last thing she ever wanted was for his insanity to contaminate her own life. She had definitely not wanted him to ruin the life of her baby. However, now that her only daughter was so much older, Janine hoped that Danielle might cope better with Edward's often bizarre, erratic behaviour.

Having now discovered that there was a chance that Danielle might come into some kind of inheritance, Janine felt justified for telling him the truth about the birth. Her decision to tell Edward did not come from greed. It was to give Danielle a chance to someday inherit what rightfully was hers.

Janine whispered, not wanting Danielle to hear, 'Hey, let's not get ahead of ourselves. We don't yet know for sure that she's yours, even though it's highly likely. We can celebrate properly once we know one way or the other. Email me soon to let me know about the test.'

She impetuously kissed his wet, haggard cheek above his greying, straggly beard before seeing him out of her home. They both waved and smiled as he walked off to catch the bus home to Moston. He needed to have his supper before his trip to the internet café nearby to send Charlie his important email.

## Groveling to Charlie

The internet café was not very busy, because there was a major football match being televised that evening. Edward found that his usual computer had been claimed by a large, sweaty man with an unconvincing comb-over and so he moved across the room to settle down at another console. He sat staring at the screen, trying to formulate a convincing email to Charlie. He loathed having to beg a favour from anyone, but it was particularly irksome to have to ask for money from someone he held a grudge against and had so much cause to envy.

'Mum's money should have been part mine in the first place. I shouldn't have to prostrate myself before Charlie and grovel for a tiny part of what I'm rightfully owed,' he thought, tapping out a draft email.

He decided to be honest and mention the actual reason for his financial request. There was no point in fabricating a reason for needing the money. If he made Charlie aware that it was to be spent on a DNA test, a positive response should be guaranteed.

'Charlie would surely not have the heart to refuse my very reasonable request if he knows it's to discover whether or not I am a father. It would make him her uncle, or half-uncle. He knows all too well that our mother acted abominably to me. It's the very least he can do to help me out under these circumstances. Last time we met, I could see in his eyes that he feels guilty for always being the favoured son,' Edward mused, as he pressed the 'send' button.

If he had owned a mobile phone or a landline, he would have preferred to have spoken to Charlie direct because he really needed to know the answer immediately, just to put his mind at rest.

'I hope the fat bastard sends me a reply soon because I really can't wait to find out if she's my kid or not. It literally means the world to me for so many reasons. Maybe I'll just nip for a half in my local down the road and then pop back here afterwards to see if he's replied to my email. I won't be able to sleep until I find out whether he agrees to lend, or preferably give me the money for the test.'

He knew that he could not really afford to buy a drink in his local pub. He justified the expenditure by reminding himself that he should celebrate the possible discovery of a beautiful daughter, albeit twenty-seven years later than he would have wished.

'I should really just go home before returning to the internet café to check if Charlie's replied to my email. It would be cheaper, but fuck it! I'm so sick and tired of watching every sodding penny, day in, day out, year in, year out. It grinds my gears! At my age, I should not be obliged to weigh up whether or not I can afford a half pint of weak lager. Charlie has never had to do such a demoralising thing in his entire life! Only the best wines for Charlie!' Edward could feel the familiar rage rising in his gullet from the pit of his stomach, a turbulent emotion that he knew all too well.

With a steely glint of determination in his eye and grinding his teeth, he strode into the pub. It was packed to the rafters with cheering football fans, all celebrating the home team's goal that had just been displayed on the enormous television screen.

Not being in any way a football fan, Edward shot them a look as if to say, 'You poor fools,' then walked up to the crowded bar and waited patiently to be served. Eventually, he carried his small, precious lager over to a table as far away from the blaring television as he could find.

'Hey there, Ed, How's it going?' a voice called out from a couple of tables away.

The voice belonged to Tommy Dolton, a local, bad boy originally from Ireland. Edward had talked to the crook several times before, as the 'Hare and Hound' was their local. Tommy was usually drunk or sky-high on drugs whenever Edward bumped into him. That evening was no exception. They had both rented rooms in the same street, so it would have been hard for Edward to have avoided bumping into the Irishman over the years.

Like an overenthusiastic puppy, Tommy always seemed overjoyed to see the less eager Edward. The only reason Tommy liked him was because Edward had reluctantly agreed to accept cash from the scruffy Irishman in exchange for occasionally hiding mystery packages at the back of his ramshackle wardrobe. Tommy had never given him any explanation for why he needed the packages to be hidden. However, it was safe to assume that the police would have been extremely interested in Tommy's clandestine activities.

As he was desperate for the cash to help him survive, Edward would not have dreamt of asking any questions, which made him extra popular with Tommy. Edward had no desire to be a criminal but had gratefully accepted the wads of twenties. When the time came for Tommy to collect the packages, Edward was always hugely relieved to be rid of them. He considered that he had more than earned the cash after all of the sleepless, anxious nights spent in bed, imagining that he could hear burly policemen outside his door ready to pounce. Edward assumed that the packages held drugs, but he later discovered that several of the packages contained other outlawed objects.

This particular evening, he could tell that Tommy probably had some more dodgy gear to offload on him. If that was the case, Edward knew that he would be happier than usual to oblige, conscious that he had even more pressing financial needs now that he might be Danielle's father. He wanted to try to impress the young woman, to make her believe that he was a person of some substance and not just a piece of dog excrement.

Snake-hipped Tommy slithered in beside him on the banquette. In a low hissing whisper, he said, 'I've got something else for you to look after for me, Ed. Are you up for it? It'd be our usual arrangement.'

'Can it wait until tomorrow morning, Tommy? I need to head back to the internet café soon to check my emails,' Edward replied, feeling slightly ridiculous for supplying such a lame excuse for not being able to immediately help Tommy.

'You can check your emails on my iPhone if you want. It'll save you a journey,' Tommy offered, wanting the package offloaded as soon as possible.

'Can I? Oh, okay then. Let's give it a whirl,' Edward said, logging into his email account after some instruction from Tommy.

Sitting in his inbox was an email from Charlie. Edward tentatively opened it, conscious that he must be looking anxious judging by the concerned looks Tommy was giving him. By the time he had read the email, Edward was smiling with huge relief. Charlie had agreed to send him a cheque for a thousand pounds to pay for the DNA test, far more than Edward had requested.

'It's probably guilt money to help salve his conscience over being the eternal golden boy of the family,' Edward thought uncharitably, although he was absolutely correct.

'So, does this mean that you are now free for me to drop a little something off at your place?' Tommy asked, desperate to shift the package that was so hot that it was burning a hole through his holdall.

Despite him soon to be sent some guilt money from Charlie, Edward still agreed to hide the illegal mystery package in his room. 'Every penny I can lay my hands on is more than welcome. Who am I to look a gift horse in the mouth?' Edward thought as the pair set off back to his dingy room.

As the unsavoury pair walked as quickly as Edward's aching back could cope with, Edward thought, 'I wish Tommy wasn't well known as a dodgy geezer in this area. I'd hate to be tarred by the same brush as this shifty Irishman, especially now that there's the prospect of parenthood in my near future. I'd never want Danielle and Janine to think that I'm a criminal.'

After a hurried discussion, Tommy unburdened himself of his mystery package and it was left to slumber in the back of Edward's wardrobe until Tommy was ready to return to collect it, brandishing another handful of twenty pound notes. Whilst he was still in his room, Edward cheekily asked to borrow the overly-tattooed Irishman's iPhone to send a quick reply of thanks to Charlie's email. It would speed up the process of transferring the thousand pounds from his half-brother's over-abundant bank account into his own meagre one.

'The sooner the money is mine, the sooner I can find out if Danielle really is my daughter,' thought Edward, unable to countenance the possibility that she was not. Throughout his entire life, he had not desired anything more than for her to be his child.

'Of course you can use my phone, man,' Tommy replied, inhaling hard on the joint he had just rolled, not bothering to ask if Edward minded him filling his small room with aromatic smoke.

Tommy sat, blurry-eyed on Edward's single bed, using a dirty plate as an ashtray. Edward resisted the temptation to fling his window wide open as he did not want to appear disapproving, although he was not interested in taking drugs himself. He had discovered whilst at university that his mental condition deteriorated whenever he smoked cannabis and had avoided all drugs ever since. When he had leapt off the Jersey sea wall whilst on LSD and permanently damaged his back and mind, it had given him further cause to shun all drugs.

His email thanking Charlie in advance was brief but sincere. If it had not been for the package lurking in his wardrobe, Edward would have slept better than he normally did that night. As it turned out, he hardly slept. Throughout the dark hours that he lay sweating in his bed, the package trapped inside the wardrobe took on massive proportions. It morphed into a bulbous, expanding, sinister monster that claimed Edward's mind that night. He struggled in vain to stuff the beast back inside the wardrobe as it battled to escape.

In the early dawn light, as he lay exhausted under the sweat-drenched, grubby duvet, he thought, 'I wish I'd not been so greedy. I should have told Tommy where he could stuff his dodgy package.'

# The DNA test

Edward had arranged with Janine for them to meet up at her house on her day off to ceremoniously open the envelope containing the DNA test results. He needed to have her near him to give him the courage to read the result. She would be there to comfort him if it broke bad news, that Danielle was not his long-lost daughter. If the news turned out to be wonderful, they could then celebrate together and work out the best way of telling Danielle.

Fortunately, Danielle would be at work on that day, which would make it easier for her mother and potential father to discuss the outcome in private. Despite being dressed in his best clothes in hopeful preparation for news worth celebrating, Edward still looked scruffy as he rang Janine's doorbell. He had tried to look his best for his potential daughter, because he would never want Danielle to look at him with disgust and disappointment when she first met him in his new role. Edward was more than aware that he was nobody a daughter could be proud of.

He was planning to take the three of them out for a meal at a local, Indian restaurant if the result turned out to be what he and Janine hoped for. He had visited his bank and excitedly slid a hundred pounds of the thousand pounds that Charlie had sent him into his pocket, solely to celebrate good news. If the news turned out to be disappointing, he planned to slink away to Moston and drown his sorrows. A daughter might make his life worth living, something he had not believed possible until bumping into Janine in the supermarket. Janine had thrown him a lifeline, a reason to live.

Ever since sending off their mouth swabs to be tested, Edward had been endlessly running through scenarios of how epically dramatic and tearfully emotional it would be when Danielle was informed that she was his surprise daughter. He had woken in the middle of the night before he was due to meet Janine, sweating and disorientated after another unsettling nightmare had gripped his vitals. In the nightmare, Edward had been thrown into a world of pain after the opening of the official looking letter had revealed devastating news. The words were a dagger in his heart, telling him that he was as childless now as he had been before spotting Janine in the supermarket queue. His own loud sobs awakened him.

'It would be unbelievably cruel for her to be snatched away from me now. It would have been better for Janine to have kept the news from me altogether if it turns out that I'm not really an accidental father after all. These warm, fuzzy feelings are foreign to me. Now that I know what I've been missing all these years, I couldn't bear to have it all snatched back,' he mused whilst wandering naked and dry-mouthed to his sink to pour and drink a glass of chemical-tasting water.

The hot sweat covering his skinny body rapidly cooled. He sat in his damp bed and shivered from the cold sweat on his body, plus the memory of his nightmare. He did not manage to return to sleep for the remainder of that night. The fear was too strong that he would be flung back into the nightmare and be forced to read the devastating bad news yet again.

Janine was feeling much the same as she lay in bed that night. She had made Danielle suspicious that evening by tidying their home from top to bottom, something that rarely happened.

'What great occasion do we owe to all this spring cleaning? Nine-thirty p.m. is a funny time to be running Henry Hoover around,' Danielle had asked, who had always hated the sound of vacuuming.

'The place is a tip and I was in the mood to do it now, okay? I've been at work all day and never had a chance to do it beforehand. Is that okay with you? It wouldn't hurt for you to give your room a quick tidy up too,' Janine replied, kicking herself for arousing her daughter's suspicions.

She had wanted their shabby house to have a better aura for the following, momentous day. Just like Edward, she was planning to spruce up her appearance for when they met. She had even had a spray tan at Danielle's workplace, cut-price of course. After a restless night, she lay in bed, grateful not to have to be setting off for work and pondered over what lay ahead for them all. Edward was due to turn up at her house for lunch at one o'clock.

They had arranged everything over email because of his lack of telephone. Each day, he had trudged to the internet café to chat to his lover from distant times over the ether. They had become friends again and she was quite looking forward to seeing his mournful face again. Her favourite dress was laying over the back of the bedroom chair in preparation for her après-shower body. It always showed her off to great advantage, although she had no intention of trying to tempt her former lover back into bed with her.

'It doesn't hurt to look desirable, even though I've been a devout singleton for years,' she thought as she dragged a wide-toothed comb through her freshly-washed, long, black hair.

Her legs were newly shaved, she smelt delicious and her makeup was as perfect as it could ever be. After admiring her reflection, resplendent in her red dress in her full-length mirror, she forced on a pair of black, high-heeled shoes. She felt like a warrior going into battle as she entered her kitchen. Her heart was beating fast with anxious anticipation.

'Two hours until he turns up and we discover the truth. I'll be an emotional wreck by then,' she thought as she paced around the living room.

If it had not been so early, she would have downed a drink of whatever alcohol was lurking in her drinks cabinet. She could not afford to supply much for their lunch, just a couple of cheese and pickle baguettes with some slightly squishy cherry tomatoes. She remembered how Edward had enjoyed cheese when they had been at university. 'Not sure we will both have much of an appetite if the news is disappointing,' she thought as she popped the part-baked baguettes into the oven for ten minutes to cook.

At twelve forty-five, the doorbell rang. When she opened the door, Edward was standing on her doorstep looking like a lost soul. He was staring at her with forlorn eyes like a boy about to ask for his football back. He tried to pluck up courage as he nervously stepped into the terraced house that looked the same as every other house in the street; rundown houses of the poor and needy.

'Janine looks a darned sight better than the last time we met,' he thought, pleasantly surprised by how good she looked in her red dress. Her fragrance was alluring and her shining, black hair no longer had streaks of grey.

'Looks like we've both made a big effort today,' she replied.

'Let's hope it was worth all of our trouble,' he said, still sounding like Eyore in the 'Winnie the Pooh' film that Danielle used to love as a child.

'Let's pour some wine and open this scary envelope together, love,' Janine suggested, desperate to take the edge off her anxiety.

'Good idea,' Edward agreed, following her like a faithful hound into the kitchen.

'It's only a cheap wine. No surprises there,' she said, handing him a large glass of red wine of dubious origin.

They sat next to each other on the sofa and looked intensely at each other. Neither wanted to be the one to look at what the letter said. Each feared how the other would react to what the letter might impart.

'You're the host, so you open it,' Edward said quietly, wishing that he felt braver. His innards were turning to water.

Janine ceremoniously opened the envelope. After reading its contents silently with Edward's pleading eyes reading her face for clues as to what was in the letter, she looked up and smiled at him. With a dramatic pause, she said, 'Great news, love. Danielle is definitely your daughter.'

Resisting the urge to cheer, Edward suddenly found that he had hidden his face behind his thin fingers and was crying like a baby. Janine put a plump, pale arm around his bony shoulders and felt her own tears welling up. They did not speak for a few minutes, both struggling with powerful, inexplicable, primal emotions that had been pent up for weeks.

Eventually, Janine said, ‘I told you that she was yours. Now we know for sure, we must tell Danielle. Try to pull yourself together by the time she gets back from work. We don’t want to freak her out, love.’

‘I feel like all of my Christmases have come at once. How do you reckon she’ll take this mind-boggling news?’ Edward asked, a little calmer after crying out his feelings for a full ten minutes.

His eyes were stinging, but he did not care because he was now a father. From that day forth, he had status and a title after a lifetime of feeling less than nothing. Without ever having a proper job because of his mental challenges, outbursts and physical disabilities, he had never had a respectable title to refer to himself as. There had been nothing impressive to scribble onto forms, nothing to be proud of in conversations with other people. From that day forward, he felt more complete than he had ever done in his entire life.

‘Hopefully Danielle will also be delighted. She’s always felt less of a proper person than other people with not knowing who her father was. The poor love has badgered me to tell her ever since she could talk. Without knowing for sure, I never wanted to even mention that you existed. It was hard to avoid her interrogations,’ she replied.

Now the truth was out, she was even more grateful that he had tidied up his appearance for the occasion. She thought, ‘Just as well he doesn’t look the way he did when I met him in the supermarket. He’s looking almost respectable today. I hope the silly sod doesn’t get overemotional again or act weirdly like he did at university. Danielle would be horrified.’

They tucked into their cheese and pickle baguettes. Edward was polite enough not to comment on the poor state of the cherry tomatoes. He washed the putrid taste away with the cheap, red wine as Janine chatted excitedly about how they might divulge their news to her only, supremely precious daughter.

Edward watched as the wine and excitement flushed Janine's cheeks and made her eyes sparkle. 'You've never looked prettier,' he suddenly blurted out, delighted to notice how she blushed and shyly lowered her eyes, brushing crumbs from the sofa into her small, pale hand.

'Thanks, love. You're not looking too grim yourself as it happens,' she replied, smiling warmly at him.

A rush of blood sped south from his brain. Taking her plate and setting it with his onto the coffee table, he lunged at her. His hand slid up her red dress. She had not had sex for years and was gratefully flattered that she could still inspire sexual desire in him. He had not had full sex with another woman since they were both at university and she had given up on men years ago.

Liberated by the red wine, Janine surprised herself by allowing him to kiss her. Conscious that their progressively sexual activity might be viewed through her living room window, she grabbed his hand and quickly led him upstairs to her bedroom. Turning the key in the bedroom door lock behind them, she let him peel her dress off her voluptuous body.

Rapidly tearing his clothes off, he pushed her gently but firmly towards the bed. The distant memory of the mechanics of sex came back to him.

'My God! I'd forgotten how awesome sex with you can be,' Edward said with an affectionate kiss as they lay panting and sweaty, arms and legs intertwined.

'I'm not sure what happened just then, but I think I liked it,' she replied, purring with pleasure, staring into his eyes. She loosely wrapped a bathrobe around her tingling body then padded off into the bathroom to wash all traces of him off her before Danielle returned.

'Do you mind if I have a shower, even if you're not having one?' Edward called out as he lay naked on the bed, listening to her fill the sink with hot water.

'Of course I don't mind. You'd better be quick though, as Danielle should be home soon. Maybe we shouldn't have enjoyed such a marathon bedroom session under the circumstances,' she shouted back, drying herself on a small hand towel.

'I wouldn't have wanted to miss a second of it,' he replied.

Edward grinned with pleasure as he noted the look of deep contentment on her face.

Janine suddenly snapped into action and said, 'I'm really worried that Danielle will be back soon. You'd better get a scoot on and have that shower before it's too late.'

It was too late. They both glanced anxiously at each other as the sound of a key being turned in the front door lock reached their horrified ears. Janine speedily leapt up and pulled on her clothes, throwing her discarded, pink bathrobe at the panicking Edward.

As he fled into the bathroom with his armful of clothes, Danielle called out, 'Hi mum, I came back a bit early. The boss owed me some hours off work.'

'Shit! This wasn't how it was meant to happen,' Janine thought, rapidly repairing her hair and make-up. She squirted on perfume to mask any smell of sex that might still linger on her body. 'I'll be down in a minute, love. Just sorting a few things out up here,' Janine called back, hoping that Edward would not be silly enough to go ahead and take a shower.

Sadly, Edward was indeed silly enough to be splashing about in her shower. He had not wanted to meet his daughter on the most important day of their lives smelling of musky sex odours. He resisted the urge to whistle, despite his rapturous excitement. He soon stepped out of the shower and towelled dry his thin body.

Both he and Janine were alarmed to hear Danielle's footsteps heading up the stairs towards the bathroom. On finding the bathroom door locked, yet with her mother clearly visible, dressed to the nines in her bedroom, Danielle looked askance at her mother and asked, 'Who's in the bathroom? I'm dying to use it.'

Edward froze, hoping that Janine could think fast and come up with a plausible excuse. He felt that it really would be unfortunate if his first introduction to his daughter was under such dubious circumstances.

'Err, um, it's Edward, love. You met him the other month, remember? He just popped round for another catch-up and needed the loo,' Janine said.

Confident that he did not look too much like he had just taken a shower, Edward considered that it was safe to emerge casually from the bathroom. He flushed the toilet in order to make it seem to Danielle as though he had been in there solely to urinate, not to destroy evidence of his very recent fornication with her mother. After washing his hands to make it seem more convincing, he cast another anxious glance in the mirror, wishing that his hair looked drier.

'Oh, hi there, Danielle. Lovely to see you again,' Edward said, noticing how the young woman was eying the rumpled bedclothes in her mother's room. He thought, 'Janine looks as guilty as hell and I'm not doing much better. What must the poor girl be thinking? She's not stupid. I reckon she's put two and two together.'

Luckily, Danielle needed to use the bathroom urgently. He left her and walked downstairs with Janine, who was whispering indecipherable words to him. He took a guess that she was scolding him for taking a shower and for prolonging the time they had played in her bedroom.

'Maybe if we tell her our big news as soon as possible, it'll deflect her attention from what we were up to earlier. It makes our behaviour more respectable if we are her parents,' Edward said hopefully.

'It'll probably freak her out all the more. Well, the damage is done now. I'll make us all a nice cup of tea and we can tell her about the DNA test result,' Janine whispered. She now felt slightly ridiculous in the red dress.

'I could do with something stronger than tea to be honest. I do feel thirsty though, so tea would be great. We can hopefully celebrate with alcohol afterwards,' Edward said, sitting on the sofa where all of the recent sexual activity had begun. He clasped his knees nervously like a maiden aunt.

'Celebrate? What occasion are we celebrating? Is it your birthday or something, Edward?' Danielle asked, startling Edward after silently entering the room.

Edward sat on the sofa, dumbstruck with shock and embarrassment. Luckily, a slightly calmer Janine entered the living room carrying three mugs of tea, a biscuit barrel and three small plates on a tray.

'Sit down, love. Edward and I have something important to tell you,' Janine said gently, sitting next to Edward on the sofa. Her words sounded like something out of one of her favourite soap operas.

Danielle looked worried as she sat obediently on the only other comfy chair in the small room. 'You're scaring me, mum. What's happened?'

Janine sensed that the words would be better coming from her own mouth rather than from Edward's. He looked deathly pale and riddled with guilt. 'Not now, Edward. Don't freak out. Hold it all together,' Janine thought, trying to silently convey it to him by her facial expressions.

'It's like this, Danielle, love,' Janine said as calmly as possible. 'I told you how, years ago, Edward here was at university with me. Well, I always suspected that he might be your father, but I never wanted to discuss this with you until we had received the results of the DNA test.'

'So, I was right to suspect that your recent strange request was something to do with a DNA test. Your excuse for rubbing a mouth swab inside my mouth didn't wash with me at all. I knew it was nothing to do with you entering us into some daft, market research into mouth infections. I'm not totally stupid, you know,' Danielle said, all the while looking at Edward.

She now knew that he was her father without the words even being said. 'I'm guessing that the DNA test says that you are my father then?' she added, directing her question at Edward.

'Yes, Danielle, you got it in one. I am indeed your father,' Edward said, smiling hopefully, wishing that he was a better prospect for Danielle to look forward to.

'I wish you'd told me about your suspicions sooner, mum. It would have been so much easier to have known who my dad was when I was at school. I received so much shit from some of the bitchier kids,' Danielle said, making Janine feel about two inches tall.

'I had my reasons for not telling you anything at the time,' Janine replied, not wishing to be more specific.

She did not want to openly admit that she thought her daughter had been too young to deal with Edward's erratic behaviour and mood swings. She hoped that at twenty-seven, Danielle would be better prepared to cope with being Edward's daughter.

'By the look on your face, you're obviously not going to tell me what those reasons were. This is a hell of a lot to take in, but I'm pleased to meet you at long last, dad,' Danielle said, standing up the same time that Edward stood. After an awkward hug, they both sat back in their seats, looking embarrassed.

To break the intense mood, Edward excitedly jumped up again and said, 'I suggest that we cement this momentous day with me taking you both out to the Indian restaurant your mum mentioned that's near here. Do you fancy that idea, Danielle?'

'I'm up for that. There's nothing better than a curry as long as it's not too hot. I'll nip upstairs and change,' Danielle said.

She was grateful to leave the tense atmosphere in the living room. Her brain was spinning in confusion as she preened herself in the sanctuary of her bedroom. Part of her was overjoyed to finally discover who had sired her, but another part felt angry and hurt not to have been told about Edward when she was a child. A third part of her, one of which she was not at all proud, felt disappointed by the man her father turned out to be. From what Danielle could discern so far, her father was a jobless, not very personable, disabled, weird, slightly scary loser.

Wearing a tight, sleeveless dress as black as her hair, bright orange, glossy lipstick and shoes that matched her fake tan and clashed with her mother's red dress, Danielle re-entered the living room with trepidation. There she found her newly-discovered father in a huddle with her mother, talking conspiratorially.

'Judging by their body language, those two were definitely having sex before I got home this evening,' Danielle thought, finding it both mildly amusing and somewhat disgusting.

'Right, girls, lets head off to the Indian restaurant. I'm starving,' Edward said, realising that his sharpened appetite was due to his recent, unexpected sexual activity with Janine. Janine shot him a glance with a cheeky grin, as if to confirm that she had been thinking the same thing.

'Luckily, the restaurant is only a five-minute walk from here, which is just as well in these heels. I've been standing all day at work whilst you two have been lolling around at home,' Danielle said, trying to wipe from her mind the image of her mother flat on her back with Edward on top of her.

The weather was balmy that evening, without Manchester's usual threat of rain. Edward's heart swelled with pride and emotion. They strolled along the pavement lined with red-brick houses, charity shops, tanning salons, tattoo-parlours and takeaways. There were only a couple of tables already occupied inside the Indian restaurant, so there was no problem with getting seated for their meal.

'This is the most important meal of my life on the most important day of my life,' Edward said, beaming with profound pleasure.

When the waiter approached them, Edward did not really need to say, 'do you have a table for my daughter, her mother and I?' to the friendly, Indian waiter. However, nothing would have prevented him from using the words 'my daughter' in as many sentences as he could manage from that day onwards. His pride was evident to everyone in the restaurant. It softened Danielle's heart towards him, although she still had many reservations about the virtual stranger who had suddenly become a major factor in her life.

'So, what do you do for a living, um, dad?' Danielle asked, conscious how odd the question sounded.

'I'm sorry to admit that I've been on disability benefit for most of my adult life. I've had certain issues to contend with, but I don't want to turn this wonderful meal into a downer. Are there any men on the scene, Danielle? I'd be surprised if there weren't,' Edward inquired, rapidly changing the subject.

He had no desire to draw attention to his mental problems, fearing that those problems might become apparent to her in the future as he had no control of when his strange moods might strike. That evening, he made huge efforts to be on his best behaviour.

'For all you know of my history, there might be women on the scene, not men,' Danielle replied with a wry smile.

'Yes, you're quite right. It was wrong of me to assume that you're not a lesbian, but you don't look like one,' Edward said with a laugh. 'It's not really my fault I knew nothing of your existence. I only found out you existed a couple of months ago,' he added.

'Go on, rub it in then. It's my fault that he didn't know all about you,' Janine chipped in, wiping a piece of naan bread around her empty plate to savour the last morsel of her chicken madras.

'It might be twenty-seven years too late, but at least I now know who my dad is. Life's too short to beat ourselves up about it all. My suggestion is that we enjoy the moment and not hark back to could have, should have regrets,' Danielle said, making both parents instantly proud of their daughter's mature attitude. It was a mighty relief that she was not going to be sulky during the meal.

The restaurant prices were cheap enough for Edward to be able to relax. There was more than enough cash in his pocket to pay the bill, even with them all enjoying a couple of bottles of red wine to accompany the meal.

'To answer your question, no, I'm not dating any men at present. I'm keeping my options open. I gave the last guy his cards a couple of months ago for being a right tosser. I can do better,' Danielle said, taking another slug of wine.

'Only the best for my girl,' Edward said, oozing paternal pride mixed with curry from every pore, giddy with wine and unaccustomed happiness.

Janine was quieter than the other two sitting at the restaurant table. She was content to watch Edward and Danielle as they tried to discover more about each other. Edward urgently wanted to find out everything he could about Danielle, to the point that she was starting to feel exhausted by his friendly interrogation.

After the meal, which had been a resounding success in Edward's opinion, they slowly walked home. Janine made them all a coffee before Edward felt obliged to make his way back to Moston. Unlike him, the two women had work in the morning. He sensed that he might be outstaying his welcome, judging by the way Danielle was yawning and checking her watch. Awkwardness seemed to be creeping back into the room.

'We will have to meet up again soon,' Edward said. He would have gladly met up again the next day if it had been his decision.

'It can't be for another couple of weeks at least. I am off to Bournemouth next weekend for a friend's hen night and the weekend after that, I'm off to Kos for a week with some girls. We've rented a villa,' Danielle said, noting how Edward's face had fallen after she spoke.

'Maybe we could meet up the weekend after that then? I'd suggest meeting in the week, but I know you both have work in the week, so we couldn't go out late. Just so that you're aware, I won't be able to afford to take us all out for slap up meals every time we get together because of being on benefits. Tonight was a special treat, for obvious reasons,' Edward said, his tongue loosened by the wine.

'We understand. You're welcome to stay on the sofa tonight. It's a fair distance back to Moston and it's getting late,' Janine offered, although hoping that he would not take her up on her offer.

'Don't worry. There's enough cash left over from the meal for me to be able to travel home. I don't want to be in your way in the morning. Drop me an email when you'll both be free so we can all meet up again. I can't wait,' said Edward, walking slowly towards the front door to make a reluctant departure.

'Of course we will. Thanks for the meal, dad,' said Danielle, giving him an awkward hug goodbye.

'It was my pleasure, love. Goodbye, you two,' said Edward, unexpectedly feeling the sting of tears in his eyes.

He gave Janine a meaningful wave, his eyes speaking volumes despite the tears swimming in them. All too soon, he found himself alone on the other side of their front door. Despite his back pain, he decided to walk all the way to Moston, in order to think and also to save some money.

'I need to save every spare penny from now on to spend on my gorgeous daughter,' he vowed as he floated on air under the now magical street lights. 'I wish that I had so much more to give her.'

## Plans change - 13:45 15th June 2015

The second bang makes Philippe's heart jump even higher off the bench than the first one had done. He had become familiar with the sound of gunshot in his late teens after spending a weekend shooting game with his father. Despite this fact, he still cannot quite believe that it can possibly be gunshot. Surely, the sound of a person shooting a gun never happens that often in real life in London. It is surely only found in films or on television?

Everyone except sleeping Mungo hears the bangs and is casually glancing around. However, the people in the park soon resume whatever they were doing before the bangs, even if they are just being lazy and doing absolutely nothing at all.

The noise has awakened a tiny, new-born baby that has been sleeping peacefully in a pram near to Philippe's bench. The wailing jangles Philippe's nerves even more than they were already jangling. However, after the baby's fleshy, black mother jiggles the pram and coos words of comfort to her first-born, the wailing ceases. Calm is briefly restored. Philippe has been contemplating heading off to attend his interview earlier than he intended once the crying started. Once the infant settles down, Philippe decides to stay in the park a bit longer. He glances at his watch.

'It's a quarter to two and my interview is not until two thirty. I reckon that I can afford to wait a little longer in the sunshine. My nerves would only get worse if I leave this bench to sit around in their waiting room. It'll be easier to convince myself that this is just a normal day if I just sit in this park and watch normal folk doing normal things,' his brain tells him.

He pulls out his packet of cigarettes from his suit pocket and lights up yet another one. Having already puffed his way through three cigarettes, his throat feels prickly, but he still inhales the acrid smoke deep into his lungs. He takes a few gulps from a bottle of water he brought with him. The sun is beating down mercilessly on his sweating head as he sits tensely on the bench.

'I'd love to drink the whole bottle down in one, but I don't want to have to look for a toilet before my interview. I'd better go easy on it.' With dismay, he realises that he needs to use the toilet anyway, due to nerves.

'I'll wait a bit then walk over to the public loos. If I go too soon, I'll only want another before the interview with the state I'm in,' he thinks.

He seeks to busy his brain with other mundane gibberish in an attempt to block out the throng of dark thoughts about his imminent interview. A few minutes is evidently too long to wait, as his bowels also start to rebel, demanding instant action. He stands up, gathers his few belongings and urgently sets off towards the public toilets, praying that they are have not been locked due to economic cutbacks. Luckily, they are open for business and as smelly as he suspected they might be.

As Philippe emerges squinting into the intense sunlight after relieving himself, he spots that the bench he had been sitting on is now occupied by an elderly woman. She is sitting in peaceful contentment watching the world pass by, as though enjoying a favourite television programme.

Philippe cannot see the spirit of her recently deceased husband, Jim, sitting peacefully beside her. However, the old lady is fully aware that her beloved soul-mate is seated by her side. She holds out her dainty, wrinkled hand to be lovingly clasped by the protective spirit of the man she loved so deeply for so long.

His words blow on the slight breeze that drifts through the trees. 'Your hand feels so bony, Maureen. You really must try to eat more. I know that you're not bothering to cook for yourself now that I'm not around anymore to cook for. Be a darling and eat, even though your heart is broken. Do it for my sake,' Jim whispers.

For decades, this has been the old, married couple's favourite park. It is close to the small, sparsely furnished, rented house where they spent most of their married life. Jim used to row her around the boating lake before he became too weak and ill to manoeuvre the oars. His widow has made a pilgrimage to the park almost every day now that the weather was decent enough. It was the place that she felt closest to the love of her life. He was in every blade of grass and tumbling leaf. Maureen never walked further afield, being a martyr to constant arthritic pain in both knees and hips.

She felt exhausted from the moment that she opened her rheumy eyes in the bed that now was too big for her, until the time that she crawled back into it. She often hears his voice and laughter blowing through the ever-changing leaves of the towering trees, which is why she always chooses this particular bench, as it is closest to their friendly protection.

She notices the good-looking, dark-haired, immaculately dressed young man looking at her on his travels from the public toilets towards her bench. He changes direction when he spots that she is now occupying his former seat.

'That handsome, young man seems really on edge. It's hardly surprising with him wearing all that fancy clobber in this fierce heat. The poor dear looks sweltering hot in his suit when most folk are wearing shorts and no sleeves. Jim, he reminds me of you when we first met. You were so energetic and full of life back then. For that matter, so was I. Remember our cycling holidays in France, where we'd stop off, sling the bikes in a hedge and make love in deserted fields? I miss those days, when everything was so much easier, before that evil bastard, cancer, ripped us apart. No aching bones, no loneliness, no cancer, no problems that we could not solve between us. I miss you so very much, my darling,' Maureen thinks loud enough for Jim's spirit to hear.

A small tear threatens to brim over her sparse, bottom lashes. To dab her watery eyes, she takes a handkerchief from her handbag. It is embroidered with a fancy letter 'J'. She treasures his collection of old-fashioned handkerchiefs, or any of his possessions for that matter. Her home is a shrine to Jim.

'Don't cry, please don't cry. You know how much it pains me. I'm still here, sitting by your side right now.' Jim's words sound either in her head or are being carried on the wind, she is not sure which.

All she knows is that she hears his voice. For Jim's sake, she pulls a tube of fruit pastilles from her handbag, sighs deeply, pulls herself together and pops a strawberry-flavoured one into her small mouth.

'Remember how we always fought over the strawberry ones?' Jim whispers gently in her ear, forcing a little chuckle out of her.

'I'm sucking this one just for you, dear,' she says, not in words, just thoughts. He feels her thoughts and smiles.

## Three months before Jim died

'The vet will hopefully soon be here. My dear wife Maureen will have to cope with it all despite me aching to be at Rocco's side to ease him gently out of this world. I want to stroke his fur and tell him one final time that he's a good boy. He was always my dog more than Maureen's, but she has been forced to look after both dog and husband since he and I fell terminally ill. I was diagnosed with prostate cancer a year ago and now it has crept into my decrepit, old bones. Four months ago, my beloved twelve-year-old mongrel Rocco, a rescue dog, also lost his appetite along with control of his bowels. It's been a rapid, undignified decline for us both.

'My patient, loving Maureen has now sadly been forced to take Rocco for his walks after I became too ill to exercise him in the park up the road from our home. I know that she finds it a chore because it makes her arthritis flare up. Walking Rocco used to be my favourite part of the day. Being permanently confined to bed, I now take Rocco for walks inside my head, picturing the carpets of bluebells, mossy paths and dappled sunlight when we were both fit, so much younger and living in the Kent countryside. Crunching through deep snow whilst Rocco bounded around like a demented kangaroo through the drifts, snapping at the falling flakes; memories like this help to distract my mind from this relentless, gnawing pain.

'As I drag to the end of my seventy-eight years on the planet, I envy my brother Michael who was lucky enough to die in bed aged fifty-nine from a brain haemorrhage. He avoided this prolonged suffering which is my fate. Michael was spared this pain and indignity, just as Rocco will soon be spared his pain once the vet eventually turns up. It will be the vet's final visit now that it's clear that Rocco cannot be cured.

'Day and night, my heavily medicated body twists and turns in this bed. Maureen has kept me up to date with my sweet dog's deteriorating condition. I am far too frail to venture downstairs to monitor it for myself. This morning's update reduced me to tears. She looked so scared and helpless when she told me how Rocco was just lying in his bed and panting, unable to scramble to his feet.

'I begged her to phone the vet straight away to ask him to come to our house and put our beloved pet out of his misery. I can't possibly tell my wife how deeply envious I am of Rocco. I can't tell her how much I wish that the vet would show me the same mercy. I can't ask him to inject me with magic liquid to carry me off into a permanent, painless sleep with Maureen gently stroking my bald head. I've lived a full, long and mostly happy life. My sole remaining ambition is to speedily end my suffering and depart this world in order to spare Maureen further distress.

'The ringing of the doorbell has just woken me from my first short nap in two days. Sleep usually eludes me thanks to this persistent pain. I'm so relieved to hear our doorbell ring. It means that dear, old Rocco will soon be released from his agony. I, his owner am sentenced to drag on, tortured and increasingly desperate. I'd pay the vet every penny I own if only he would be merciful and also give me a lethal injection. There's obviously no point in asking him. Humans are supposed to be more civilised than dogs, yet I'm denied the same consideration and humanity that is being shown to my pet at this very moment. I hear the vet's car drive away and rejoice, knowing that at least one of us has been spared and released from such cruel, relentless pain.'

## Thoughts of Neil

Every few minutes, Philippe checks his watch and discovers that it is still too soon for him to set off for the nearby retailer's head office for his interview. Wondering why the old lady on the bench nearby is chuckling to herself, he rehearses answers to any possible questions his interviewers might soon be asking him. Mingled with these rehearsals are wonderings over the cause of the recent loud bangs, but they do not unduly concern him. Once he has satisfied himself that his interview answers are word perfect, his mind turns to Neil.

'How am I ever going to convince that silly sod that I've no intention of running off and finding a younger, more attractive lover than him?' he ponders, knowing that he is lying to himself as well as to Neil.

He had already betrayed his older lover, although his sexual activities had never been serious or committed. Nevertheless, he was aware that there was no excuse for his cheating. Philippe had no intention of permanently replacing Neil with another man. The sex on the side was always just a bit of fun in Philippe's eyes. Deep down, he knew very well that it would break Neil's heart if he ever discovered the truth of what his younger lover had done and with whom.

For a wealthy male who was reasonably attractive in a suave way, Neil's level of insecurity was worryingly high. It was starting to impinge on the quality of their lives and making Philippe feel suffocated. The Spaniard suspects that even attending this job interview will trigger Neil's fear that he might meet and become involved with a new, sexier man. Neil also used to also fear that Philippe would hook up with a customer or fellow employee at his old job. As it turned out, Neil had been right to worry, although he had as yet not discovered the scandalous truth.

Neil had been relieved when Philippe walked out of his last job. It meant that the couple could be together twenty-four hours a day. It was Neil's idea of heaven but was becoming increasingly hellish for Philippe. His hot-blooded lover started to spend days with him at Neil's art gallery, but Philippe eventually became bored with that.

After months of living in perpetual close proximity, Philippe knew that he must stop that restrictive, stifling arrangement. He started looking for a job, first in secret and then, when he started to receive letters calling him for interview, with Neil's full knowledge. When he discovered Philippe's plan to escape back into the work force, Neil threw another massive sulk. However, he eventually had to ungraciously accept Philippe's decision to seek out new employment.

His dislike of constantly being around Neil added extra pressure on Philippe to put on his best performance during the interview. He loved Neil dearly, but could cheerfully strangle him whenever the man displayed his jealous insecurities. He knew that when he returned, Neil would probably quiz him over how attractive his interviewers had been. He was used to such annoying inquisitions because it happened every time Philippe set foot alone outside of Neil's flat. He was heartily sick of it.

During their row late the previous night in their oversized, luxurious bed, Neil had once again tried and failed to justify his frustrating behaviour. 'It's just that you always look so sexy that I'm convinced that any man with eyes would want you as much as I do. I'm looking so much older these days. You could do so much better than me.'

Philippe had sighed deeply then replied, 'Oh, for Pete's sake, I'm not looking to become involved with anyone else. How many more times must I reassure you? The only thing that'll drive me away is all of this insecurity bullshit you keep hammering me with every day. It's the worst kind of Japanese water torture. It's just not on you know. We have a great thing going for us, but you're going to ruin it all.'

'I know and I'm trying really hard not to be a jealous pain, but it just sneaks out. I promise that I'll be good from now on,' Neil said, leaning over and kissing him.

'A likely story,' Philippe thought as he turned away irritably from Neil and attempted to sleep. He had needed to be fresh and well-rested for the interview the following day and his boyfriend had put an end to that. Eventually he managed to lose consciousness.

Neil felt affronted and rejected by the way his lover coldly turned his back on him, but knew that he deserved it because of his jealous fears. His suspicious jealousy was like an illness, much harder to shake off than secure, self-confident people could ever imagine. He also feared that the illness might turn out to be chronic and therefore incurable. Unless he worked out how to slay the green-eyed monster, he would undoubtedly lose his Spanish lover, just as he had lost Daniel, Pierre, Simon and so many other fine young lovers. The phrase 'his own worst enemy' must surely have been constructed with Neil in mind.

'Perhaps I should pick an older, less handsome lover in future if it all ends with Philippe. Maybe then I'll be able to relax and quit all of this jealousy nonsense,' Neil thought. He dismissed the idea immediately, unable to picture himself with a man of his own age. 'I'm going to die a lonely, old, gay guy if I'm not very careful,' he mused.

Neil finally fell into a fitful sleep which was populated by erotic dreams of young lovers from his past allowing him to do disgraceful things to them.

## The unfortunate postman

The second bang is the sound of Edward shooting a ginger postman called Stuart. Mercifully for Stuart, the bullet only tears into his bare, ginger-haired thigh, narrowly missing a main artery. Because the postman is wearing shorts, the blood runs freely down his bare leg and turns his white sock red.

The middle-aged man has been sweating profusely delivering letters to a large house four doors away from where Edward has snuffed out Sam's short, unproductive life. Stuart soon has more than his heavy post bag to contend with. He has just been traumatised by witnessing the horrific image of a young, trendy-looking, plump, youth losing the top part of his skull.

Fear transfixes him so forcibly that he cannot move to escape the gunman's line of fire. Stuart is aware of sprawling head-first down the three steps leading up to the house. He needs to scream out in terror and pain, but resists the urge, scared to draw further murderous attention from this madman stalking the London streets. Stuart bites his hand to silence himself in a desperate attempt to save his life.

'I'm going to die. I'm going to die. I'm going to die,' Stuart mumbles, praying that the swivel-eyed lunatic only yards away from him will disappear. The two men look quizzically into each other's equally terrified eyes.

Suddenly, Stuart discovers that he might be alone. He hears the sound of the traffic in the distance and the toot of a horn. As soon as he gratefully hears retreating footsteps on the pavement, Stuart emits a piercing scream, followed by a second and then a third. He drags himself and his bloodied, excruciatingly painful leg down the steps headfirst until he huddles awkwardly on the gravel below. As well as one leg being painfully punctured by a bullet, both of Stuart's legs are now badly grazed along their entire length from scraping the concrete steps on his awkward descent. Writhing in agony on the gravel, Stuart stares at the blood gushing from his wounds and screams louder for help.

The ornate door of the building where Stuart has just posted a bundle of letters tentatively opens. An anxious, inquisitive, blonde girl, called Gill looks down from the top step at the war zone below. A young man, obviously dead judging by the large piece of skull that is missing, sprawls motionless on the pavement. An older, ginger-haired man, who she has often noticed delivering letters is screaming like a girl, blood pouring out of nasty-looking leg wounds.

She now knows that the bangs must have been a gunshot, although their volume has been muffled thanks to the building's triple glazing, plus the fact that she has been wearing a headset. She has been busy transposing an interview that she recorded two days previously. Gill works as a journalist for an agricultural magazine and had recently been interviewing a dairy farmer in Wales. The farmer's Welsh accent had been difficult to understand over the headphones, especially as the man talked fifteen to the dozen. He had been shamelessly flirting with her throughout the interview, a hazard of the job when a woman is as good-looking as Gill.

The postman thankfully stops screaming, not wishing to look cowardly in front of such an attractive female. He urgently shouts in a whisper to her, saying, 'Please, please help me. I've just been shot by some crazy guy. I think he's gone now, but I'm not totally sure.'

'Christ!' Gill says, looking around fearfully in case she is next on the gunman's list.

'On second thoughts, go back inside and ring emergency services in case the gunman is still hanging around somewhere. I'm not sure you should or could move me anyway,' Stuart shouts in a whisper.

The street is eerily empty, although several worried faces are appearing in windows from a few of the surrounding buildings.

'Okay, I'll phone the police and ambulance and get them

here as quickly as possible. Just lie still. I'm Gill, by the way,' and with that she disappears back inside the office building.

Automatically watching her shapely legs and pert bottom departing up the steps, Stuart thinks, 'I don't care what your bloody name is, even if you have got a cute bum. Just get me some help.' He pulls a wad of tissues from his short's pocket and presses it over the wound to staunch the blood flow.

Back inside her office, one of Gill's colleagues asks, 'What the hell's going on?' Only two journalists are working in the office today, as the editor and sales team have stepped out for a boozy lunch with a potential advertiser.

'There's a gunman on the street ... tell you more later ... must call police and ambulance,' Gill replies as though she is a Dalek talking in Morse code.

She grabs a phone and punches in 999. Several people who have been watching the action outside from various buildings have already dialled the same number. Gill's telephone call proves to be surplus to requirements, but she is unaware of that and considers herself to be a bit of a heroine from that day on.

## No going back

Edward staggers wildly along the pavement with the postman's screams still ringing in his ears. Pure terror makes it easier for Edward to ignore his usual stabbing back pain.

'I could easily have killed that ginger guy, but I like postmen. I just needed to stop him from possibly tackling me and preventing my escape.'

He glances over his shoulder to quickly evaluate the damage in his wake. At least his main mission is complete now that his nephew Sam lies dead, surrounded by a widening pool of blood.

'That'll teach him to try conning me out of what's rightfully mine. I told his father that I'd make everyone sorry if anyone ever tried to diddle me again. Job done! I really should have killed that postman though. He saw my face and can identify me,' Edward thinks as irrationally as ever.

He forgets that his face has already been captured on multiple CCTV cameras. Rational thought is the last thing that he is capable of. He feels like an actor in some random American action film, with nobody to call cut. He is out of control yet omnipotent for once in his life.

As he walks away from Sam's body, glancing at it to check it has not suddenly sprung back to life, he thinks, 'Doubtless I'll be dead soon too. I might as well take as many people with me as I can before some copper's bullet ends my sorry life. That's what happens to baddies in films. I'm the baddie now. I might as well be really, really bad. They might have forgotten me all of my life, but nobody will forget Edward Le Cornu after today.'

He knows that most people will be found inside the park that he passed on his way to kill his nephew. He is now heading there, making no attempt to hide his gun which feels heavy and slippery with sweat in his hand.

Edward had wanted to get hold of a semi-automatic pistol

but had only managed to purchase two, antiquated revolvers from Tommy. The seedy Irishman had luckily not inquired about the reason for Edward's purchase. The crook had not cared, just so long as he earned a decent amount of cash to feed his drug habit. Edward had bought no extra bullets from Tommy, but the chambers of both revolvers had been filled. They were now gradually emptying to devastating effect.

Edward had not been able to indulge in any target practice before today, not wanting to waste the bullets. Drawing attention to himself by attempting preparatory target practice would not have been wise. Today, he knew that he must use his bullets wisely, keeping a few for self-defence when the time comes.

'I'm already two bullets down. With luck, both these guns will soon be empty.' His mind is a hot soup of hatred and confusion. 'No mercy will be shown to anyone who gets in my way. Why should I show mercy? Nobody has been merciful to me throughout my entire life!'

As he feels for the second handgun inside the deep pocket of his shorts, he mutters, 'Boo hoo me! Boo hoo me! I'll show them all that no more will I take shit from all and sundry. For however long I have left to live, I will be God personified. Edward Le Cornu shall decide who shall live and who shall die.'

An image of his brother's florid, bloated face floats into Edward's mind's eye. He wishes that his brother was still alive so he could see what Edward has just dealt out to his only son, Sam, the youth that foolishly tried to cheat his only uncle out of what was rightfully Edward's, his mother's property in Jersey.

# The agreement

Ten years following their mother's demise, Charlie and Edward had eventually come to an agreement. They signed papers that stated that proceeds from their deceased mother's house in Jersey should be shared between them if Marcus died before them. As Marcus was rapidly drinking and eating himself to death, much like his son Charlie, his imminent death was highly probable.

As the two half-brothers floated on their backs in Charlie's pool in his spacious, neatly manicured garden in Cornwall, Edward had turned to Charlie and unexpectedly said, 'You know very well that I did nothing to warrant such a drastic, cruel punch in my solar plexus. Being punched in the stomach is exactly how it felt when I discovered what our mother had done to me. The feeling has never worn off. Mum was as mad as a box of frogs, always loving to cause trouble between us two. You know what I'm saying is true.

'Yes, the old lady sure loved to cause shit storms,' Charlie agreed.

'I wish I'd possessed the emotional strength to contest her Will as soon as I heard what she'd done to me. I was too destroyed and completely floored by her inhumanity to her own flesh and blood. She wanted to cause division between you and I, even beyond the grave. Her betrayal and then Sam's betrayal made me so ill. She wanted to cause me pain for reasons best known to her, being the sadistic witch that she always was to me, never to you.'

Charlie stared at Edward for a while over his rotund belly as he floated, whale-like in his pool. After some consideration, he said, 'Only you and I know what mum was really like. She hid her craziness pretty well from the outside world. I think the way she singled you out might have had something to do with the way you look so much like her first husband.'

'Exactly! It was hardly my fault that I looked so much like

him was it?' Edward replied, surprised that Charlie was being so receptive to his words. At the very least, he had expected a firm rebuttal from him.

Charlie added, 'She never forgave Gregory for cheating on her with that barmaid. It was hardly your fault that you inherited his genes and looked the spit of him. I never met your dad, as he obviously died before I was born. I've seen enough photographs of Gregory to see the strong resemblance between you two. I totally agree that you did not deserve to be punished for something that you had zero control over.'

'I'm so relieved that you understand what I'm saying. I will never, ever recover from what our mother did to me,' Edward replied bitterly.

'If I were you I'd probably feel exactly the same way. By the look on your face, I can see there's no point in me telling you to try to forget it. I'd not be strong enough to put it all behind me either,' Charlie said, seeing clearly how being disinherited was driving Edward further out of his mind than he was already.

'I've tried to bury the pain that she's caused deep inside me for too many years. Every time I thought about what she did, the pain would become so unbearable that I'd bury all the shit even deeper inside me. I need to formalise our agreement whilst I am mentally strong enough to go through a meeting with a solicitor,' Edward said, gritting his teeth with resolve.

'Tell you what, whilst you're staying in Cornwall, we must book an appointment with a property lawyer that I've used. I'll come along too for moral support if you like,' Charlie replied, flipping over onto his front in the pool and blowing a spout of water out of his mouth.

'I'd appreciate that. Hey, I reckon you'd better climb out of the pool soon. You're turning a bit blue around the gills,' Edward said anxiously.

'Good idea. I've had several sharp chest pains and tingling fingers over the past six months,' Charlie replied. He struggled to haul his bulky carcass out of the pool, but eventually lay panting on the hot paving slabs.

'Christ, Charlie! You really should see your doctor to check that out.'

'I know, I know, but I hate doctors,' Charlie replied.

'I'm the same, but whilst I'm down here you must book an appointment to see your GP about your worrying symptoms,' Edward said sternly.

'Okay, boss,' Charlie replied sulkily. Even whilst he was gasping for breath, he reached over to his poolside table and withdrew a cigarette from its pack. Edward shook his head and sighed in disbelief as Charlie inhaled deeply.

Charlie's visit to his GP on the following day eventually revealed that Charlie had a severe heart condition. His doctor instructed him to cut out everything that he enjoyed in life, namely eating, drinking and smoking to excess. Charlie chose to ignore this advice. He also continued to indulge in his love of golf, thinking that the exercise would improve his health.

Although not a golfer, Edward had reluctantly joined him on the golf course the day after their meeting with Charlie's solicitor. As the wind whistled and the grey, leaden skies threatened rain, the pair plodded on bravely around the course.

'I'm freezing,' Edward complained as drops of rain plopped onto his face.

'You're so skinny; you feel the cold more than me,' Charlie replied, whose ample padding of flesh was keeping him warm.

'That meeting with your solicitor was a bit disappointing. I hoped that it could all be sorted out much easier than it turned out. Damn Jersey law! She was such a young solicitor that I wonder if she's experienced enough to handle it,' Edward said through chattering teeth.

'Well, at least she admitted that she's not an expert in Jersey law. Pretty little thing, though. She'll get back to us once she's picked the brains of her boss at the firm. He's more au fait with Jersey law. From what I could understand from the meeting, the solicitor will draw up the Deed of Assignment of

Reversionary Interest and we'll both sign it in front of witnesses. It should all be sorted out once a bit of research into the weird machinations of Jersey property laws has been carried out. At least you've set the ball rolling,' Charlie said, taking a swing at the golf ball which promptly careered into a sandy bunker. 'Bugger it!' he shouted.

'Speaking of setting the ball rolling, you really screwed that shot up didn't you, ha?' Edward observed mischievously. 'Do you think it'll be necessary to get Sam to sign a similar document to us? It would ensure that he doesn't assume ownership of Mum's house as your closest relative if you happen to snuff it before I do? I'm not made of money, far from it. All this legalese is going to cost me over a thousand pounds which I haven't got.'

'Well, I'm sure that Sam is well aware of the situation. He remembers all too well what a crackpot his granny could be. I'll inform him about what we're signing and what my wishes are. Although he's a bit of a bread-head, I'm pretty sure my son would never stitch his uncle up. It wouldn't be cricket, would it?' Charlie said.

He privately had to admit that he had often been disappointed by his son's morality when it came to money and many other things. 'Sam will be well taken care of in any case, being sole inheritor of my estate and restaurant here in Cornwall.'

'I honestly couldn't take being screwed over for a second time by yet another relative,' Edward said looking pained.

'Look, I can't vouch a hundred percent that Sam won't stake a claim to Mum's house when I snuff it. You know how he's always been interested in money, even from early childhood. I'd certainly hope that he'd do the right thing and let you have mum's house. I don't really want to legally ban him from claiming it. That would be a bit of a slap in the face to him for me to mention that I even slightly doubted that he would do the right thing,' Charlie said to Edward, who was looking more and more worried by the minute.

'If someone else even tries to stitch me up again when it comes to my rightful inheritance, I won't be responsible for my actions. It was almost unbearable for my own mother to disinherit me, but, if it were to happen a second time …,' Edward replied, his words trailing away with heavy intent.

Charlie was shocked. He searched Edward's face for assurance that he was not really issuing a threat against his son, but he found nothing. Edward realised that he might have said too much and with too much force. However, he had meant every word of his implied, menacing threat.

# A final betrayal

With Edward being the oldest offspring, it was natural to assume that Edward would die before Charlie, but it proved not to be the case. Not having the money to buy copious food, alcohol and cigarettes, Edward was not unhealthily overweight like Charlie, neither were his lungs as damaged. Smoking a packet of cigarettes per day, an excess of rich food and alcohol, especially after his divorce from Lara, had raised Charlie's blood pressure to dangerous levels and put too much strain on his heart. Just as Bing Crosby before him, Charlie dropped dead on a golf course when his son Sam was twenty.

Sam had not known or cared that Edward had at the time it happened been far too emotionally distraught at being disinherited to contest his mother's Will. Edward's character and demeanour changed for the worse following the blow. Although always suffering from depression, irrational anger outbursts and ennui, their severity worsened immeasurably following the reading of the Will.

Edward had even developed a debilitating case of psoriasis after three weeks, triggered by having been disowned. It was an ailment that he had never previously suffered from and increased his sense of alienation from society. He hid away for months so that the disfiguring, flaking skin and sores could be hidden from disgusted eyes, knowing how nauseated he was when looking at his disappointing reflection. The condition eventually disappeared after several embarrassing months and luckily never returned.

'This nasty psoriasis is the only inheritance my mother left me,' he thought one night as his tears soaked into his pillow.

His self-pity irritated Edward, but his spirit had been pushed down so low under water that he could not crawl out of his drowning pool of despair. Many years passed before Edward could even start to come to terms with being publically, legally disowned by his mother. There were so many ramifications that followed on from her heinous act of betrayal. By the time he felt strong enough to attempt doing something to rectify the situation by contesting the Will on the grounds of his mother's mental instability, it was far too late. Not only had time run out to legally challenge the document, his mental stability had been irretrievably shot to pieces. Edward was in a helpless, self-pitying, destructive, downward spiral.

Due to Edward's self-inflicted solitary life, nobody official or medical had been aware how great a danger his mental decline had become to himself and to others. His inability to function in public might have come to light if he had received his decades of government handouts solely for his mental illness.

However, he received the bare minimum to exist, not live on, because of his severe back problem which had been triggered by his drug-induced leap from the sea wall in his youth. The injury had caused him long periods of excruciating sciatica and chronic pain. When the sciatica was at its worst, he was forced to stay in bed for months on end, with various carers popping in to see to his daily needs. The chronic pain slowly drove him even madder than his mother's cruelty and less than perfect genes had already made him.

His uncaring carers and sparse number of relatives had always considered Edward to be an eccentric with mental issues. Like his mother, he had learned how to mask the full extent of his true, dark nature under a cloak of self-deprecating humour. He tried to act the part of a sane person when necessary, but inside his head he was becoming increasingly crazed. His erratic, unstable behaviour increasingly broke out in public, causing many fearful, critical stares from strangers forced to witness them.

The interior of Edward's brain was like Louis Wain's cat paintings which had turned increasing bizarre and psychedelic the deeper into insanity that Louis Wain had fallen. Rational thought began to trickle away like sand through Edward's fingers from the day he was callously disowned until, standing in a Battersea park at sixty-three there were only a few grains of sanity remaining.

When Edward was sixty-two, his nephew, Sam committed the most far-reaching faux pas that he had ever made, unbeknownst to him; Sam became ultra greedy. Not satisfied with having taken possession of his deceased father's house and successful restaurant business in Cornwall, he set his sights on also claiming his grandmother's property in Jersey.

'I'm still a young guy. Who knows how much money I might need in my lifetime? I have expensive tastes. Cocaine doesn't come cheap,' Sam thought as he power-swam lengths up and down his Cornish pool in an attempt to shift some weight to make himself more attractive to Trixie.

Not wishing to waste his time working as owner manager of the seafood restaurant, he had employed a manager to do most of the hard work. Sam only bothered to drift into the restaurant once or twice a week to make sure everything was in order.

One of the main reasons he drove down there was to discover if there was any decent female talent in the bar or dining alone. Before the death of his father, Sam had often dreamt of a grope and much more with Siobhan, the most attractive, young waitress working in the restaurant. However, he had thought it wiser not to anger Charlie by abusing his position of owner's son, so had resisted making a move on her. Now that Charlie sadly was no more, there were no barriers to prevent Sam's desire for Siobhan running amok.

There were obvious barriers that would have prevented more moral people from taking advantage of their employees, but Sam had no time for morals. It never occurred to him that he should respect his staff in any way. A lack of financial worries went to his spoilt, young head and brought out the playboy in him. Sam was now responsible for paying the staffs' wages, not his father and felt that his employees were as good as his own, personal property.

Luckily for Sam, on becoming sole owner of the Cornish restaurant in his early twenties, he was delighted to discover that Siobhan had the morals of an alley cat. After he had first trapped her inside his office after hours one night, Siobhan did not once consider pressing sexual harassment charges against her employer. He had planned the whole seduction meticulously.

After most of the staff had set off home, he called her into his office under the pretext of chastising her for coming in late to work. Her suspicions were aroused after Sam locked the office door behind her as she sat waiting to be verbally chastised for her tardiness. She had not expected to be physically chastised, but she found him attractive enough not to object. The dark-haired, flirtatious, Welsh girl was flattered to be manhandled on top of her young employer's large, walnut desk.

Over the next few months, Siobhan allowed Sam to do whatever he liked with her. The ambitious siren hoped that he might eventually be unable to do without her and make her his regular girlfriend. There were monetary advantages to being Sam's girlfriend. Unfortunately for Siobhan, she was usurped by an even prettier, blonde girl, called Trixie who worked in a hair salon in town. Sam had met his new fancy at a club and after discovering that she had superior sexual skills to his current girlfriend, he never locked the office door behind Siobhan again.

Unable to stomach having to watch Sam and Trixie with their hands all over each other in the restaurant, Siobhan handed in her notice. She soon found another waitressing job in a rival restaurant. Having learnt nothing from her upsetting experiences with Sam, she became the willing plaything of Jonathan, the new restaurant's much older, married owner. The arrangement progressed more smoothly than her disaster with Sam had done because Siobhan managed to prize her married lover away from his dull wife. Siobhan and Jonathan married a few years later and spent a contented life together. Two years later, Jonathan's ex-wife met a far more suitable partner, so Siobhan had unwittingly done everyone a favour.

Sam had acquired an increasingly expensive cocaine habit after discovering that his sexual performance was greatly enhanced under its influence. He especially liked the way that Trixie morphed into a snarling beast in the bedroom after she had snorted a few lines. He was buying the drug daily with no regard to the expense. He was a wealthy man now that he owned the restaurant, his father's house and all of his assets. It was never a problem to pay for copious amounts of the drug for him and Trixie to enjoy. They considered themselves to be the power couple of Cornwall, splashing out on cocaine, expensive clothes, more cocaine, luxury foreign holidays, even more cocaine and top of the range, flashy cars to pose around all of the trendiest areas.

Splurging money had become as addictive a drug as their cocaine habit had become to Sam, and especially to Trixie. She had wormed her way into his bed, his mind and his life. She eventually managed to convince him to live with her at his deceased father's house situated a short drive from the restaurant. Having skilfully dispatched Siobhan, Trixie was now free to work on making herself indispensable to her new lover. Sam was so besotted with Trixie that he was blind to the fact that his relationship with Trixie was shaping up to be an identical setup to the marriage of Charlie and his cheating mother. That marriage had not worked out at all well for his father.

It was Trixie that had first suggested to Sam as they lay in bed after a marathon cocaine bender, that he should make a claim on his grandmother's house in Jersey now that Charlie was no more.

She said, 'Babe, you know your grandmother's place in Jersey? Well, I've been thinking. Didn't you tell me that your Gran had cut your uncle Edward out of her Will?

'Yes, she did, for reasons best known to herself,' Sam replied.

'Well, doesn't it mean that the property should pass down to you? Imagine what we could do with all the money from selling it. If we have a kid one day, that money could make life so much better for all of us.'

'Life's pretty good for us right now, isn't it? You've been able to give up your job at the hairdressers and now you're living the life of Riley with me every day. Isn't that good enough for you?' Sam asked, snorting another line of cocaine to delay coming down from his earlier hit.

'Didn't anyone ever let you in on a little secret? Didn't anybody ever tell you that you can never have enough money?' Trixie replied, knowing that she had him firmly in the palm of her well-manicured hand.

'I must admit that I have been thinking about staking a claim on Grandma's house. I just have never got around to doing it yet. I've been far too busy having a great time here with you. I do hear what you're saying though. Uncle Edward will be absolutely livid. Dad and he had some sort of written agreement between them, but dad died before he could go halves on Grandma's house with my crackpot uncle. I've never been asked to sign anything saying that I have to share the house with him.'

'So, you're in with a chance of owning the property?' Trixie asked.

'I guess so. Now that you mention it, I really should get my act together and visit a solicitor to discuss the matter,' Sam replied, suddenly enthused by the idea. He became more fired up and animated the more he thought about it, but that was partly due to the cocaine he had just sniffed.

'I suggest you think seriously about it, babes,' Trixie said, tossing her long, blonde hair over her tanned, bare shoulders so that it cascaded in waves down her shapely back.

She wriggled down his overweight body. Trixie had learned from her vast sexual experience how to best control her men.

'I'll see the solicitor as soon as I can book an

appointment,' Sam said, settling back to enjoy the ride.

True to his word, Sam made an appointment to meet with his solicitor on the following Tuesday. Sitting across the desk from the senior partner in the solicitor's firm, Sam said, 'You know that I'm now the owner of my father's home and business in Cornwall. Well, I need to ask your advice about my grandmother's property in Jersey. Following her death, it passed on to her second husband, Marcus until his recent death which took place three months after my father's fatal heart attack.'

'I'm sorry that your family has been touched by so many sad losses. You have my sympathies,' said the elderly, male lawyer who was well used to death, but felt obliged to make comforting noises.

'Thanks. Yes, it's not been an easy couple of years for the family. There's not many of us left. My grandmother never intended that my half-uncle Edward should ever own her home after her death, which is the reason why she excluded him from her Will. For whatever reason, she chose to disinherit and disown him. It would make a mockery of her dying wishes if the house ever became my uncle's property and make a complete travesty out of the entire Will process. She must have had a really good reason to keep Uncle Edward of her Will.'

'Do you have any suspicion as to why your grandmother chose to disinherit your uncle?' the solicitor asked.

'I have absolutely no idea because it was never stated in her Will. She did not even mention his name apparently. For all I know, he might be a gambler who Gran did not trust to have ownership of her money after she died, fearing that he might fritter it away. Or maybe he was a sex offender or something equally unsavoury, someone who she did not think deserved to inherit her wealth and property. I have no clue what made her do such an unusual thing.

'She must have had her reasons and who are we to question her motives? Disinheritance happens more often than one might imagine,' the solicitor said.

‘To put it mildly, my half-uncle has always been a bit strange. He is a lot like my Gran in that respect. Maybe that’s why she wrote him out of her Will, believing that he was too unstable to make sensible use of the sudden wealth after a lifetime of poverty. Christmases and summer holidays at Grandma’s house in Jersey were legendary because of the way she behaved around my uncle Ed if he was there. If my uncle had wished to contest her Will on the grounds of her mental instability, he should have done so at the time, surely?’

‘Was anything ever put in writing between your father and uncle concerning your Grandmother’s property in Jersey?’ the solicitor inquired, stroking his moustache.

‘Not to my knowledge,’ Sam lied, knowing that he had burnt the agreement letter after finding it in his deceased father’s office drawer.

He had also found a bunch of keys in Charlie’s drawer, labelled ‘Mum’s house.’ He had already arranged with Trixie that they would visit the Jersey house in a week’s time so that she could admire the property for the first time.

‘If there was no witnessed, written agreement between your father and uncle, there’s not much your uncle can do to stop you claiming the property, especially as he was never mentioned in your grandmother’s Will. It would normally have passed on to your father. As he is now sadly deceased, it would become yours as part of his inheritance as the closest relative. Your mother has been divorced from your father for years, so she would find it hard to make a claim on it,’ the solicitor said.

‘She always stated that she wanted no part of my father’s life or inheritance. I very much doubt she would change her mind on that. She’s always felt guilty for running off to Portugal with her new man, Geraldo and leaving me far behind. I think she would definitely want me to inherit the property rather than her, to salve her conscience,’ Sam said.

# Just like Lara

As Sam strolled out of the solicitor's office that rainy Tuesday morning, he mentally rubbed his podgy hands with glee at the thought of all the extra luxury that he and Trixie would soon be indulging in, once his Grandmother's house was sold. Trixie was waiting for him inside a nearby upmarket bistro opposite a prosperous harbour where they had agreed to eat lunch.

'Hey, babe, the meeting was a piece of cake. I reckon we should move into the Jersey house for a while, to make it clear that we are staking our claim,' Sam said, his nose running from snorting a line of coke in the toilet before settling down to eat.

'Possession is nine-tenths of the Law, and all that jazz,' Trixie replied, somewhat distracted.

She had been enjoying the close attentions of a tall, dark and disgracefully handsome waiter at the almost empty bistro whilst she was waiting for her much less attractive Sam to arrive. Trixie had become very aroused by the waiter's titillating presence and the sexy way that he had breathed on her bare shoulders when bending to pour her wine. Stalker-like, she planned to return alone to the bistro in the near future to see how far she could progress with the waiter whilst Sam was busy at the restaurant.

'It's a shame that Sam hardly visits his restaurant these days. It's so hard for me to sneak away from him when I strike it lucky with a guy. That hunk over there can't take his eyes off me. He should be an easy enough conquest, just like Sam was. I reckon if I wear the sexy, very revealing, little black dress that I bought on Saturday, that waiter will be putty in my hands. God, he's so sexy. Such a tight bum, unlike Sam's flabby backside,' Trixie thought, shooting the defenceless man a dazzling smile whilst Sam was happily looking out at the boats bobbing and clanking about on the glinting waters of the picturesque harbour.

Trixie was very much like Sam's cheating mother, Lara, in looks and character traits, but sadly for Sam, he had not yet realised the ominous resemblance. All the way through the lunch, Trixie and the waiter made meaningful eye contact whilst Sam waffled on.

'Just think, Trixie, soon I could be owner of not one but two, luxury properties plus a restaurant, without really having to lift a finger. I'm so glad that I had the foresight to employ such an efficient restaurant manager to take care of the day to day restaurant business,' Sam said, whilst his girlfriend faked interest.

When Sam disappeared to the toilet for yet another hit of cocaine, the waiter walked over to Trixie's table. He placed a masterful hand on her tanned, bare back as though he knew her. Bending down, he whispered in what sounded like a French accent, 'I'd love to see you soon. I finish at one tomorrow afternoon if you'd like to meet up with me here. I could drive us out to Falmouth where I rent a houseboat.'

'I'll dream up some excuse so that I can be here at that time,' she quickly whispered before Sam returned.

'I look forward to it,' he replied, boldly running his fingers down her bare back, making her tingle from his animal magnetism and the promise of sex. Sex was a drug that she was deeply addicted to and she sought it out constantly.

Sam returned to the table, oblivious to his girlfriend's flirtatious scheming, although the waiter's obvious good looks were making him feel visually inferior. No matter how much money Sam had, it irked him to know that he would never look as handsome as the waiter.

'I'll book our flights to Jersey this afternoon. I can't wait to show you the island,' Sam said. He took a pair of binoculars from his jacket pocket and scouring the ocean to savour the exciting sight of a stream of yachts that were involved in a race around buoys.

'And I can't wait to see it,' she replied, smiling her dazzling signature smile directly at the waiter and winking whilst Sam was distracted. The swarthy, young waiter smiled and winked back, then licked his lips obscenely, fairly confident that the stunning, wealthy looking blonde was not referring to the Channel island.

Before they left the bistro Trixie said to her lunch date, 'I'm just popping to the ladies. Back in a mo.'

As she walked down the winding corridor leading to the toilets, she crossed paths with the dark-haired, animalistic waiter carrying a tray of steaming dishes coming out of the kitchens. Sparks flew as their eyes met and they smiled broadly at each other. When she emerged from the fragrant toilets, the waiter was waiting just outside the door. He thrust a small piece of paper into her hand.

Before she returned to the table, Trixie glanced at the note. It simply said, 'You will be mine. I cannot wait. Clémont xxx'

'Classy,' she thought. 'I do love a man who knows his own mind and takes control.'

# Devious

Edward had no clue that Sam had destroyed the missing agreement that he and Charlie had signed. Sam had already found and destroyed his father's copy months before. This treacherous act had come about after Sam had fabricated a reason for visiting his uncle with the sole purpose of finding and destroying the agreement letter.

'There's a chance that this document might be held securely somewhere away from my uncle's lodgings, but it's a risk we have to take. He is such a scatterbrain. I'm guessing that he's holding a copy somewhere in his room,' Sam told Trixie as they boarded a plane to Manchester.

'A room? Are you telling me he lives in a room?' Trixic replied, shocked that a man who looked at least sixty would only have a rented room to his name.

'Uncle Edward has his little challenges. You'll see what I mean when you meet him. We're just going to turn up there, as I doubt that he would agree to meet me if we gave him warning of our visit. We were never close,' Sam replied.

Edward was completely thrown by the surprise visit, as his nephew and Edward had never before shown any interest in each other. He put the visit down to Sam perhaps wanting some contact with his family now that their numbers were dwindling. As they had sat awkwardly making conversation in Edward's room, Sam and Trixie had cast their eyes around it to guess the most likely hiding place.

Trixie spotted a heap of letters sticking out from under Edward's single bed. When Edward left the room to use the toilet on the third floor, she grabbed half of the letters and handed the rest to Sam. With a pounding heart, Sam quickly rifled through his pile and boom, there it was. With his heart beating fast, Sam stuffed the vital document into his pocket and shoved the other letters back under the bed, seconds before Edward re-entered his room.

Edward had paid no attention to the beads of perspiration on Sam's upper lip or Trixie's guilty expression. He was only wondering how to be rid of the young couple as soon as possible, having nothing to say to them. As the pair sat on his bed wearing their expensive, immaculate designer clothes, they looked comically out of place in his down-market, badly decorated room.

'Sorry I haven't got a telly to entertain you both. The bugger broke over six months ago and I can't afford to replace it. My only form of entertainment at present is guessing what the Bengali family in the next room might be cooking by judging the number of pings of their microwave and the smells filling the house,' Edward said despondently.

Trixie laughed nervously, thinking that he was being witty, but he shot her a look to let her know that he was being deadly serious.

'Oh, poor you,' she replied then realised that she had yet again said the wrong thing. She had no idea what damage that six months of just listening to the voices in his head had done to Edward's insanity with no television to help drown out the babbling gibberish.

'Do you fancy a meal out somewhere nice, Uncle Edward? My treat,' Sam offered, desperately wanting to escape the claustrophobic, smelly sock ambience of his uncle's room.

'That's good of you, Sam, but to be honest, I have a splitting headache. Don't let me stop you two from hitting the fleshpots of Manchester though,' Edward replied. He did not actually have a headache, but he was damned if he was going to be made to feel beholden to a spoilt kid a third of his age.

'Well, if you're sure, Trixie and I will head off back to our hotel. There are a few great restaurants around there and I for one am starving,' Sam said, standing up, eager to escape. Trixie scrambled up onto her tottering five-inch heels, flicked her blonde hair triumphantly and followed her boyfriend out into the evening air.

They couple hopped into a cab and sped back towards their

luxury hotel. When they drew up outside, before entering the impressive building, Sam wandered along the pavement in search of a waste bin. Once he found one, he took a lighter out of his pocket and lit the corner of the pilfered document.

'That really could not have gone any smoother,' Trixie said gleefully, rubbing her hands together.

Sam was disturbed by how the reflection from the flames dancing in her eyes made her look like a cold-blooded vixen from Hell. All that remained of the signed agreement between Charlie and Edward were ashes in a trash can. The couple turned on their heels and went out to celebrate. Sam knew that nothing now stood in his way to prevent him from claiming the Jersey property as his own.

# The fuse is lit

Over the following months, Edward managed to visit his newly-discovered daughter and her mother several times, although they did not meet up as often as he would have liked. He would also have very much liked to repeat his sexual activity with Janine. However, the opportunity never arose because Danielle was always in the house whenever he turned up. It seemed disrespectful to share a bed with Janine whilst his daughter was in bed in the next room. Edward knew that Janine was particularly vocal during sex; he was not confident that he could quieten her down.

Janine also wanted to keep some emotional as well as physical distance from her former lover, seeing the same old craziness escaping from him, much to her dismay. Edward would lose his temper at the most innocuous things, ranting over the rising price of bus fares, the Government, foreign aid, but mostly about the way his mother had disowned and disinherited him.

'Yes, we get it, love. Rejection is a terrible, painful thing. You don't have to go on and on about not getting your rightful due. If there was anything that I could do about it, I would. It's over and done with now and you should move on. Try to enjoy what remains of your life as you're not getting any younger,' Janine said as the three of them sat in a pub eating greasy burgers and chips. They shared the cost of the meal because the two women were well aware that they were the only ones earning wages, albeit minimum wages.

'We three could have been a perfect family unit if only he had been a normal man, not mentally and physically impaired, unemployed and just plain weird,' Janine thought, hoping to ensure that she was never left alone with him again. 'Danielle is polite enough to her dad, but I sense that she's disappointed in who her father turned out to be. Who could really blame her? He's hardly anything to boast about to her friends. She'd die of embarrassment to introduce him to them, but at least she won't be bugging me to tell her who her dad is any more.'

Four months after she was first introduced to her father, Danielle witnessed just how deranged he could be. Edward had turned up at their house in a towering rage, brandishing a letter from Sam's solicitor which stated that his half-nephew was now residing in Edward's mother's house in Jersey. Sam had wanted to publically stake his claim as soon as possible to deal with any objections sooner rather than later.

Sam and Trixie could have just stayed in the house without informing Edward, but they both wanted to sell the Jersey property as soon as possible. Trixie was particularly eager to add the money from the sale to their already impressive horde of wealth. They were both burning through their cash at an alarming rate, what with their constant drug use and expensive life-style.

Before Edward had scarcely walked through Janine's front door, he raged, 'Look what that fat bastard has done to me! He's stitched me up like a kipper! I'll slaughter the prick!'

'Slow down, slow down! Let me close the front door. The neighbours will be wondering what the hell all the shouting is about,' Janine said. Danielle rapidly backed away from him, horror written all over her face.

'Come and sit down, dad. Have a nice cup of tea and try to calm down,' Danielle implored as Edward stumbled into the coffee table, such was his disorientation brought on by his seething anger.

'I'm far too bloody upset to calm down any time soon,' Edward replied, pacing around the room like a caged panther. He thrust the letter under Janine's nose and screamed, 'Read this, then you'll understand why I'm so bloody livid!'

'I will do, but only if you stop punching my wall,' Janine said, desperate to calm him down so as not to terrify her daughter any further.

Having read the letter, Janine could see why Edward had erupted, especially knowing his history all too well because he never shut up about it.

'What are you going to do about what Sam has done?' Janine asked, looking up at him with concerned eyes from her seat on the sofa. She feared that anything that came out of her mouth would worsen his ferocious temper.

He sat beside her and snatched the letter from her, giving her a small but painful paper cut. Janine sucked the wound silently, fearing that if she mentioned it, Edward might cry with guilt or something equally upsetting.

'I'll rip that fat slob's head right off, that's what I'll do!' he yelled, making Janine wish that she had kept quiet. 'There's nothing much that I can do. I had a letter signed by Charlie that stated that he and I would share the proceeds from the sale of the Jersey property. But, can I find it? No, I bloody can't! My room is a tip at the moment and my filing system has always been non-existent. I've turned the place upside down looking for the damned agreement letter. I must have flung it out by mistake. That conniving shit Sam will doubtlessly have destroyed his father's copy of the letter. I can't afford a solicitor to contest what bloody Sam has done. My brain is in complete turmoil,' he said, suddenly putting his head in his hands and crying noisily, as though his heart would break. 'I'm at my wit's end.'

The women were both thinking that they preferred a crying Edward, distressing as it was to behold, rather than a ranting, possessed one.

'It's only money,' Danielle said unhelpfully. Her ill-considered words set Edward off again on another venomous torrent.

'That's just the thing. It isn't 'only money.' It's the fucking principle of the thing. It was my mother's house and it should now belong to me, not some sodding nephew! If it wasn't for my evil witch of a mother bloody disinheriting me for no fucking reason, I'd be living over in Jersey right now. It would have solved all of my financial problems,' he raged, spittle flying from his mouth.

‘I’m sorry, that was a stupid thing for me to say,’ Danielle said, wishing that the evening would end.

‘Sam is robbing not only from me, but he’s also robbing from you, Danielle. As my daughter, you’d have inherited the Jersey property after I snuff it. That cunt has knifed you in the back too!’ Edward shouted, making both women gasp with shock.

‘Language, Edward!’ Janine said.

‘I’m sorry, but Sam is a cunt, plain and simple,’ Edward replied, wishing that he knew an even stronger insult. ‘He’s worse than a cunt, because at least a cunt has some use. I can see no useful purpose for him.’

‘Enough! You’re in such a bad frame of mind right now that I reckon we should cancel our plans to go out for a curry. Under the circumstances, I’d prefer to order a takeaway to be delivered instead,’ Janine said, hoping that food might help to quieten Edward down.

She had no desire to be embarrassed in public by his alarming behaviour. Like Danielle, she wished that he would just disappear, because her head was now splitting from all of the unbearable stress.

Looking slowly from Janine to Danielle, Edward could tell from their worried expressions that he had completely destroyed what could have been a pleasant evening.

‘This solicitor’s letter has upset me so much that I’m not really hungry. I’m so sorry, but I reckon it’d be better for all concerned if I set off back home. Nothing and nobody can rescue me from the way I’m feeling. It’s plain from the look on your faces that you’d be happier for me to just disappear,’ Edward said, stuffing the offending letter into the pocket of his charity shop jacket and heading towards the front door.

Neither woman raised any objection to him leaving, so he gave them both an awkward hug and set off homeward, still raging inside. Their living room seemed to sigh with relief the second after Edward vacated the premises.

‘What a ghastly evening. I’m so sorry that you had to

witness all that drama, love' Janine said to her shell-shocked daughter.

'Trust me to be the one to have a madman for a father! I do understand why he's so upset, but he just takes everything too far,' Danielle replied.

'He always has done. His bad attitude doesn't seem to have changed much from when I first knew him. I think we should leave it a fair while before we all meet up again, don't you?' Janine said, knowing exactly what her daughter's reply would be. She was not surprised when Danielle nodded vigorously.

## Tommy helps out

Still giddy with rage, Edward trudged purposefully towards Moston. However, instead of going home to bounce off the walls of his room like a furious Tigger, he took a detour to his local pub. He decided to use the cash that he had taken for his share of the aborted meal with his daughter and Janine to buy a much needed pint of lager instead. He urgently needed to speak to Tommy and hoped that he would be in the pub and not out somewhere wheeling and dealing.

A plan had been formulating in Edward's jumbled brain during his long, painful walk back from Janine's home. He knew that he could not legally defeat his nephew, even if he had sufficient funds to employ a solicitor.

'I can't be fussing around with bloody lawyers. This needs direct action. Lessons need to be taught. I am so pissed off right now, I'll gladly teach them all not to mess with me. I warned Charlie what would happen if Sam stitched me up and unlike Sam, I'm a man of my word,' he said out loud to the wind as he limped determinedly towards the pub.

'I mustn't let on to Tommy why I need a gun, or maybe two. The less he knows about my plans the better. I'll tell him I need the guns for a friend, no questions asked. I'm pretty sure the heavier packages I stash in my wardrobe for Tommy are guns. They seem to be a very popular commodity around this area. The lighter packages are probably drugs, also easy to sell. There are still several hundred pounds left over from the money Charlie gave me for the DNA test, plus what Tommy owes me for the goods I'm hiding for him at the moment. I'm a sort of mate of Tommy's, so he should give me favourable mate's rates to buy the guns and bullets. Judging by the look on their faces, I think I've blown it with Janine and Danielle. I've nothing left to lose. They'll be proud of me for ensuring justice is served. My future actions will show the world that I've got balls and won't be walked over like lesser men.

There'll be no pussyfooting around when it comes to right, wrong and Edward Le Cornu.'

Tommy was sitting on his usual sticky banquette in the pub, trying to chat up a skinny, tattooed, red-haired girl with a ring through her nose. Judging by her disinterested, bored expression, Tommy was not getting very far with the girl. When Edward marched up to Tommy's table to ask for a word, she eagerly took the opportunity to slide off the seat and headed over to her friends at the bar.

'Thanks for nothing, mate. I was well in there,' Tommy said as Edward took her place next to Tommy.

'Doubtful. Hey, never mind her. I need a private word with you as soon as you can manage it,' Edward replied, fired up with angry resolve.

'Is it private enough in here or should we shoot off to your place?' Tommy asked, seeing that Edward meant business and would not be taking no for an answer.

'It might be better if we went back to mine,' Edward said, abandoning his plan to buy a lager. What he needed to discuss could not wait for him to buy and drink alcohol. He wanted to sort it all out before he lost his nerve.

Blowing the flame-haired, tattooed temptress an exaggerated kiss that she ignored, Tommy pulled on his stained, light-blue denim jacket over his faded Metallica T-shirt and the two, shifty, seedy men slid out of the door into the night.

'Do you mind if we pick up some fish and chips on the way? I've got the munchies,' Tommy asked, swerving into the chip shop before Edward could answer.

Although not in the mood to eat, Edward humoured him. He bought a small portion of chips for himself and felt obliged to buy Tommy's haddock and chips as he was about to ask a huge favour of him.

'Cheers mate. You're a star,' Tommy said, dropping greasy chips into his gaping mouth like a baby bird being fed by its mother.

'No problem, Tommy,' Edward replied, forcing himself to nibble on a floppy, unappetising slice of undercooked potato; the local chippie would never win any culinary accolades.

The smell of vinegar blotted out the rank odour of dirty, male laundry in Edward's room, which looked like it had been burgled. The chaos in the small room was a result of Edward's fruitless search for his agreement letter with Charlie. He had not had the heart to tidy it all away after his crushing disappointment and horror at not being able to unearth it. Little did he know that all that remained of the letter were now ashes on a council rubbish tip.

'Jesus, Ed! I thought my place looked bad, but yours looks like a bleeding bomb's hit it,' Tommy said.

'I was looking for something. It's a long story. I'll clear a space on the bed for you to finish your chips whilst I fill you in on my little problem,' Edward replied, shoving piles of paperwork onto the floor to join the rest of the rubbish.

'That's just what I need; someone else's problems, ha! Don't you reckon that I have enough problems of my own?' Tommy joked. 'No, seriously, how can I be of service?'

'Well, it's like this. I have a mate who really needs to get hold of a handgun for someone. You and I have never discussed what is in the packages that I occasionally hide for you. I am guessing that some might contain guns? Am I right?' Edward asked, hoping he was not wrong.

'Possibly. Let's be honest, there's no friend involved, is there? It's you that we're talking about here, isn't it, mate? I don't care why you need the gun. I never ask why my punters need a gun, as it's none of my business. The less I know, the more I like it,' Tommy said, wiping chip grease from his chin. Most of his guns were sold to warring drug gangs, which Manchester had never been short of for decades.

'I'm a lousy liar. Ask me no questions and I'll tell you no lies. I've only got a set amount of money. You can tell from my surroundings that I'm not exactly rolling in dosh. I need mate's rates if you can manage it,' Edward said, encouraged that Tommy seemed unfazed by his unusual request.

'Of course it'll be mate's rates. I'll even throw in an extra handgun, as it's you. You've helped me out no end with my little enterprise. All I ask is that you don't get caught. I don't want to lose my little hidey hole at the back of your wardrobe. When I next come round to collect the packages stashed inside there, I'll bring round a couple of shooters and ammo for you. I'm actually expecting another delivery tomorrow from my source,' Tommy replied, much to Edward's relief.

Edward luckily had enough money left over from Charlie's gift for the DNA test. With the money that Tommy owed him for hiding dubious goods in his wardrobe, plus his disability money, he would have enough to meet the cost of the discounted firearms and hopefully carry out the rest of his plan. The poetic irony of Charlie's money being used to dispose of Charlie's own son was not lost on Edward.

True to his word, Tommy delivered the pair of matching handguns and ammunition to Edward's room at the end of the following week, taking away most of Edward's money, plus the packages that had been hiding in the wardrobe. Not much was said; no questions were asked.

'Nice doing business with you. Keep safe,' Tommy said, after counting out the wads of cash.

'Cheers, Tommy,' Edward replied, thinking that there was every chance that he might never see his underworld friend again. Judging by the meaningful way that the Irishman had looked at him, Tommy had been thinking exactly the same as Edward.

## Plotting under duress

'I wish I'd managed to keep a bit more cash back in my dealings with Tommy, despite the huge discount he gave me. I've bugger all left to live on and God knows how I'll get to Jersey to polish off that fat pig of a nephew,' Edward pondered as he lay in his dirty sheets soon after Tommy had left.

He had rifled through his piles of paper for the umpteenth time to see if he could miraculously find the elusive agreement document. Every time he looked and it could not to be found, he punched a wall or kicked the wardrobe in frustration, swearing at himself loudly for being so careless. He only just stopped short of punching himself in the face as punishment.

The young Bengali family living in the next room wondered what all the banging and shouting coming from the next room was all about, but were too afraid of him to investigate. They had all kept as far away as possible from the crazy-eyed, shabby, old man whenever they bumped into him on the stairs or in the corner shop. His appearance had degenerated rapidly over recent weeks. He smelt bad, not having the money to launder his clothes. He had lost the will to wash or nourish his body, his weight burning off due to his endless pacing as he schemed late into the night.

'Desperate times call for desperate measures,' he said out loud to himself as he tossed and turned in bed.

As the early light peeped through his ill-fitting curtains, he had managed to formulate a rough plan to lay his desperate hands on some urgently needed cash. Not wanting to witness the look of disappointed disapproval on Janine's face if he were to ask her for a loan, and unable to earn the money, he was left with little alternative. He would simply have to take it.

'As long as I pinch it from someone who looks like they can afford it, I can live with the guilt. My needs are greater than the needs of most people,' he said to his reflection as he dragged a comb through his straggly, greasy, greying hair after pulling on the same grubby clothes that he had worn for the past ten days.

Later that morning, he walked to the Co-op shop three streets away from his room. He needed to restock with cheap teabags, because hot, black tea was all that he had consumed throughout the week. Milk in his tea was a luxury that he could no longer afford after his gun purchases. He had sat staring at the two firearms for half an hour before setting out into the high wind and rain. He often sat gazing at the guns as they lay on the bed before him, thinking into the future, wondering how on earth he was supposed to operate objects so foreign to him.

With his teabags stuffed into his deep pockets to save them from the rain, he followed a large, blonde woman out of the shop. She looked more affluent than most of the inhabitants of the area. Puffing and panting as she struggled up the deserted road, the woman was laden down with two bags of groceries, an umbrella and a large shoulder bag. Limping ten feet behind her, Edward had singled her out as the one to tackle. He glanced up and down the street, then up at the windows to check that he was not being observed.

After a sudden rush of blood to his disjointed brain, he pounced. There was a narrow alleyway running up the back of the Indian takeaway that had recently been closed due to unhygienic practices. The overweight housewife did not catch a single glimpse of her assailant before he shoved her face down into the overgrown grass, weeds and dog mess of the alley.

Before the startled woman could recover from his forceful push, Edward had grabbed the heavy shoulder bag and fled. His escape was not as swift as he would have liked, due to his usual back pain and sexagenarian body. Fortunately for him, he made a clean getaway. It was as though the gods had for once been looking down kindly on him. With the stolen shoulder bag tucked under his coat, he raced home as fast as he could, considering all of his impediments.

With his body still surging with adrenaline, he withdrew

the bulging, burgundy shoulder bag from under his jacket like a magician producing a rabbit from a hat. 'Voila!' he shouted, not caring who heard him. 'It looks promising. Let's hope there's some cash in here.'

Without a thought for how the woman in the alley was faring or whether he might later be apprehended, Edward unzipped the bag and tipped its contents onto his bed. There before him lay a veritable treasure trove. Before the unfortunate housewife had entered the shop, she had withdrawn two hundred pounds in twenty pound notes from an adjacent cash point. She had planned on slipping the money into a birthday card for her son on his eighteenth birthday. As she had used her debit card in the Co-op, the entire two hundred pounds was still intact.

'Thank you, God! What a haul! First problem solved. There's even another thirty quid in change in her purse. Bull's eye! I could get a taste for this mugging lark. No, maybe not. I think this has been an unusually smooth mugging. Don't think I could pull it off again with so little hassle. God knows that I'm a good person at heart and that I only did it because I was desperate. You know that, don't you God?' Edward asked, looking upwards at a crack in the ceiling. The madder he became, the more frequent became his conversations with God, even though it was always a frustratingly one-sided conversation.

Not interested in the rest of the shoulder bag's contents, Edward tipped it all into a plastic bag and bundled it into the back of the wardrobe where he normally stashed Tommy's illegal goods.

'Now I must embark on to my next and most difficult task. I need to track down that cunt Sam as soon as I can, whilst I have enough money. Best way to discover what he's doing and in which location is to use the internet café and investigate his Facebook page,' Edward said. He pulled on his wet coat and set out of the door with a couple of freshly pilfered twenties in his pocket.

He had already ascertained that Sam had a Facebook page, much like most people on the planet. It luckily had not been set to private, because Sam and his girlfriend enjoyed bragging to all and sundry about the high life they were enjoying.

'If I don't find out what Sam's doing from his Facebook page, I'm sure that his girlfriend, Trixie will oblige. Those two don't even fart without updating their profile statuses to boast how loud it was and how special it smelt,' he thought, settling into a chair in front of his favourite console.

'Bingo! So, it says here that the wanker is in London on a management course. Just as well I looked at Trixie's page. The stupid cow has taken a selfie, showing too much cleavage, looking sad because she's missing him whilst he's away for a week. Good old Facebook have even put the name of the place where he's studying. Thank goodness for Facebook's location services. What's this? The insensitive tart has had the nerve to post a photo of her half-naked body lying next to the pool that should belong to me. Well missy, we'll see who has the last laugh.'

## Trixie enjoys Jersey a little too much

With Sam safely in London for a week, far away from his grandmother's house that he now called his own, Trixie flew her new lover, Clémont over to join her in Jersey. She had been meeting him on his houseboat in Cornwall every chance that came their way. She had fallen hopelessly under his Gallic spell ever since the day that she had lied to Sam and told her podgy, live-in lover that she had a dental appointment. The only filling that happened that day was nothing to do with her teeth.

'Bonjour, sexy fox,' Clémont had breathed in her ear when she had arrived at the bistro.

'God, you look so hot in those jeans and white shirt,' she cooed back as he confidently flicked his long, dark fringe out of his electric blue eyes.

She drove them to his charmingly quirky houseboat which was moored in a quiet part of the river. He had not been able to keep his hands off her on the drive over there. They had both worked themselves up so much that they were both naked soon after stepping onto the boat. All of the curtains were pulled tight shut to keep out prying eyes. They were enclosed in a bubble of passion and deceit.

An hour later, they lay exhausted on his narrow bed, sensing the boat lift and fall whenever another boat chugged by. They each knew, without discussion that they would soon be meeting up again.

'Sam is going on a night out with some of his old, rugby chums on Thursday. Can you wangle any time off work that evening? I can pay you if seeing me means that you'll lose out on wages,' Trixie asked, feeling no shame in fundamentally buying his services.

'I could throw a .... how do you say? ... sickie?' Clémont replied, also feeling that there was no shame in accepting her money for his time. He had taken money for sex on several occasions, but it was usually money from far less attractive, less sexually accomplished women than the beautiful, youthful Trixie.

The couple met again on the following Thursday after Clémont had lied to his irritated employers and faked an attack of gastroenteritis. They put the three hours on his houseboat to great use. Trixie's shrieks of pleasure were clearly heard by the inhabitants of a neighbouring houseboat.

'Looks like Clémont has another satisfied customer, Jane,' Clémont's balding, bespectacled neighbour said to his blousy, auburn wife as they ate Bourbon biscuits and sipped steaming mugs of cocoa.

The bored woman merely nodded, deeply jealous of the fortunate woman that the Frenchman was pleasuring, having had a crush on him ever since they had been introduced. Little did the middle-aged wife know that if she had paid enough money, it could have been herself with the handsome man, not Trixie.

As she raced homeward through the dark, winding lanes in her immaculate, white sports car, Trixie hoped that she would have time to shower before Sam returned from his drinks with his rugby club friends. She could smell her new lover on her body and she bore his bite marks. Trixie prayed that Sam would not notice the teeth marks, having no reasonable excuse for them being there.

'If Clémont has bruised me, I'm in big trouble,' Trixie thought, examining her naked body in her bathroom's full-length mirror. 'I must fake sleep when Sam returns. Hopefully he'll be too drunk to want sex with me. I'm shattered and it's all that Frenchman's fault.'

Her hair was badly tangled and there was a dull ache in her back. 'It was all worth it though,' she thought, reliving frame by frame the last few lust-filled hours.

Instead of a shower, she filled the large, walk-in, white, marble bath. She climbed in and let the jets of soothing water caress her porn star body.

‘Good as new,’ she lied to herself, rubbing scented moisturising lotion over her breasts, hoping that it would lessen the incriminating, red bite marks.

She snuggled under the crisp, clean sheets of the enormous bed and tried to fall asleep in preparation for Sam’s return. Pleasurable thoughts of Clémont were still drifting through her mind when she heard Sam’s key turning in the lock. She lay under the sheets silently faking sleep whilst he crept into their bedroom. Luckily, Sam was too drunk to perform that night and was too badly hung over the following morning to need her services.

‘My poor baby. Is his poor head hurting him then?’ said Trixie in an annoying sing-song voice that oozed false sympathy. She stroked his hair after bringing a cup of tea upstairs for him as he suffered in their bed.

‘’Fraid so. It’s thumping like the drums of Hell. I’m as sick as a rabid dog,’ Sam moaned. ‘I had to leave my car at the pub and caught a cab home. Can you drop me off later so I can pick it up?’

‘Yes of course. You know that I’d do anything for you,’ she lied, bending over to kiss his sweaty forehead, making sure that her luxury bathrobe completely covered her bruises as she stooped to console him.

Trixie was beginning to regret that she had moved into Sam’s luxury home in Cornwall now that she had met her new, far superior French lover. On top of that, she was not looking forward to the forthcoming scheduled trip to Jersey for Sam to show off his dead grandmother’s home to her. The primary reason for the trip was so that, by moving into the house with her, it would be staking his claim to the property.

‘If you like the island and the house enough, we could even sell the Cornish house and restaurant business and relocate to Jersey, if the residential laws allow. I know there are certain constraints over who can and cannot live on the island. I’ll ask my solicitor to look into it,’ Sam said over breakfast one morning.

'Let's not jump ahead of ourselves. What about all of my family and friends in Cornwall?' Trixie replied. 'Especially my hunky Clémont,' she thought. She could not stand the thought of being cut off from her new, exciting love interest.

'I'll have to leave you alone over in Jersey for a week because of the management course in London that I booked last year,' he reminded her.

'Can't I come back to the mainland whilst you're away? I'll die of boredom stuck over in Jersey. Can't you cancel the course?' she moaned. A seed of an idea of how she could keep herself amused was beginning to form in her devious brain even as she spoke.

'I really need to attend the course because it will help me deal better with the restaurant or any other business I decide to involve myself in,' he said.

Just prior to his death, Charlie had been nagging Sam to take the business side of the restaurant more seriously. 'I made dad a solemn promise that I would enrol in a management course and it does make perfect sense. If you can stand it, I really need you to stay on at Gran's house to maintain our claim over it. It has its own pool and the house is near to the beach, so you can keep your tan topped up nicely. It'll only be for seven days and then I'll be returning to you forever and ever. Surely, you can stand being away from me for that long?'

'I suppose so,' she replied with a martyred sigh. All the while she was itching to telephone Clémont to arrange for him to take leave from his job for a few days to join her over in Jersey whilst Sam was otherwise occupied in London.

Leaving Sam in bed to recover from his hangover, Trixie walked out of the house and off down the leafy lane to ensure that nobody could overhear her conversation with her over-sexed, French lover.

Irritated by Clémont not answering her call, she left two, long voicemail messages, outlining her plan for him to join her for a few days of debauchery, all paid for by Sam. 'Text me back if you agree that this is the best plan ever. Don't worry about the cost of the flights to and from Jersey. I'll pay for your ticket, as long as you promise not to bite me next time,' she said, confident that he would be sure to agree to a free holiday.

Before she had even walked back up the lane and into the house, she heard the ping of an incoming text.

'Of course I'll join you. Text me flight details. See you soon sexy xxx,' said Clémont's text.

Sam revelled in showing his stunning, blonde girlfriend all around the island he had visited so often throughout his twenty years on earth. He had so many happy memories of spending weeks in summer at his Grandmother's house with his father and mother Lara, before she took off forever with Geraldo, her Portuguese lover. Coincidentally, Geraldo had been a waiter when he had met Lara, just as Clémont was a waiter when he met Trixie. History was repeating itself, unbeknownst to Sam, although Trixie found the coincidence was hilarious.

Trixie acknowledged that the island was indeed beautiful, with so many character-packed bays interlaced with intricate, narrow, winding lanes. The French names of so many of the roads reminded her that her French lover would be in her arms within days. Her mind would often drift off to hot thoughts of Clémont as Sam was prattling on with his tales of the happy times he had spent on the island.

As they sipped cocktails by the pool after Sam had shown her proudly around the sprawling property, Trixie said, 'I can tell this property is worth a packet, but it's such a spooky, dark, old house. I'm not sure that I'd want to permanently live here. I prefer modern.'

'If you feel that way about it, maybe we should sell it and pour the money into the Cornish property and business. It seems a pity though. You don't come across grand staircases like that every day of the week,' Sam said, pointing through the patio doors to the wide, ornate stairs which divided the expansive hall in two.

'But those stairs lead up to so many creepy bedrooms and

antiquated bathrooms. I'm sure the place is haunted. I popped my head around one of the doors and there were about twenty porcelain dolls all staring ominously at me from the bedspread. They completely freaked me out,' Trixie said with a shiver.

'Oh, that's my grandmother's room. She loved those old dolls. I know what you mean. They used to creep me out too when I was a kid. They still do actually. They can easily be sold off because I'm sure they must be quite valuable. You do approve of the small copse over there though, don't you?'

'To be honest, even that has a haunted feel about it, almost as though people have been hung from the branches in ancient times,' Trixie replied, her eyes as wide as saucers as she looked at the dark trees leading off from one side of the property.

'Don't be daft. Your imagination really is a worry sometimes,' Sam said, disappointed by his girlfriend's negative response to the house. 'Are you sure you won't mind being left alone here for a few days if you find the place so creepy?'

'Oh, I'm sure that I'll survive. I've brought my iPad to amuse me,' she replied. She had no intention of cancelling her plans to fly Clémont over to join her, so decided to limit her objections to the house in case Sam cancelled his management course out of chivalry.

As Sam flew out of the island, Clémont flew in, like the changing of the guard at Buckingham Palace. As there can occasionally be flight cancellations due to Jersey often being fog-bound, it was lucky for Trixie that there was not a wisp of fog that week. The Frenchman's excitement was almost as intense as Trixie's as his taxi drew up into the grounds of the old house. He could smell money as soon as he set eyes on the property.

Grabbing his small suitcase from the cab driver, he raced into her over-eager embrace. After a lingering, appropriate, French kiss, she virtually dragged him upstairs to the bedroom that she had shared with Sam the previous night. She had the decency to have changed the sheets, but that was the only decency shown over the next few days. The couple christened every room, every floor, the swimming pool and even the wide staircase.

To help throw Sam off the scent, on her second evening with Clémont, Trixie updated her Facebook status with, 'Enjoying Jersey, but missing my Sam so much whilst he's slaving away in Battersea on his management course. Come home soon, darling.'

She had used her selfie stick to take a photo of herself lounging by the pool sipping wine to illustrate the point. Her Gallic lover was naturally keeping well out of the shot and was inwardly laughing at her trout pout pose.

If Sam had looked very, very carefully at the photograph, he might have seen Clémont's hairy toe at the end of his sun lounger reflected in the patio doors. Trixie noticed the toe reflection later that day when she was counting how many of her friends had liked her photograph.

'Bugger it! I never noticed your toe when I uploaded my photo. I look so good in it that it seems a shame to delete it, but I really must. Sam might also notice your toe,' she said glumly.

'Just crop me out of it and upload it again, silly girl,' Clémont suggested.

'Brilliant. Good thinking, Batman,' she replied, setting about the task. 'It'll give me the opportunity to upload it again on everyone's newsfeed in case anyone didn't see it the first time. More likes. Good oh,' she thought.

Within days, Trixie would have much more to think about than how many likes she had received on Facebook.

## Meanwhile, over in Manchester

Trixie was oblivious to the fact that her Facebook status update was about to trigger a far-reaching catalogue of horrifying events. Edward had been visiting the internet café near his home every evening to track the whereabouts of his nephew.

'Sam's woman has some nerve, posting half-naked selfies from my mother's poolside. I'll teach her to rub my nose in their theft of what should rightfully be mine. So, it appears that dear Sam is in Battersea on some management course. I'll Google management courses available in Battersea, but first I'll take a peek at Sam's profile page to see if he mentions exactly where he is,' Edward said under his breath, not caring that he was attracting quizzical looks from a spotty Goth sitting at the next console.

'Bingo! Here's a photo of Sam with a few guys smiling like idiots inside the management building. He must have his location services switched on in his phone settings because the name of the management training business is shown on his page,' he thought, chuckling and rubbing his malnourished hands with glee.

The young Goth decided to move to a console at the opposite end of the room to the gibbering, obviously disturbed, old man who smelt like a sewer. Edward noticed the youth glare at him, stand up and retreat across the room. Edward knew that he must be the cause, but did not care. 'At least I don't look like I've just been dug up from some graveyard,' Edward mumbled at the back of the departing Goth, just loud enough for him to hear.

'You smell like you have been, though,' thought the youth. He could have said it out loud, but he did not want to further enflame the wild-eyed, crazy, old man.

Sam's caption to his group photograph informed the world, 'Working hard for the first time in my life. Not sure if I like it,' which infuriated his half-uncle all the more. Like so many other people of his generation, Sam had the habit of informing all of the thousands of people on his Facebook and Twitter accounts of his every move and thought. Being as boastful as his girlfriend, he wanted the world to witness what a fabulous life he enjoyed. He had never considered it prudent to set his profile's privacy settings to 'friends only.'

'Sam, you don't have to underline the fact that you're spoilt, lazy and have never had to work for all of the luxury you enjoy. I already know that's true, you damned thief! You didn't have to rob me of my one and only chance of living an easier life when you already have been given more than you need,' Edward muttered, writing the full address of the management trainers onto an envelope that the disability benefits office had just sent him.

Earlier that day, Edward had received a letter from the disability benefit people to inform him that his benefit claim was about to be reassessed after the Government was taking measures to crack down on benefit fraud across the nation. Despite being fully entitled to the paltry amount of money that he had been receiving, the letter calling him for interview at some inconveniently situated, hostile building had pushed Edward even further towards the perilous precipice of despair. That cold letter could not have arrived at a worse time, although there is never really a good time to receive such a worrying summons.

'Now they're even going to take away the little I have,' he had thought on opening the upsetting letter.

If it had never arrived, Edward might not have felt so sharply that he had nothing more to lose, nothing more to live for. With his daughter and Janine not seeming as eager to meet up with him after his recent outburst at their home, he no longer felt on a high after discovering that he had a grown-up daughter. That evening, he had noticed the look of fear and disappointment in their eyes. He now knew that he was an unwanted embarrassment to both women. That night, Edward felt more despondent, let-down, angry and betrayed than he had ever felt. Like an enormous raspberry ripple of hate, this new whirlwind of pain mixed in with his old, eternal whirlwind of pain caused through the Will debacle.

The only challenge left to tackle in his life was to right another terrible injustice. He could not countenance doing nothing about being disinherited for a second time. He needed to focus, so he set about the task with as much gusto as his troubled emotions could muster.

With the management course office's address safely tucked inside his jacket pocket, he limped out of the internet café, having kicked the Goth's chair leg harder than he had intended on the way.

'Prick!' Edward had said loud enough for everyone to hear.

The white-faced Goth had stayed sitting rigidly upright, choosing not to turn around in order to discover who had kicked him. He knew from the acrid odour exactly who the culprit must have been. The aura surrounding the scary, old man had already troubled him enough. 'It's much safer to let that freak leave this place unchallenged,' he rightly thought before returning to his online chat with his wraith-like, Goth girlfriend.

As soon as Edward reached his room, he rummaged around at the back of his wardrobe for the two handguns and the remaining cash. He bundled it all into a cheap holdall along with some mouldy clothes. After eating three limp biscuits, which was all that remained in his food cupboard, he set off towards the railway station.

'My rent's overdue, but if everything turns out as I expect, I will never have to pay rent ever again where I'm going.' This random thought strangely lifted his spirits as the train raced through the ominous darkness.

# Edward has a visitation – 13:57 15th June 2015

An image of Charlie's florid, bloated face floats into Edward's boiling brain. The disembodied head floats above Edward as he walks along the pavement clutching his guns, looking down at him in a glowering, Shakespearean, ghostly way. Part of Edward wishes that Charlie was still alive so that he could discover that Edward has just carried out his threat to punish anyone who dared to cheat him out of his inheritance for a second, unforgivable time. He wants to explain to him all of the myriad reasons for his extreme actions. He needs to justify why he has minutes before committed the unspeakable act of destroying his half-brother's only offspring.

'Your evil son made me do it, Charlie. Surely you realise what a spoilt, conniving, back-stabbing little prick he always was. Sam never lived in mum's house like you and I did, or played on the nearby beaches like we did. Do you remember when we were kids how we both used to love taking our nets to catch prawns at low tide? I want to do that again. Owning mum's house would've meant bugger all to Sam, not like it would mean to you and me. I have history with the house, just as you did. Sam would never have wanted to live out his days in Jersey like I long to do. Doubt I'll get the chance to live there now, or anywhere else for that matter.'

Charlie's energy whirls screaming in tormented rage around Edward's grey head as he continues speaking to him. 'Sam was not even my full nephew; he was only a half-nephew, as you were my half-brother. It made Sam's eventual betrayal even more galling because I know that only I, Edward was a full, blood relative, the first-born. It was I who should have become the rightful, new owner of the Jersey house. I'll probably be dead soon, Charlie, then I'll be able to explain it all to you better. I could not allow myself to be disinherited twice in one lifetime. It's the principle of the thing. I'm a bit busy right now, but soon I will be able to explain.'

Edward is deafened by the noises in his head which could only be the bellowing wails of a grief-stricken Charlie. 'Stop screaming in my head, Charlie. If I hadn't shot Sam, he'd have soon sold the Jersey house as a means to grasp far more money than he's ever seen in his over-indulgent life.'

Intent on more bloodshed, he walks the couple of hundred yards towards the park entrance. In the distance, he can see the impressive, decorative wrought-iron park gates are flung wide, welcoming him inside. One second the gates remind him of the finely engraved drawing of the gates of heaven in his battered, old school hymnbook. Next second, they take on the look of sinister cemetery gates. He shivers in the sunshine.

The pavements are unnaturally empty because any pedestrians who have spotted him have wisely immediately fled. Everyone knows that a crazed-looking man carrying a handgun cannot possibly be a good thing and needs to be avoided at all costs. Edward wonders whether or not to fire at their backs as they run up the street away from him. He decides that he is not confident enough of hitting them and should conserve bullets.

'I don't reckon I'm a good enough shot to hit them from here. Need to save bullets for the park. Once I'm inside those gates, it'll be like shooting fish in a barrel. Not long now.'

Although he has not quite reached his destination, he can hear the incongruously happy sounds of children playing on its grass. It reminds him of the long ago sounds of Charlie, himself and their friends as they enjoyed their time on the seaweed-strewn, Jersey beaches. For a split second, he wonders if he should perhaps forget about shooting anybody else.

'Maybe I can just run away, disappear and forget that this ever happened,' Edward thinks, stopping in his tracks, suddenly panicking. Watching the terrified pedestrians running from him informs him that he is not invisible. His actions have been well noted and will undoubtedly soon be acted upon by those equipped to do so. He is just sane enough to realise this much at least.

'I don't want to kill those kids playing in the park. I'm not a monster. If Sam had not been such a vile, grasping shit, I might possibly have had qualms about shooting him. He was only twenty-one, but evil is evil whatever the age. Shooting that postman was just a glitch, a bit of an afterthought.'

As the transparent, bobbing image of Charlie's head hovers above him, the last vestiges of reality finally abandon him. He says, 'I would never have sold mum's house so it could be torn down for some sodding hotel to be built in its place. It's my rightful heritage, Charlie and you know it is. I can't wait to see my old bedroom again. Remember when we were kids and you climbed out of your bedroom window, crawled along the roof and in through my bedroom window one Christmas Eve? Remember how we carefully opened up all of our presents in bed? I remember as clear as day how we wrapped them all up again so that we could pretend we'd never seen them before when we opened them on Christmas morning in front of mum and dad? Well, your dad, anyway. My dad was long dead by then. I'm so thirsty, Charlie. I wonder if there's a café in the park where I can buy a can of drink. Do you fancy one too?'

In the grip of his mania, Edward hopes to placate his brother's spirit, visibly incandescent with rage, by offering him a can of soft drink. Before he can receive a reply from Charlie's screaming, bloated, floating head, it disappears from view. The piercing wails of distant sirens chase Charlie's tortured spirit away from London. Charlie suddenly decides to abandon plans to return to his beloved Cornish home. Instead, he streaks on southward at lightning speed, ripping through the air back to his mother's Jersey property.

The vengeful energy of Charlie resolves to wait in readiness for the possible return of Edward's spirit so that he can deal with him as he sees fit. Having been dead for months, the essence of Charlie is now used to travelling with far greater ease than when he was weighed down by his heavy, overstuffed body. He slices through the air like a hot knife through butter, using the thermals to speed him all the more.

Having just witnessed the scene of his son's shockingly brutal and bloody murder, Charlie's turbulent, furious passage south briefly stirs the leaves in the trees through London, Kent, and every county until it reaches Jersey's shores. As the troubled, angry spirit descends onto the lawn of his mother's house, a whirlwind of garden debris whisks high into the air, much to the alarm of a flock of seagulls perched on top of the shed roof of the property. They fly screaming into the air, thrice circling Florence's house before deeming it to be too dangerous a place to congregate now that it is occupied by Charlie's malevolent spirit.

The large, grey and white birds fly off in confusion to the comparative safety of the beach area, orange beaks raucously cawing a warning to any other birds to stay away from the now malevolently haunted property. They strut about in their eternal search for food to scavenge. A young boy's dripping strawberry ice cream cone falls prey to one of the seagull's bomber attacks, leaving the distressed child wailing inconsolably to his mother.

'Damn these birds! They're costing me a bloody fortune,' his mother moans, trudging off with the grizzling child to buy him another ice cream from the beach café.

# James takes action – 13:58 15th June 2015

By now, it has become crystal clear inside the cluttered offices of the literary agency where James works, that a dangerous but gripping drama is unfolding in the streets below them. The closed windows are lined with anxious faces attempting to glean information. Worried eyes scan up and down the unusually empty pavements. Whilst sitting in front of their computer terminals, they have all heard the first two, muffled gunshots. However, their building does not directly overlook the scene of the two shootings, but are positioned ten buildings away from the action.

Their office windows are never opened because the heaps of submitted manuscripts from hopeful authors would have been blown around like autumn leaves in a gale. The air conditioning is the only source of air for the agents to breathe, albeit, germ-riddled, recycled air.

Monica, a blonde, plump literary agent in her twenties has a desk situated closest to one of the windows. She is relating a running commentary to her colleagues as she stares outside, 'Guys, there's a dodgy-looking guy in shorts limping towards the park. I don't know if he's the cause of those bangs. I reckon so, because nobody else is in the street. He's staring around weirdly, as though he's lost Oh fuck! He's looking up here and his eyes look really scary. He's holding something in each hand. Might be guns I suppose.'

'No shit, Sherlock,' says James. Monica's dreamy, slow nature has always irritated him, but never more than today. He rushes to unlock the large window then flings it wide open.

'Whooooa! Watch out Jimbo! All the sodding manuscripts are blowing off our desks,' Peter admonishes, looking irritably over his unfashionable glasses.

Thus far, Peter has paid no heed to the excitement in the street, being too involved in a gripping manuscript that had been submitted earlier that week from a crazy-sounding woman from up North. Her book dealt with a shooting in London and showed some promise, although it was highly unlikely that his agency would accept it onto their bulging author list. With only a few spaces on the list each year, her work would probably end up in the heap of rejected manuscripts destined to be recycled, in keeping with his company's environment-friendly policy.

'Sorry Peter and everyone! I need to look up the road,' James replies, thrusting his head and shoulders as far out of the window as safety allows. 'I'm scared that Claire might still be in the park on her lunch break.'

His pregnant fiancée occasionally failed to return to work on time if the weather was too inviting. James usually met her for lunch, but two days ago he had magnanimously volunteered to swap his lunch break with a colleague who had a dental appointment. Without even knowing the full severity of the situation, James shivers with unease, sensing some malevolence as yet identified could be threatening Claire.

His fears increase on hearing the piercing wail of sirens speeding ever closer. He says, 'I just pray that Claire is sitting safely in her office up the road and not still in the park. Oh God! She might be walking back to work right now and bump into this guy. I'll send her a text to check she's safe at work.'

When he receives no immediate reply, panic kicks in. Not caring about the increasing piles of manuscripts now lying scattered on the floor, he leans ever further out of the open window. There are many other people leaning out of their office windows all along the street, targets of their colleague's wrath as paperwork blows around.

Too stressed to remember to close the window, James walks towards the desk of his employer, Eugenie. As the damage is now mostly done, with a paperwork carpet now covering the original one, other agents take James' station over by the window. They crane their necks to find out what is happening, just as James has been doing.

'I'm going to dash outside to check what's happening out

there. Claire may be in danger and I must make sure she's okay,' James says, not giving a damn whether Eugenie objects or not.

She is vainly attempting to hold down her scattering paperwork and hoping that she looks girlish to James as her bleached, straggly, fair hair falls coquettishly over one eye. James barely looks at her, so her effort to look vulnerable and in need of help is completely wasted on him.

In order to gain favour, Peter rushes over to Eugenie's desk and helps her to restore some semblance of order, picking up clumps of scattered manuscripts. He starts to sort the pages into numerical order, occasionally glimpsing down Eugenie's blouse as she bends to scoop up more pages.

Peter has always imagined having sex with his boss. As a thirty-five year-old, below average-looking boffin type, Eugenie was almost out of his league. Despite the odds against him, he considered that he might be in with a slight chance of bedding her, knowing how uncharacteristically uninhibited the spinster became when inebriated.

'Creepy brown-noser,' James thinks, not for the first time where his colleague Peter is concerned.

Bob had been performing his normal, comparatively dull taxi driving duties, having cut back a little on his secret, porn star activities. He was beginning to feel his age, worn out by the physical exertions of satisfying the constant stream of young women that paraded through his taxi to be filmed having sex with him. He had decided to limit his porn days to twice a month in order to recover.

His popularity amongst the girls, film crew and millions of porn subscribers meant that the company paying him were keen to keep him on their books. He was flattered that they were attempting to woo him, trying to convince him not to give up his lucrative sideline entirely. If it was not for his vanity, he might have relinquished his porn star life completely, for Pauline's sake. She thankfully was still unaware of her husband's secret, disreputable life. However, Bob knew that she might discover what he had been up to when he should have been driving ordinary punters around London's streets.

Bob was more than aware that some of his all too willing porn star conquests were young enough to be his grand-daughter; it was a fact that he was becoming increasingly uncomfortable with. His filmed filthy dalliances with the eager girls had a whiff of paedophilia about them, which Bob struggled to banish from his mind because both he and the general populace naturally despise paedophiles.

Bob relished his many flashbacks to his favourite highlights of his filmed adventures on the back seat of his cab. Thinking about time spent performing on camera with certain, exceptional girls helped pass the time when his cab was chugging in long queues at traffic lights, or whenever Pauline forced him to watch a boring television programme. His guilt at having hoodwinked his wife as they sat side by side on the sofa did not stop him thinking back.

'Are you okay? You look like you're in a dream during the best bit of the programme. You've missed who got voted through to the next round of X Factor,' Pauline had said.

He had said, 'Don't bother telling me who got through, because I actually couldn't give a damn.' They had both laughed, just as they often did whenever they were together.

## Bob's unease

Bob's out of control gambling habit forced him to keep his sleazy activities going, to fund his addiction. He wanted to make as much money as possible over the next year or two, so that he could carry on gambling and hopefully retire early from the world of porn and the world of driving taxis.

'I can't wait to retire with Pauline,' he thought as he wandered into the bookies to lay on another bet.

Despite losing the bet, he knew that he would be back tomorrow to repeat the process. Failing that, he would be betting online. Pauline was as oblivious to his gambling addiction as she was to his sexual activities. As an accountant, she was an intelligent woman, but she had unwittingly married a deeply flawed, masterful deceiver.

Bob and Pauline had often discussed the possibility of selling their house and retiring early to Spain. Part of his reason for picking Spain was because he needed to get far away from the possibility of being recognised by one of the girls he had met during his regular porn work. Such a meeting could have proved more than awkward if Pauline had been with him. Although it might still be possible to bump into one of the women on a Spanish beach, it was less likely to happen there than walking around the streets of London.

Once, fortunately when he had been alone and not shopping with Pauline, he had been recognised by one of the girls stacking shelves in a large hardware store when he was in there buying gaffer tape.

'Hey, Bob, small world,' the short, dark-haired girl had said, sidling up next to him. He had been so engrossed selecting the perfect product that the girl's voice startled him.

At first he had not recognised the girl, dressed as she was in an ill-fitting, red overall.

'I'm sorry. Do I know you?' he asked brusquely, irritated at being interrupted when he had limited time to shop. He felt guilty, as though he had been caught with his hand in the till. He should really have been out in his cab picking up fares, but had decided to take a short break to purchase the tape.

'It's me, Noreen. Don't you recognise me with clothes on?' the girl enquired with a mischievous grin on her elfin face. Luckily the store was fairly empty, so mercifully nobody other than Bob heard her remark. 'We 'met' a couple of months ago in the back of your cab,' she added, heavily emphasising the word 'met' and adding a wink.

He stared at her for a few seconds and then it all came flooding back to him.

'Ah, yes, Noreen. I remember you, you little devil,' Bob said to the short, pretty girl. 'How's it going?'

'I'm still doing porn stuff occasionally, but there are so many other girls doing it now that I have to also work at this place to pay my bills. I'm very new to porn, but hopefully I'll manage to make a name for myself in the profession so that I can give up this bloody boring shop work,' said Noreen, secretly hoping that Bob might be able to put in a good word for her to his bosses.

'Noreen, you're wanted in aisle four. There's been a spillage,' a male, shop supervisor called out to the girl, who immediately looked disgruntled.

'See what I mean? The sooner I'm out of this dump the better,' Noreen said to Bob over her shoulder as she walked off to deal with aisle four's little problem.

'Good luck, Noreen,' Bob said.

As he paid for the gaffer tape and walked out of the store, he felt sad, but could not work out why. He could not work out if he felt sorry for Noreen that she worked in such a dull shop or whether he felt sad because her ambition was to be a successful porn star.

'I really must get out of this soul-destroying porn business soon. It's messing with my head and could easily ruin my marriage,' Bob thought as he climbed behind the wheel of his cab to pick up his next fare.

Five minutes later, he was looking in his rear-view mirror as he drove away with an obese, sour-faced old woman sitting in the back of his taxi.

'I'd have my work cut out for me with that one,' he thought with a shudder.

## James steps up

The breeze from the open windows, flung open by the concerned literary agents after the loud bangs, had made a terrible mess of all the piles of submitted manuscripts. The floor was now awash in A4, white paper. Chaos reigns in the office.

'Thank God we insist the authors submitting work to us number, name and title each page they send us. James, please make sure that you're extremely careful out there. I can't afford to lose my best agent,' Eugenie replies.

Her feeble attempt at humour in a potentially life-threatening situation badly rubs James up the wrong way and he inwardly grimaces. Eugenie has always had a soft spot for James and secretly lusts over him from behind her desk in the corner of the office. He would have been horrified to learn about his employer's desire for him because Eugenie is twenty years older than him and he is deeply in love with Claire. Eugenie's age is not such an issue with his colleague Peter, who frequently wishes that he was James. Peter is often eaten up with jealousy after witnessing Eugenie's eyes glinting with obvious desire when she looks at James.

Leaving the chaos in his office behind him, James takes the lift to the ground floor. He walks gingerly out into the sunshine and into a new kind of chaos. The sun rapidly warms his arms through his shirtsleeves. The air conditioning in his office was deceptively chilly, making the wall of heat that hits him in the empty streets a surprise.

'Must keep both eyes peeled if there really is a gun-happy lunatic roaming around. He might be up that side street or lurking in one of those doorways. I'm really not cut out for this lark. Claire's muscle-bound ex-boyfriend, Mark would be far more up for this sort of excitement. Mustn't start thinking about that fool, not now. I must keep focussed.'

James has a bad habit of talking to himself and today is no

exception. 'Claire hates me talking to myself. Oh damn, there I go again, talking to myself. I just wish I knew what was going on.'

He quickens his pace, glancing anxiously around him in case of an ambush. 'I feel really vulnerable in just this shirt and trousers, not that wearing a coat would save me from a bullet, but it would have made me feel more protected. It's all psychological.' He looks out for potential hiding places, just in case the unknown gunman suddenly leaps out from the shadows to shoot him.

'If it wasn't for the fact that Claire might possibly be in danger, I'd never be walking along this street, like a poor man's Clint Eastwood. With my future wife and unborn child in jeopardy, I have zero option,' he thinks, sweating profusely as though walking into the Minotaur's labyrinth.

His lilac shirt now has wet, purple stains under the arm pits and another sweat patch is gradually turning the back of his shirt purple. Wrenching his restricting tie to one side, he removes it and thrusts it into his trouser pocket. His underpants feel unpleasantly damp as his temperature rises courtesy of the sun's heat and from pure fear.

Frantic, efficient, professional activity is taking place further down the road, in the opposite direction of the park. James is still oblivious to the full severity of his situation, as it is happening just out of range of his vision. He is well aware that something bad might have happened, but has only a vague idea what that might be. Going into the unknown is a scary undertaking to all but the brave and foolhardy; James is in no way an adrenaline junkie. The closest he has ever come to danger has been to cross the road before a pelican crossing bleeps and the light turns to green, or occasionally to eat food a day after its expiry date.

Speeding, wailing police vans and ambulances have just arrived to deal with Sam's body and several officers are sternly cordoning off the scene of his murder. Other policemen are urgently collecting useful information from shell-shocked witnesses. They fear that the killer is still at large and now have a good description of the suspect. They pinpoint where the gunman is and the direction in which he is travelling. Armed reinforcements have now been summoned and will eventually scramble into place to resolve this dangerous situation. It all takes precious time; police reactions to a crime can never be instantaneous, giving time to would-be killers to continue killing for a while longer.

With such a high density of population inside a London Park on such a sunny day, the stakes could not be higher. The police hear the third and fourth gunshot even as they rush towards the sounds of the new crime scene, all too aware that each second they lose would likely mean the loss of more lives.

James intends to just dash into Claire's office to check that she is safe and secure.

'I know that I'm probably being over-cautious, but I'll never be able to keep my mind on my work until I know what's happened and that she's not in any danger.'

The sound of what must be gunfire forces James to change his plans. Instead of entering Clair's office building, he sprints towards the park from where the sound seems to be coming. He sees a couple of policemen wearing bulletproof jackets running ahead of him towards the park, trying to discuss tactics as they pound the pavement. They stretch out their arms to try to grab his as James races past them, but he just manages to shake them off.

'I'm checking that my fiancée is okay,' James yells as he hurtles through the park gates. He plans to dash towards their favourite bench, the likeliest place to find her if she is still in the park.

## Edward – 14:02 15th June 2015

'What's that noise? Sounds like sirens or something. Fuck, they must be coming for me! I'd better get a move on before it's too late,' Edward says, his heightened panic automatically setting his feet back in motion.

His arthritic hands feel cramped from clutching the unfamiliar handguns and the pain pulls him back into the moment. His curdled mind has been wandering off to a dark, unknown and unfathomable place. It snaps back rapidly, making him dizzy with terror.

'Oh shit, they're coming for me! I can't escape or breathe,' Edward mutters.

Into his consciousness springs a gory image of Sam's head, missing the top part of its skull. Edward staggers at the horrific sight, leans against the park railings and vomits profusely onto the pavement, gripped his guns tightly, ready for action.

'Now I'll probably get a fine for littering the street,' he thinks, wiping his foul-tasting mouth on his bare forearm.

He briefly leans, panting against the hot, pealing railings. Nobody inside the park has yet spotted him through the railings. As he enters the park, one or two people glance in his direction and take urgent, intense interest in the strange, scruffy, armed man. It takes the witnesses only a few seconds to comprehend the peril they are in.

Those who are not too busy to notice Edward, take in the image of a tall, thin, sweating, grey-haired man in his sixties, wearing baggy shorts and a sleeveless top. His crazed eyes are staring out of a pale, petrified, hunted, haunted face. As his arms hang limply by his sides, not every witness realises that the man is carrying two guns.

Pauline is the first to spot the guns. 'He's got guns!' she yells urgently, pointing at the stranger. She drags her heavy frame from the bench and grabs Claire's delicate arm so they can try to make a hasty retreat. Pauline's nails dig into the blonde girl's arm and Claire glares angrily at her in disbelief, until she too spots danger approaching ominously through the park gates.

Pauline's loud, warning shout prompts Edward to automatically spring into action. As a knee-jerk reaction, he raises his right hand, takes random aim at the largest target in the shape of Pauline. He fires and a woman's scream rings out. As he squeezes the trigger, an image of his dead mother maliciously laughing at him floats in front of his eyes. Although the woman looks nothing like his mother, she seems about the same age and height as he best remembers her. As the third gunfire of the day rings out, Pauline falls to the ground, dragging Claire with her. They both sprawl on the grass, one shot, the other shocked but unhurt.

'Pauline, speak to me, speak to me! Are you okay?' Claire says, shaking the still fleshy body of her new friend, who is all too obviously far from okay.

Seeing the blood flowing from an ugly hole in the side of the woman's neck, Claire realises that her new friend is either dead, or shortly will be dead from a single bullet. As the realisation hits Claire that there probably will be more bullets flying around the park at any second, she instinctively stands up to run from the deranged gunman. She and her unborn child might have stood more of a chance of staying unharmed if she had stayed prone.

Edward is now living inside a horrific, slow-motion nightmare, a cross between a fantasy land of blurred edges and a gory video game. For a perfect score, he must destroy the blonde girl attempting to run from his aim. Her blonde hair reminds him horribly of both his treacherous mother and of Lara, his adulterous sister-in-law who years before had attempted to seduce him.

He raises his right arm again and fires haphazardly in the young woman's direction. Claire feels a sharp, burning pain in her upper arm and collapses in a heap. Motionless on the grass, she feigns death, her bloodied arm across her belly where her foetus is nestling, oblivious to the drama unfolding in the world outside its womb cave.

Through her pain, Claire mouths silent words, so the gunman cannot hear and finish his work. 'Not my baby, not my baby, please, not my baby.' Baby sleeps. Claire's overriding maternal instinct kicks in, forcing her to decide to save herself and her unborn child rather than try to unselfishly assist Pauline.

'There's a time and a place for heroics. Other people in the park can help the poor woman. I reckon she's dead in any case. My priority is this life inside me. I daren't look up to see what's happening. This lunatic might shoot me again. Play possum,' Claire thinks.

She wants to vomit from the pain in her arm and it takes all of her will power not to raise her head to find out exactly where the gunman is and what he is doing. Although not religious, Claire shuts her eyes and prays.

Luckily for Claire, her ploy to play dead pays off. Edward assumes that he has done for her and moves on in a blood lust dream, in search of fresh meat.

'So many to choose from, but so little time left to me,' he says out loud, to Claire's horror.

'Don't let it be me. Just leave us alone. Why doesn't someone kill the lunatic? Where are the police? Surely they must be watching all this?' Claire thinks, unaware that the police are frantically discussing the situation whilst knowing that the longer they delay, the more members of the public will surely die.

A group of armed policemen are squatting below the shoulder-high, park wall. They are frantically signalling to each other in an attempt to work out the most efficient way to exterminate this vermin, who is so intent on committing mass murder. In the few seconds delay before the police marksmen aim and fire, more people find themselves in the wrong place at the wrong time. Edward uses the second handgun, knowing he might as well because there will not be adequate time to use all of his bullets anyway.

'Any second now I'll be dead, just like you, Charlie,' Edward says to the backs of the panicking, fleeing civilians trying to escape his bullets.

Only one person lies oblivious to it all, Metallica blaring through his headphones as he sleeps with a slight smile on his lips. Four feet away, Edward spots the viable, easy target in the shape of Mungo.

'I can't stand his sort,' Edward says.

He instantly sums up the mixed-race youth blissfully sleeping on the grass at his feet. Edward categorises Mungo as a drop-out, judging by his hair style, nose ring and tattoos. Edward takes aim and fires one deadly shot directly into Mungo's bare chest.

Mungo is blissfully unaware that he has been shot dead, or the reason why it has happened. Luckier than most, he has suffered a stress-free, easy, instant death. Billions of people throughout history would have envied Mungo such a speedy death, shot through the heart in a sunny, London park, whilst dreaming of the torrid night he has just spent with Francesca.

His leather bag bulging with drugs is still nestling under his curly, black locks, ready to be discovered by the police. The drug squad will soon be looking on these findings with extreme interest, realising that only a drug pusher would have such a vast array of drugs on them.

Mungo's spirit floats up into the blue, cloudless sky. Being a rootless wanderer at heart, he has no particular place to return to. He wanders haphazardly over the earth, always restless and never knowing what it is that he seeks.

Edward has no time to stand and gloat over the recumbent, gory body of the young man who, apart from his oozing wound, appears to be peacefully sleeping. Edward instantly raises both arms. Without singling out anybody in particular, he fires two more random bullets into the panic-stricken, fleeing crowd.

## War zone

The chaotic scene that greets James pulls him up short. People are fleeing all around him, trying to keep low to the ground to avoid the bullets. About fifty yards away, he spots a tall, scrawny man in his sixties wielding a handgun in each hand, who is heading away from James, in pursuit of a group of fleeing human targets. Ignoring the threat of imminent death as much as he can, James desperately searches for Claire. He loses count of the number of shots he has heard. Each time he hears another bang, he fears the worst; that Claire is now dead.

He is almost relieved when he sees that a plump woman is lying motionless on his and Claire's favourite bench, because the woman is not Claire. A split second later his relief changes to horror. Half-hidden by the bench, he takes in a sight that makes him cry out in terror and disbelief. Although he cannot yet see a face, and the apple-green skirt is new to him, James recognises the familiar, fair hair of the woman carrying his child. Shooting a quick glance to see what the gunman is doing, James rushes to crouch down beside Claire's motionless, bloodied body.

'Claire, darling, speak to me. It's James,' he whispers, gently brushing the hair from her pale face and looking at her ominously closed eyes.

He quickly scans up and down her slim body, searching for other possible wounds. The ugly, red hole in her bare arm draped over her appears to be the only source of the oozing blood as far as he can tell. He prays that this wound is not hiding another, more serious shot into her belly. There is so much blood soaking her top from where the deep wound in her arm has bled over it that he fears it might mask another more serious injury. The gunshot might have destroyed his greatest loves, Claire and their unborn baby. So as not to draw the gunman's attention, he crouches down near her behind the bench which seats the motionless, slumped body of the older woman. James prays that the lunatic keeps walking in the opposite direction to their bench.

Claire's eyes slowly open on hearing her lover's voice. Despite her intense pain and the lurking danger, she smiles bravely up at him from the grass. 'Shush, don't move a muscle,' Claire whispers urgently, barely audible. She knows that the guns could be trained on them both at any second, depending on the gunman's whim. 'I think only my arm is wounded. Hurts like fuck, but mustn't move.'

'Woman on bench looks dead. She's not breathing,' James whispers, noticing that the desperate-looking gunman appears to be moving further away from their bench hideout. He scarcely dares to look at the madman, fearing that if their eyes met, his and Claire's life would be terminated.

'Christ, no! She was such a friendly lady. We were only talking minutes ago and now look at her,' Claire thinks, too terrified and in pain to whisper a response.

James feels an urge to pick Claire up and run with her through the park gates. He resists the temptation, not confident that the gunman will ignore them. 'He could shoot us from where he is if he is an accurate marksman. Better stay put. Surely the police will shoot him soon. Oh shit, more gunfire! Some poor bugger has drawn his attention. Please, don't let it be us. Shoot anyone else, but not us. Leave us alone you bastard! Shoot him! Somebody, hurry up and shoot him! Claire might be bleeding to death right now for all I know,' James thinks, stroking Claire's hair as she lays grim-faced on the grass.

Claire's eyes close and the blood flows freely from the wound in her arm, a sight which fills James with dread. He dares not lift her arm to check her torso is intact for fear of hurting her, drawing the gunman's interest, plus fear of what he might find beneath. He endures the unbearable uncertainty over whether or not Claire is carrying a more serious, possibly fatal wound beneath the arm that she has placed so protectively over her womb to shield their future child.

## A merciful release

Only one other person does not run from the steely-eyed gunman. Even if she wants to run, Maureen knows that she will be unable to, even if someone were to bribe her with a million pounds to do so. Her arthritis is far too severe to do anything more than hobble. Her eyes have been closed as she has been dreaming of Jim in the dappled sunshine. They immediately jerk open on hearing the sound of Edward shooting a bullet into Mungo's chest twenty feet from her bench reverie.

Maureen sits motionless, resigned and aware that she cannot run from the crazy-looking stranger. Seconds later, she slumps sideways onto the bench, fatally shot in the neck, her long life instantly wiped out.

Edward never intended to shoot her, but his random bullet finds her nonetheless. As soon as he sees her slump over, he gasps and halts in his tracks, distraught at being responsible for murdering a sweet, dignified, old lady.

'No!' he screams in one, long, fading breath, taking a few steps towards her oddly peaceful-looking body.

Maureen is unconcerned by Edward's scream of remorse. She is experiencing a wonderful release from her arthritic pain, floating weightlessly up into the towering, leafy tree overlooking the bench towards the essence of her much-loved husband, Jim. She feels his smile mingling with hers as their glowing energies combine in a single, warm embrace. Ignoring the tragedy and bloodshed unfurling beneath them, their joyous delight at being reunited outweighs and transcends absolutely everything else in the world.

'My love, how wonderful to feel you moving through me and inside me after all this time apart,' Jim says, without words.

'I've missed you so much, you darling man,' Maureen breathes all over him. Intermingled, they float together through the balmy air, oblivious to the drama below.

To spare her further distress, Jim leads his wife away from the negative energies in the park to soar together in the sunshine back to the old house that they once shared with their dog, Rocco. The dog has been keeping his master company ever since being released from pain by the vet's merciful injection. Dog and master's reunion had been heart-warming enough when Jim eventually died, but was naturally not as joyous as Jim's reunion with his beloved Maureen. Rocco's essence is curled up under the dining room table in their house, awaiting the return of his jubilant masters.

'Down boy,' says Jim, sensing Rocco's delight as their faithful dog leaps through and around them in warm, over-eager greeting.

'What a wonderful surprise to feel you here, Rocco. The three musketeers, reunited once more,' Maureen wordlessly says, protected in Jim's endless embrace.

Their old house has been cold and miserable since the deaths of Jim and Rocco, but now it is warmed with the heady concoction produced by their three, golden vibrations. They all know that once the dark, negative forces have disappeared from the park, they will all return to their tree next to the bench. The love energies of Jim, Maureen and Rocco oozing from the bench area will soon dispel some of the park's negative energies.

Future visitors to the park who are unfamiliar with its tragic history will experience an unexpected tranquillity when they take their ease on that particular bench under the majestic tree. As the strangers rest, although they will be unaware that the breeze in the tree above them holds three, blissful souls, they will mysteriously feel better than they ever had done before, replenished and recharged by Jim's, Maureen's and Rocco's positive, loving vibrations.

## Guilty parties

'We are receiving reports of fatal shootings in the Battersea area of London, including one of the parks. Four people are believed to be dead and several have been wounded. The extent of their injuries is as yet unknown. We will keep you informed of events as soon as we find out more,' says the radio newscaster with their velvety voice displaying just the right amount of concern.

'Battersea? That's where Pauline's new employers are. She told me the other day that her new office building is near a park. God, please let her be safe,' thinks Bob.

He has been eating a tuna Panini in a pleasant café in Hempstead during a late lunch break. He quickly reaches for his mobile phone and calls Pauline's number. Desperate for an answer, he listens stony-faced as it rings and rings.

It eventually switches to her voicemail, which makes Bob's stomach lurch with fear. 'Maybe she's too busy at work to answer it. No need to panic,' he thinks, panicking anyway.

He has a porn job over in Camden to head over to shortly. He has been questioning the wisdom of his choice of tuna Panini for lunch as the raw onion and fishy smell would not please Ronnie, the girl he is scheduled to be paired with later. As soon as he hears the news report, all thoughts of Ronnie disappear.

'I'll phone the bosses and see if they can reschedule, or get some other geezer to work with her. I'm off to Battersea to visit Pauline's office to check that she's okay. I'll carry on texting and phoning her along the way. Finding out whether my wife is safe is infinitely more important than being fined for using my phone whilst driving. She might text me back any time now, then perhaps I can still make it over to the porn shoot. I don't like to let the guys down,' Bob muses. He is suddenly disgusted with himself for even thinking about porn shoots when his wife might be injured, or worse.

As he steers his cab towards Battersea, Bob thinks, 'Please God, don't let Pauline be in any danger. Please don't let her be one of the four dead people. No reason to fear the worst, but I do. If you make sure she's okay, God, I promise to knock all the porn nonsense on the head. I was going to give it up soon anyway. You know that I was planning to quit so that I can look Pauline in the eye without wallowing in guilt. Deal God? Just make sure she's safe for me, okay? I'm serious. I swear that I'll give up all of the girls if Pauline is as fit as she was when I left our home this morning. There are several parks in Battersea, so it doesn't mean it all kicked off in the one near her office. Christ, please don't let it be that one!'

Bob soon realises with a sinking heart that the incident has indeed happened in the same park near to Pauline's office. Before he even attempts to pull up outside her building, he sees acres of flapping police incident tape all around the railings of the building where Sam was earlier murdered. Police vans and journalists' vehicles are lining the road leading up to and beyond the ill-fated area. The strong sun still shines incongruously in the blue, mid-afternoon sky, imperiously overseeing the tragedies. Its rays seem to be mocking Bob from on high.

Everyone in the vicinity, including Bob looks shell-shocked. Faces look stunned by all of the deaths and injuries in the warm sunshine. Office workers are now milling around in anxious packs on the pavements, hunting for information and reassurance that nobody they know has been killed or maimed. Until all of the casualties have been formally identified, the police naturally refuse to release any names; this protocol naturally frustrates Bob and all of the other people who are aching for reassurance. The police discover Pauline's name from rummaging around inside her handbag and discovering her debit card, but her body needs formal identification before they can release her name to anyone.

Pauline's body has been taken to a nearby hospital mortuary. Within a few hours, amidst floods of tears and guilty regret, Bob has identified his dear wife's body. As he looks at the face he has lived with for decades, he realises just how immense his love has always been for her.

'I wish I'd told you more often how I truly felt about you,' he says in floods of tears. Mixed in with his guilt about his undercover porn career is a relief that Pauline never discovered his secret, then an awful thought hits him.

'I know it's irrational, but maybe now you're dead, your spirit might know everything that I've been doing behind your back. I'm so very, very sorry, darling. I mostly did it to make both of us money for our retirement. I'm so bloody sorry,' Bob tells Pauline without words as he stares down in disbelief at the discarded husk that once was his wife.

Only that morning, they had shared a rushed breakfast together before both setting off to work. Remembering her proud excitement over her new accountancy job in Battersea releases a fresh torrent of tears that flow down Bob's cheeks and drip onto the floor.

'It's so unfair. I deserved to be killed, not you! What did you ever do to deserve such a tragic, terrible end? Not one damned thing! I hope that fucking bastard suffers an eternity of unspeakable tortures in the fiery pits of Hell for this atrocity. What made him single you out and rob me of my wife? I don't know his name yet, but when I do, I need to understand why he thought he could snatch you away from me and everyone who loves you. Oh God, what will I and the kids do without this woman? I'm all alone and don't know what to do next,' Bob whispers to Pauline's body, his face wet with tears. He prays that she will understand, not that he understands a single thing at this grim time.

For a split second, he decides to return home to see Pauline, before he remembers he will never see her ever again and that his home will forever be different. He wipes his dripping face, blows his nose, kisses his wife's icy face one last time, strokes her hair and walks like a zombie out of the room. Bob never touches another woman or places another bet ever again.

The police know Sam's name from his raft of credit cards, but he also needs formal identification. One of his only remaining relatives who would have been able to identify him is ironically also his murderer, his half-uncle Edward whose body now resides in the same bleak mortuary.

At the exact time of Lara's son's murder, she is contentedly sipping wine in Portugal with Geraldo, the new man in her life. She is oblivious to the gruesome manner in which her estranged son has died. When she finally learns what her brother-in-law has done to her spoilt, only child, Lara suffers a complete nervous breakdown. Her distress is partly caused by her guilt at having selfishly deserted her son, leaving him to the mercies of a vindictive murderer, a relative that she had always suspected of being worryingly unstable. Although Charlie had thrown her out of the marital home over a decade previously, Lara will forever blame herself for having cheated on Charlie in the first place.

'If I had avoided Geraldo, Sam might still be alive,' she thinks more often than is healthy for her mental stability and for her second marriage.

Some pains never disappear no matter how many years pass. For the rest of her life, Lara periodically, longingly turns the pages of her photo albums. She tortures herself by flicking through images from Sam's brief life. Lara will forever shed endless tears whenever she catches sight of his cute, five-year-old face smiling back at her, a lurid parrot perched on his strawberry-blond hair, or doing cartwheels on a beach in the Maldives during a family holiday. She punishes herself with thoughts of how her boy might still be alive if she had not selfishly chosen to have sex with Geraldo behind her dull husband's back.

Geraldo eventually tires of the way his wife mopes around and starts to blatantly cheat on Lara, seeking out any willing women on holiday in Portugal. Most evenings he wanders into the bars and clubs of the nearby holiday resort to seek out whatever women are on offer that week. His good looks and charm ensures that he strikes lucky more often than not and he spends many nights making love to random females of various shapes, ages and colours.

Lara becomes so weighed down with guilt and regret that she will never have the strength to complain about Geraldo's blatant adultery. The unhappily married couple will live out their days together in Portugal, but will forever be as distant to each other as the moon is to the sun.

# A gleam of light in the dark

As soon as Edward's lifeless body drops onto the grass, the unbearable tension in the air eases, to be replaced by an icy blanket of extreme shock.

James sees that it is now safe enough to carefully lift Claire's arm to check for other wounds. Intense relief washes over him when he can find no worse injury than a bloodied arm with a bullet in it, although that is bad enough as she is losing blood at an alarming rate.

'Lie still whilst I get help for you. I think your friend on the bench is sadly beyond any help,' James tells Claire, who is now crying from the pain of the gunshot wound. James runs towards the ambulance crews entering the park, pulling a couple of them over to tend to his fiancée and Pauline.

After checking Pauline for signs of life, they cover her body and carry it off on a stretcher to be transported to the nearest hospital mortuary. Her essence has already floated weightlessly back to her living room to await Bob's eventual return. Mercifully, she is spared the discovery of her husband's appalling secret life.

Five years pass before the couple are properly reunited, after a grieving Bob is fatally knifed in his cab whilst challenging a group of drunken youths when they try to escape without paying the taxi fare. Unhampered by his body, Bob knows that he does not deserve to find happiness with Pauline after living a secret life of porn and gambling, but he finds it with her anyway. On Pauline's suggestion, they decide to start afresh now that the world for all eternity is their oyster. They merrily float off to spend an eternity island hopping in the Caribbean. It had been their favourite holiday destination when they had both been tied down and restricted by their bodies.

The ambulance crew quickly check Claire then urgently whisk her to hospital to be treated. James accompanies her in the back of the ambulance as its wailing siren clears the traffic out of its way. Claire is hooked up to a drip as she has lost so much blood and it sways as the ambulance takes the corners at speed.

'What about the baby? Never mind about me. I need to know our baby is okay,' Claire cries, trying to sit up.

'We will check the baby is fine as soon as we reach hospital. We're almost there. Just lie still and save your strength,' the fatherly ambulance man says soothingly.

With his head bursting from so much stress, James jogs behind the stretcher as Claire is carried into the hospital. Her gunshot wound is tended to before any attention is paid to the state of her pregnancy. Once the bullet is removed and her arm is bandaged and in a sling, the doctors discover that the tenacious foetus is still alive. The young couple collapse on each other sobbing tears of relief.

Another person much relieved is Neil, Philippe's boyfriend. He has been awaiting his Spanish lover's return following his job interview, oblivious to all the drama that has so recently unfolded. He never listens to the news as it depresses him, so when a hysterical, shocked Philippe turns up at their flat later than expected, he knows nothing of the shootings.

'What's up with you, love?' Neil asks, surprised to see Philippe collapse in floods of tears onto their bed.

'Didn't you hear?' Philippe replies through his shuddering sobs, almost accusingly.

'Did the job interview go badly? Why all of these tears?' Neil asks, trying to guess the cause of his lover's distress.

'No, it not about the damned interview. I never went. There was a terrible, mass shooting at the park that I was waiting in. A crazy guy shot a sweet-looking old lady I'd been sitting near. Police shot the bastard as I was legging it away from the mayhem. I turned around and that's when I saw him shoot her stone dead. I don't know who else was shot, but I'm guessing that there were quite a few. I caught a cab home after police questioned me for an eye witness report after all the shootings. That's why I'm home so late.'

'God! I can't take it all in. You poor, poor thing. I can hardly believe it. No wonder you're so shaken up,' Neil says, pouring a large brandy to revive Philippe.

'The old lady, he shot the old lady,' Philippe says, weeping inconsolably.

'Drink this. I'll look after you. You're safe now,' Neil lifts the glass to his lover's quivering lips.

For well over six months, Philippe is struck down by severe post-traumatic stress disorder because of what he has witnessed in the park. Repeated severe panic attacks prevent him from leaving the house, which suits Neil just fine. For those six months of gradual recovery, Neil has never been happier and more relaxed because he no longer has to worry about what his lover is getting up to whilst at work.

During this anxious, troubled time, Philippe is incapable of looking for a new job or holding one down. He often wakes in a blind panic at night, crying inconsolably, after suffering horrific nightmares which mainly feature the shooting of the old lady.

The haunted Spaniard eventually manages to recover enough to seek out a new job in men's fashion retail, where he continues to secretly cheat on Neil with one of his new work colleagues. Neil's paranoia quickly returns and predictably drives Philippe out of his life forever, to be replaced by a string of similar young, attractive, male lovers. Neil eventually dies alone and unloved, a victim of his own worst enemy; his paranoia.

## Dealing with the dealer

The police are at first uncertain of Mungo's identity, as he is carrying nothing on him to identify him. They know that he must have been a drug dealer due to the large quantity and wide range of drugs inside his holdall pillow that had been found squashed under his peaceful-looking, handsome death mask.

'One less scumbag to bang up behind bars,' thinks P.C. Delaney whilst placing Mungo's copious drug stash into plastic bags and meticulously labelling them.

The policeman labelling Mungo's drugs thinks about dead Edward in much the same way. 'That's one less murdering crackpot to deal with. No need to waste taxpayers' money on feeding, clothing and boarding him in jail for the rest of his sorry life. A bullet in the heart soon sorted that waste of space out. Cheap at half the price!' P.C. Delaney is obviously well overdue for a spell of leave.

Mungo's girlfriend is naturally distraught to hear the news of her lover's violent death. This is partly due to having to move out of the flat they shared, as she will not be able to pay the rent on her own. The police contact her at the flat on the evening of his murder. They want to inform her of her boyfriend's death, plus search their lodgings for illegal substances. Another stash of drugs is unearthed from under the bed. No amount of protestation over her innocence prevents Francesca's prosecution for drug possession, although she escapes a more serious charge of drug dealing, as this could not be proved.

Francesca's constant need for sex will soon outweigh her need to grieve over Mungo's murder. Within a week of his death, the heartless girl will be starting to date one of Mungo's more unusual drug customers. This smartly dressed, dark-haired businessman in his thirties will take a fancy to her when he visits the flat to score his usual cocaine. He will expect to find Mungo opening the door, but it will be opened by Francesca, interrupted by his knock from packing boxes in preparation for vacating the flat. Francesca will recognise him from his previous visits to score off Mungo.

It does not take long to explain the situation, how Mungo has been fatally shot and how there are no drugs in the flat. The opportunist banker tries to comfort her over Mungo's death. He kisses her and within minutes, they are exploring each other's bodies. Within the hour, Francesca and the banker are rolling around the very bed that she so recently shared with Mungo. Indecently soon, with a new, virile partner in her life, she forgets all about her murdered boyfriend. Mungo had no living relatives to mourn his demise.

Within a few months, Francesca is living with the banker, who finds another drug dealer. Soon, it is as though Mungo has never existed. The only name he has ever managed to make for himself is as a drug dealer and as one of the victims of multiple shootings in a London Park. Having no particularly strong emotional attachments to any places or people, rootless Mungo now wanders the world forever, just drinking in the incredible scenery, as laid back as ever.

# Hell

Before distraught, unhinged Edward can reach Maureen to try to apologise for his inaccurate aim, a far more accurate police marksman's bullet rips into his chest. It instantly kills him as dead as Maureen, Sam, Mungo and Pauline discover themselves to be. Edward has fully expected to be killed and so he meets his fate with little surprise, more of a huge sigh of relief. The pain in his back mercifully disappears after making his life a misery for so many decades.

Edward feels impossibly light and pain-free now that he is unhampered by his disabled body, cured by death, the most powerful analgesic. He slowly ascends majestically into the air, high enough to be able to briefly survey the scene of devastation laid out below him like some gruesome tableaux sewn into the Bayeux tapestry.

Edward is being magnetically drawn away from the chaos that is of his making. He rushes through the air, zooming across southern England, swooping over frothy waves, tiny boats bobbing below him like bath toys. Within minutes, he is shocked to find that all that is left of him is floating above his mother's garden in Jersey.

'No. Not here. I don't want to be here,' he wails, all too fearfully aware who might be awaiting his arrival.

'You evil, fucking bastard!' screams a male voice which seems to be emanating from all around him. The voice is ominously familiar to Edward.

'Charlie? I know it's you,' Edward says, sensing that he is in deep, inescapable trouble.

He cannot see his younger sibling, but can sense Charlie's raging energy, burning red and threatening near the fishpond. It hovers above the pampas grass, prepared to attack. Edward's energy is suddenly splintered by Charlie's tornado of released fury, hell bent on destruction. For what seems like hours, Charlie pounds and tears at every invisible energy strand of

Edward's soul, all the while berating him for murdering his only son. Shattered into a million pieces, Edward is in no shape to justify his actions. Instead, he has to resign himself to suffer the relentless beating.

Next door to their dead mother's house, an elderly neighbour called John Le Maitre is busy mowing his lawn. The bald, sprightly, retired stockbroker cannot identify the feeling of unease and foreboding that he is suddenly experiencing. He cannot see Charlie's revengeful attack on Edward's energy source, but he senses it.

As the living exist in a different dimension to the dead, John and every other living human being will never see the physical representations of the spirits coexisting with him. However, his nerve endings tingle from their sudden unsettling presence. All is definitely not right, despite the perfect weather and despite him having no reason for his increasing anxiety.

John hurriedly finishes mowing the lawn and scuttles indoors. On such a beautiful day, he normally would stay outside to drink his afternoon tea and eat a few biscuits, but not today. John can discern an invisible yet malevolent turbulence whirling like a dervish close to his tranquil garden. Once indoors, John is forced to turn on day-time television to divert his mind. At dusk, he wanders outside and is relieved to find that, although there is not quite a tranquil aura, the turbulent energy has slightly abated.

At dusk, Edward finally manages to be heard amidst Charlie's wailing which is gradually easing off. Although Charlie desperately wants to continue with his onslaught on Edward, his energy is depleting through venting so much high-octane anger. Edward's energy strands are given a desperately needed, brief chance to regroup and reform. He knows that he will only have a brief window of time to state his case before his half-brother recovers and resumes his vicious, vindictive attack.

'It's now or never,' Edward thinks.

If he had possessed hands, Edward would have grasped his

opportunity with both of them, but instead he shouts, 'Charlie, I warned you what I'd do if I was disinherited again. Out of pure greed, your son, Sam chose to ignore both of our wishes and stole what is rightfully mine. I'm a man of my word. Sam wasn't. He's not here is he?'

Edward senses Charlie's voice drifting through him, carried on the slight summer breeze, saying, 'Sam will no doubt be along shortly to tell you exactly how he feels about you blowing the top of his skull off. Mum will be beyond disgusted by your foul actions. She probably won't be able to stand to speak to you. She floated down to Anne Port Bay this morning as the tide would be perfect about now. God help you when she gets home!'

Edward remembers how Anne Port Bay had always been his mother's favourite beach. He tries to gain himself more recovery time by saying, 'I'm surprised that she still visits any beaches at all after her tragic drowning debacle at Grouville Bay.'

Charlie replies, 'She says she still feels happiest when hanging out on a beach. The beach energy is perfect for her. She likes to amuse herself by just watching the holiday makers or lying in the sun with them, despite not having a body to tan anymore. Old habits never die,' Charlie suddenly realises that Edward is trying to distract him from attacking him with idle chitchat. He shouts, 'Nice try at changing the subject! She will be back soon enough to help me to sort you out good and proper, you murdering cunt!'

'You won't be using language like that when mum returns,' Edward says. He realises with horror that he cannot escape this garden. He thinks, 'I seem to have been transported here by some force to be punished. I must have been brought here because I always wanted to return here to live when I had a body. I'd have never come back here if I'd realised what I'd be in for.'

Soon, his nephew Sam's spirit will return from the bloodied pavement, whisked along on the breeze. Its sole purpose will be to attack Edward in alliance with his father and grandmother. Edward fears that Sam's vengeance will be as great, if not greater than Charlie's fury. The understandable anger of father and son combined would surely be impossible for Edward to withstand.

'Is this to be my endless purgatory, my punishment, my personal Hell?' Edward wonders, just before the combined energy that is Sam and Florence storms through him with angry screams of foul abuse.

Edward's energy strands are yet again torn asunder by wave upon wave of terrifying, vitriolic pummels, kicks and screams, screams that only the spirit world can hear. The deadly trio of Edward's relatives take turns to vent their fury on what is left of him. For three brutal days and nights, Edward can grasp no respite, unable to defend himself against the relentless battering.

To make matters worse, Marcus also turns up on the third day to lend a hand after hearing on the ethereal grapevine of his grandson's murder at the hands of Edward. As he has always strongly disliked his step-son, Marcus needs no excuse to join in the fray.

For three days and nights, John Le Maitre can sense an unidentifiable disturbance in the ether, even greater than what he had first experienced in his garden. Thoughts of exorcism enter his troubled mind. He organises an urgent visit to his irritating sister in Bude, solely to escape the indefinable malevolence that has ruined his precious home's tranquillity. John knows that the bad energy weirdly seems to emanate from his neighbour's property, but he cannot understand why. It is beyond all human comprehension.

The day after the shooting, whilst reading his daily newspaper's headlines about the murder in the park, John is stunned to recognise the familiar names of Edward and Sam Le Cornu.

'Jesus, that's Florence's son and grandson! The story in the paper mentions Jersey, so there's no doubt that it's them. So,

Florence's son murdered her grandson then went on a killing spree. Who'd have thought? I hope the weird vibes coming from next door have nothing to do with the murders, but it would explain a great deal if they are behind it,' John thinks. An icy finger traces down his old, crumbling spine and he shivers as his body hair stands to attention.

John has always believed in the possibility of ghosts and spirits. When he was about ten, he suspected that he had seen a ghost at the end of a dark, sombre corridor on a visit to his great aunt's spooky house in the parish of St Saviour. A brief brush with a guru in his twenties also gave John an appreciation of positive and negative energies, making him particularly susceptible to the invisible, but potent group of spirits berating the essence of Edward. He senses that members of the Le Cornu family in whatever form, may very well still be occupying the neighbouring property. He feels powerless to know how to resolve the problem.

Unfortunately for John Le Maitre, Edward's strands of energy automatically reform after each surge of attack from the spirits of his vengeful relatives. Tormented and exhausted, whenever each attack subsides, Edward's aura floats limply over to a patch of grass under the weeping willow tree to regain strength. There seems that there will never be any lasting peace for him. After a few hour's rest, the intense attack of powerful grievances resumes and Edward is torn asunder once more, disturbing John's peace of mind into the bargain.

Eventually, John's nerves can no longer stand the oppressive, negative energy. He contemplates selling his beloved home and moving to a more peaceful area. However, the surprise entrance onto the turbulent scene of the spirit of Gregory, Edward's dead father, works in John's favour and ends Edward's purgatory.

For decades, Gregory's energy has been basking in the Tropics but he suddenly senses all is not well. In the blink of an eye, Gregory is transported to his former home in Jersey, where he had met his painful, cancerous end. He had long ago realised that he could do nothing to help his only son whilst Edward was still alive. Through a shift in the world's vital energy flows, he has sensed that Edward has met a bloody end and is now part of the spirit world, just like him.

Gregory has found the experience of being dead far more enjoyable than living unhappily with Florence, but he can see that Edward is a spirit in deep trouble and under vicious attack. Gregory feels an exquisite rush of love for Edward as he remembers how even as a young child his son had cared for him far more diligently than Florence had ever done when he was dying painfully from cancer.

It soon becomes clear to Gregory that, just as in life, Edward is at the mercy of the negative energy sources of his mother, step-father, brother and nephew.

'What's all this then? Four of you bullies all ganging up against just one? That's hardly fair! Leave my son alone right now, you evil bastards!' Gregory screams as he swoops through all four of them, splitting their energy strands to smithereens with his righteous, pent-up rage.

An ecstatic Edward seizes his chance. With a supreme effort, he flies up into the air to mingle with his long-lost father's powerful energy. Gregory rapidly pulls his grateful son away from the confusion.

'Hello, Edward. You're coming home with me,' Edward feels his long-lost father say.

Gregory sets course towards a more tranquil, permanent existence on an island in the Tropics. Beneath them, he and Edward notice with concern that Florence, Sam, Charlie and Marcus seem to be attempting to regroup in order to attack the fleeing couple again.

Screaming like a banshee, Sam begins to set off in pursuit, intent on continuing with Edward's relentless persecution and punishment. Charlie calls out to him and unexpectedly rushes ahead to restrain his son, saying, 'Let those two wastes of space go, son. I think we've made our feelings perfectly clear to Edward. We can't punish him forever and I'm bored with it all now.'

'Okay. To be honest, I'm getting fed up with all of the screaming and shouting at him too, pops. All of that angst is so bloody exhausting. I doubt that we'll ever be seeing either of those two bastards again. Come on Gran and Gramps, I vote that we all head down to the beach for a change of scenery so that we can recharge our batteries.'

The unpleasant quartet mingles together until it forms into a swirling, invisible ball of negative energy. Comet-like, they shoot off on a rapid course towards Anne Port Bay. Peace is thankfully restored once more at John's house next door, never again to be disrupted, except by the squawking of seagulls that now deem it safe to return to Florence's property.

Thousands of miles from Jersey, Edward and his father have never been happier. Reunited once more, they bask peacefully together in the balmy air of a tropical island, more than content to spend eternity in each other's loving company.

# Books by Joy Mutter

## A Slice of the Seventies
### Book One of the Mug Trilogy

This first book in the Mug Trilogy tells the story of Jersey-born Mug, a rape victim from a recently broken home. It covers her time as a sixteen-year-old at the Isle of Wight Music Festival in 1970, the year she followed a guru and follows her tumultuous experiences as an art student in Coventry. The book then details her torrid relationship with fellow student, David and the dramatic events that lead on from their graduation. Available on Amazon in paperback and Kindle editions.

## The Lying Scotsman
### Book Two of the Mug Trilogy

The words in this book were triggered by the entanglement between Mug, a recently divorced, disinherited, temporarily sex-obsessed woman and Michael, a complex, mendacious, Scottish baggage handler. Destiny threw this Gordian knot her way one night in early 2004. She was an honest, trusting, troubled woman in her late forties. He was an enigma in his late thirties who was hiding many shocking secrets. Her original plan was to write about their unusual story as a gift to him, taking the opportunity to describe her life prior to their meeting as it shaped how she felt about him, why she tolerated what others might deem unacceptable and dictated how she lived her future life. The purpose of her book changed into a desperate effort to make sense of unfolding, bizarre events and to help them both deal with the aftermath. Available on Amazon in paperback and Kindle editions.

## Straws
### Book Three of the Mug Trilogy

The aftermath of Mug's torrid time, whirling in The Lying Scotsman's vortex. This third book in the Mug Trilogy documents her epic struggles to achieve a happy outcome in her turbulent relationships with men, family, work and life in general. Available on Amazon in paperback and Kindle editions.

## Random Bullets

After shooting and killing his nephew, a gunman runs wild in a London park. What drives Edward to commit such a heinous act? Who will survive yet another of his moments of madness? Set in 2015, *Random Bullets* is a contemporary thriller with a fantasy twist. Available on Amazon in paperback and Kindle editions.

## Potholes and Magic Carpets

The main action in this book takes place in rural Kent and London. It is set in 2015 and looks at the dramatic incidents, challenges and temptations in the past and present lives of four couples of varying ages, professions and sexual persuasions that are all linked by either blood or friendship. Just as in life, the negative, selfish nature of some of the characters in 'Potholes and Magic Carpets' wreaks havoc on both the innocent and guilty alike. Available on Amazon in paperback and Kindle editions.

## Living with Postcards

This non-fiction book describes my close relationship with old postcards, mainly fantasy ones. I have collected them since the seventies and now own over two thousand of these charming, beautiful, historic items. I started fanatically collecting them whilst writing my thesis on Fantasy in Postcards at Art College, where I was studying for a graphic design degree. My thesis won me a first with distinction, whereas my graphic art annoyingly gained me only a 2:2. I was asked by my art history tutor to lecture on the subject of Fantasy in Postcards, but as I was only twenty-one at the time I did not feel ready and declined. The cards in my book are from my own collection. Available on Amazon in paperback and Kindle editions.

## Her demonic Angel

*Her demonic Angel* is a collection of all of my short stories written thus far. The stories have been written in a variety of genres so hopefully there should be something for everyone. Some tales are stranger than others, but all could be said to be different shades of dark. Despite its somewhat suggestive title *Her demonic Angel* is not erotic fiction. Available on Amazon in paperback and Kindle editions.

# About the Author

Joy Mutter was born in Jersey in the Channel Islands and lived there for eighteen years. She lived and worked in Kent as a professional graphic designer for twenty years after gaining a Graphic Design Degree at Coventry University. In 2012, Joy moved to Oldham and has been writing full-time there ever since.

Joy has written seven books since 2007. Her first three books are mainly autobiographical and form *The Mug Trilogy*. Her fourth book, *Potholes and Magic Carpets* is contemporary fiction and she recently published a non-fiction book called *Living with Postcards*. *Random Bullets* is a contemporary thriller with a fantasy twist and was published in September 2015. *Her demonic Angel* is the author's first collection of short stories in different genres and was published in 2016. She is now working on another contemporary thriller called *Hostile* and has many ideas for future books.

Joy Mutter's book information and blogs can be found at joymutter.com. All of her books are available to buy on Amazon in paperback and Kindle editions.

Random Bullets
Copyright: Joy Mutter
Published: November 2015
Publisher: Joy Mutter
The right of Joy Mutter to be identified as author of this Work has been asserted by her in accordance with sections 77 and 78 of the Copyright, Designs and Patents Act 1988. All rights reserved. No part of this publication may be reproduced, stored in retrieval systems, copied in any form or by any means, electronic, mechanical, photocopying, recording or otherwise transmitted without prior written permission from the publisher. You must not circulate this book in any format.

Printed in Great Britain
by Amazon